play me to *infinity*

THE BROKEN MEN CHRONICLES

book three

carey decevito

This book is an original publication of Emberlust Press.

Decevito, Carey
Play Me to Infinity / Carey Decevito – Paperback edition
ISBN-13: 978-1-988806-03-7

Cover photography by Eric David Battershell
Cover design by Clarisse Tan, CT Cover Creations
Cover model: Johnny Kane

ACKNOWLEDGEMENTS

This book couldn't have come to fruition without the help of some amazing people.

To my entire production team: you truly are amazing gems and I feel blessed to have been able to work with you all.

Eric, Johnny, and Clarise, without you three, Mike's journey would be without an amazing cover. Thank you for your expertise, your professionalism, your talent, but most of all, thank you for your support and friendship. You are truly extraordinary people.

Laurie and Marissa at Pub-Craft, you lovely ladies rock! Words cannot convey my appreciation for what you ladies do.

And last but certainly not least, to you, my wonderful readers, thank you for your kind words, your reviews, your support, and for your love of literature. Without you, I would be writing strictly for myself (and that's okay), but you sure warm this lady's heart by enjoying the journeys put forth before you. In this case, Mike's.

CHAPTER 1

I sat at Fairfax, checking out the flavors of the evening while unwinding from a grueling day at the office. It was slim pickings in the crowd, but the night was still young.

Sitting in the back corner at a table by herself, I spotted her. Nicole. I might have turned her unsavory attitude around where my brother-in-law, Jake, was concerned, but the woman now had a gun out for me.

Okay, so you've surmised that I'm single, perhaps even a player, and I'll admit that you're somewhat right.

I enjoy my bachelorhood…well, sort of. I wouldn't say that it's the lifestyle I'd have chosen for myself, more like one chosen for me, thanks to my ex-fiancée.

Loving Tracey with everything I had hadn't been good enough. Despite the numerous warnings from friends, I had been living by the 'denial is bliss' adage until one day, the flip of her hair, the wiggle of her tight ass, and the batting of her lashes no longer clouded my perception.

After six months of dealing with her deceit, I shredded my devoted fiancé card and moved on. I've been playing the field for a year and a half since.

Truth be told, I don't have time for a relationship, as much as I'd prefer one. I'm the CEO of Withers International, a multi-million-dollar company that specializes in public and government relations. Need I say more?

Ben knocked me back into the present as he dropped himself into the seat across from me. "Rough day?"

"Rough few months is more like it." I huffed out a breath. "I need a new assistant."

The man's brows furrowed. "You still haven't gotten rid of Karen?"

A dry laugh escaped. "You mean Tania." I didn't have the gall to look at my friend, knowing I'd be met with his disapproving look, and rightly so. As of late, there was quite the revolving door where my PA's were concerned.

"Why do you do this to yourself?"

Okay, so I may have overstepped the boundaries on employer-employee relations. In my defense, they were the ones who approached me, not the other way around.

Ben shook his head at me. "Tracey really did fuck you up. This is ridiculous."

I took a swig from my beer and let out a loud tension-filled sigh while leaning my bottle in my best friend's direction. "You don't know the half of it."

It was late, and despite the fact that I'd made it out tonight, my interest in entertaining a possible suitor to cap off my day was lost once Ben returned to his bartending duties.

What about Nikki? As soon as the thought occurred, I almost choked on my last sip of beer. I would have to be desperate—no, insane—to even approach that man-eater.

Despite my intent on ignoring the woman who had eyed daggers at me all night, I turned my gaze toward the table she had been occupying to find that she was no longer there.

Nicole was a beautiful woman, and I'd be lying if I said I didn't remember much about her from our childhood. Hell, she'd practically been a sister; and harassing her and my sister had been one of mine and Ben's favorite pastimes. In our later years however, she became skittish, always quick to leave the room as soon as I entered it. The teenager I'd been had always wondered about the possibility of her having a schoolgirl crush. I have to say that I enjoyed cornering her to see that blush, especially that last summer before Mom and Dad picked up and moved us all to Austin.

Shaking the memories from my mind, I left my empty

bottle on the table. As I turned to leave, I plowed into a tiny body. Bracing my hands on the soft skin of slim shoulders to prevent the person from toppling over, I found myself staring down into bright green pools laced with flames that were Nicole's eyes.

What color do they turn when… I groaned at the imagery that flashed through my mind. Forget it, bud, there's no way in hell that you want to go there.

"Watch where you're going."

"Sorry," I mumbled, my voice a few octaves lower than normal.

"D-do you mind moving?"

Her unsettled demeanor had me smirking. "Do I make you nervous, Little Nikki?"

As I let go of her shoulders, she stepped back.

"No." She gave me a saccharine smile, but her eyes showed mischievousness. "You make me nauseous. Now, get out of my way."

As she made to pass me, I grasped her elbow. "You know," I leaned toward her ear, the subtlety of her scent clouding my thoughts momentarily, "if you're ever looking for someone to help you get that stick out of your ass, I'd be more than–"

The claws came out. "Bite me!"

"I'd love to, sugar." I grinned, pulling away just in time to see her face turn a delightful shade of pink. Yes, that blush was still as much fun to bring about now as it was back in the day.

As quick as our interaction occurred, it ended when she turned and trotted off.

My gaze turned to follow her exiting the bar. I let out a low whistle as I watched those hips sway in that skirt of hers. Her rounded ass filled the material to perfection and images of that luscious derrière, bent over as I took her from behind began playing in my head.

Damn! It's too bad she's as cold as ice.

And that was my cue to head home.

I came to a stop in front of my large four-bedroom house and sighed. Purchased to avoid the cramped lofts and high-rise condos, it was a constant reminder of the dream I once had of a home filled with children and a woman to worship. Nowadays, all I had to look forward to was the cold beer in my fridge, my comfortable furniture, and a house filled with silence.

Silence. It was always there when you didn't want it, and never there when you needed it.

Over the last eighteen months, I kept my new façade intact, my machismo held close to the vest in an effort to mask that I was a family man to the core. Being honest, I was miserable. Lonely.

Maybe it's time to take a chance? It had been two years since I'd left Tracey, a year and a half since I chose to have absolutely nothing to do with my ex.

Danica, Jake, and so many others disagree with the casualness with which I treated my suitors, but they understood why I did it. Well, most of them, with the exception of my sister's judgmental best friend, Nicole that is.

So why wasn't I going for it after two years?

The answer was simple: I was scared.

As I settled into bed, I came to realize that maybe it was time I let go of my pessimism where relationships were concerned.

CHAPTER 2

At six the following morning, I was in my office. It was my favorite time of the workday. It gave me time to think. It gave me time to analyze where I was taking this company that my father built from the ground up and then, before he could run it into the ground, left it to me and Danica.

After bumping into Nicole last night, I had a replay of her ass swaying from side to side, her bare shoulders, and those legs of hers capped in four-inch heels, playing on a continuous loop in my mind.

And this morning, the thought of those…

Snap out of it, man!

The sudden twitch below the belt had me groaning. These reactions of mine had come way out of left field, and I'd be damned if I paid them any heed simply because Nicole now appealed to a certain member of my anatomy.

With that said, I could only deal with craziness one person at a time.

And that brings me to another woman that plagued my thoughts as of late: my personal assistant.

I needed to do something about my current work predicament—and fast. Burning the candle at both ends, I was putting in longer hours lately while my sister, and Withers International's CFO, was at home by dinnertime, enjoying life with her husband, their son, and her very pregnant belly.

Ben was right. And I quote, the measure of a great personal assistant is how well she tends to your schedule, files, paperwork and the like, and not how she blows you from beneath your desk. Crass, I know, but true all the same. It was time I got rid of Tania. She was incompetent and she gave me more grief than help on the best of days.

Thinking of my sister, I picked up the phone, figuring she could be of help with my current predicament, but thought better and set the receiver back on its cradle. She'd be in the office within the hour anyway.

Danica and I have gotten closer since my move back to Jacksonville became permanent. We had weekly dinners at her place and she always stopped by my office for a chat first thing every morning.

Like me, she found her way into work a tad earlier than most, unless my brother-in-law found a way to hold her back.

Jake and I have bonded more, and I love the man as if he were my own brother. He got me, for the lack of a better description, and with the way I've been living my life lately, that's something Ben and I haven't been able to relate to. Jake was worse than me a short time ago, but when it came down to his relationship with my sister, I never once doubted his intentions. I knew the man loved her. Everyone knew it. Though years had kept them separated, their love had never faded; no matter how stubborn they had been when Danica moved back, or how my father had conspired to keep them apart.

I released a tension-filled sigh, regaining my focus on the present.

A look at my day's itinerary left me with a burning sensation in my gut. After a nearly a month and repetitive requests, the damn thing was still predominantly blank with the exception of those appointments I had entered myself in recent weeks.

I grunted my annoyance and looked toward the pile of files on the edge of my desk that had only grown instead of finding their way into one of the mahogany cabinets in the far corner.

I was more organized doing everything solo before she came along.

Yes, it was official. I was fed up.

Despite the warnings and reminders, Tania had had her opportunity to prove her worth. Her probationary period wasn't over yet, but I'd be dammed if I allowed her to wreak more chaos over my office for another day. Knowing what I had to do next, and probably should have done yesterday if not last week, I picked up the phone and dialed.

I waited for the woman in question to pick up.

"Hello." She sounded half-asleep.

"Tania."

"Mike?" Her voice came out squeaky.

"Yes." I took a deep breath.

"What's wrong?"

"Tania," I cleared my throat, "I'm sorry to do this, but I won't be needing your services any longer."

"But…"

"I need someone who's organized and knows what she's doing; someone with more experience and who does what I need them to do. I'm saying things need to be seamless and they're not. I think you know what I mean by this." I began to guide the mouse over my computer screen. "I'm looking at my calendar right now and the four meetings I asked you to confirm and add to my agenda before you left yesterday aren't in there. Simple things like that, I shouldn't have to clarify at this point in your employment. I'm sorry but I can't keep you any longer."

"But, Mike!" Her voice grated on my nerves.

"Your belongings and relevant paperwork will be waiting for you with HR by this afternoon. I trust that a week's severance is ample enough seeing as you've only been with us for under a month. When you come in, please ask for Emma in Human Resources. She'll handle everything. Again, I'm very sorry and I wish you luck. Take care of yourself."

I hung up before she could say anything else and took a deep breath.

Putting in a call to Emma in HR and leaving a voicemail with what I needed from her later, I hung up the phone.

Getting up, I grabbed a banker's box from the small supply cabinet in my office and walked to Tania's former quarters and cringed. There were photo frames on the desk; I counted five pairs of shoes, three jackets, a couple of pashminas, and that was excluding whatever personal items would most likely be stored in the desk drawers. I didn't envy Emma at all for what she'd have to do when she got in this morning.

On a groan, I leaned forward with my elbows on my desk and massaged my temples. My mood had taken a downward spiral, and I hoped that the rest of my day didn't follow in the same fashion.

"What's got you down, big brother?" I startled, not having heard Danica come in. My sister waddled toward me with a cup of coffee in both hands.

"That better be decaf." I gestured to the drink she kept for herself after she handed me mine.

"Every morning you ask me that question and every morning I give you the same answer." She smirked, then stuck her tongue out at me. "You know it is."

"Just making sure." I smiled, but the gesture wasn't reciprocal. Instead, she assessed me from top to bottom.

"You look tired." She took a seat in front of my desk.

"Because I am."

"You're working too hard. You need to get out and live a little."

I shrugged my shoulders. "I get out."

"Finding a woman to warm your bed on occasion isn't considered 'getting out'." She was right, but would I tell her that? Hell, no! Just like I wouldn't tell her that the only bed-warming there'd been in the last month, aside from the one time with Tania a few weeks ago, had been done by me alone.

"I know you don't agree with it sis, and I don't need this right now." I ran a hand through my dark brown hair. "I had to fire Tania and, to be honest, I have no clue what's on my agenda for today, plus I have to coordinate with HR to get a new posting out there, and deal with interviews, and..." I sighed.

"Calm down, I know someone who'd be great for you."

Well that got my attention. "Who?"

"Just someone." She gave me a wry grin. "I can say that fucking her won't be a problem for you, which means that her attention will be on her work the entire time. She's the best I know, and if she'd been free when I was looking for my PA, I would have snapped her up myself."

She knows?

She snorted. "Yes, I know about your latest tastes in personal assistants, big brother."

"So who is it?"

"I'll have to speak with her first, see if she's interested." She tapped her index finger on her chin. "As for who it is, I'll leave that surprise to her." She winked. "I'm sorry, but I've got to run. You remember not to expect me in the office after this morning, right?"

I laughed, but my excitement of acquiring a new PA without much effort dimmed as worry for my sister kicked in. "I always said you worked too hard. You need to take it easy, you're due any day now. Your husband's right to worry, you know. We all do."

She laughed, but the humor in her eyes faded and her expression softened as she reached out a hand to me. "Come help me out of this chair and give me a hug." I rounded my desk and helped her up. "I need to get some work done before Jake comes back to pick me up in a few hours. I hate that I can't drive thanks to this belly of mine." Her hands clasped her stomach that held two of the most precious of cargos.

"Hey, that's my niece and nephew you're talking about in there." I gave her belly a rub.

I kissed the top of her head and she moved into my arms

to hug me. "So, you'll think about the PA I have in mind for you?"

"Go ahead and send her in." I released her. "I need all the help I can get." *The sooner, the better* was left unsaid.

"Okay!"

CHAPTER 3

"Not now, Joe!" If it was the man in question, I swear I would tear him a new one. I had had more than enough of running interference for him in order to rectify his latest fuck-up.

As you can gather, my day had followed the same route it had started on: with a shitload of incompetence.

A softer knock came as a reply to my grumbling acknowledgement of the initial disturbance.

Didn't anyone get what a closed office door meant? With a huff, I got up, wrenched the knob inward and barked a, "What?"

"Oh hell, no! Not you!" she said.

"Nicole?" I smirked as she started to back up, never taking her eyes off of me.

"I need a job, but not this bad."

Her withdrawal from me was quite amusing, so I leaned against the doorway, my arms crossed at my chest. My day could use a little divertissement, and Nicole's presence was sure to make it entertaining. "So you're the PA that Dani's been boasting about?"

She huffed. "Yeah, and you're the arrogant executive prick that's in dire straits. Funny how your sister left out the prick part."

Feisty! I liked my women that way, but then again, I always knew Nicole had the knack to bite back, despite her shyness.

My feet moved me toward her and she kept backing away. "Nicole." I stifled a bout of laughter when her butt hit the desk behind her and her eyes grew panicked with the realization that she was somewhat cornered.

"Jackass!" she spat, maneuvering away from her trap.

Feisty and skittish all at once made for an interesting combination. Now I saw a glimpse of both of the Nicoles I'd enjoyed so much over the years, and that fact only egged me on.

"It would be Jackass Boss to you," I paused for dramatics, "if I give you the position. Why is it that my sister thinks that you'd be perfect for the job?"

"It doesn't matter. I don't need it."

"Yes you do. You said so just now."

She blushed. "Well I– What I mean to say is…" She pinched her lips and a frustrated sigh escaped seconds later. "Yeah, I need a job, so what?"

"I'm currently hiring," I said with nonchalance.

"So I've heard. And?"

"And, do you want the job or not?" Annoyance laced my words.

I gauged her demeanor. She was stuck between a rock and a hard place. She needed money, but I could tell that the last place she wanted to be was anywhere near me.

Nothing new there.

The woman, even as a girl, had always found a way to give me a wide berth, even at family events, which she seemed to always be in attendance.

"I'll think about it." She turned to walk away.

"You either do or you don't, Nicole. I'd like an answer now so I don't feel as if I've wasted my time."

She spun on her heels to face me. "Oh?" She crossed her arms and spoke with so much disdain. "Did I just waste your precious time finding a slut to satisfy you tonight?"

My eyes narrowed on her. "Keep your voice down. And where the hell did that come from?"

"You know where it came from!" She marched toward me and jabbed her index in my chest as she looked up at me. "You're a sleaze! You're all over a woman one minute and onto another the next. I wouldn't be surprised if you screwed your former PA." Her almond-shaped eyes widened when I didn't hurry to defend myself. "Oh my God, you did, didn't you?"

"N-no I didn't!" Yeah, that wasn't as convincing as I'd hoped.

"Did so!" She cupped her forehead with a single hand. "I can't believe I was about to agree."

"You were?" I thought there'd be no shot in hell that she'd agree to work for me unless I got down on my knees and begged. And there's no way that was happening.

"Forget it!" She waved her hand, brushing off the idea of working with me, then made a mad dash for the elevators, grumbling. "I'm going to kill Danica for this."

She summoned the elevator before I could peel my eyes off of her ass and legs.

"Wait!" I rushed to her, but the doors started closing with her inside. My final glimpse of Nicole was one of her wiping at what looked like angry tears from her face.

Well now you've done it!

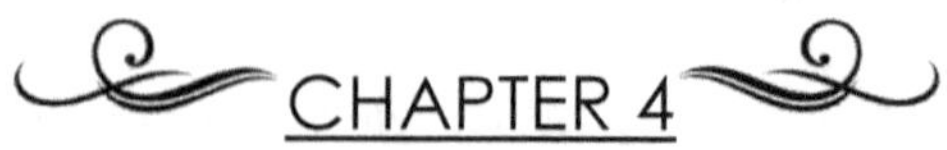

CHAPTER 4

Later that night, I had a rather pissed-off, about-to-pop sister knocking at my door.

"Sis…" I kissed her on the cheek, then smiled, hoping that the combination of both would help ease the brunt of her wrath.

"Oh cut the sis bit, Mike! What the fuck did you do to her?"

"To who?" I thought twice about playing dumb. "To Nikki?"

"Yes, to Nikki, you idiot! She showed up at the house, pissed off that I hadn't told her who she'd be working for at WI. I know you two have never really gotten along, but I didn't expect it to be like this."

"Like what?" I was losing my patience. "Where she attacked me by accusing me of making a habit of seducing my PA's?" She arched her brow, crossed her arms, and tapped her foot. "Okay…fine, I've done it, but–"

"But what?"

"But there's no way in hell that…" I decided to go with the obvious. "She's your friend and she hates my guts and–"

"And what?"

"It's Little Nikki." I shrugged my shoulders. "She's gorgeous and all, but like I've said, she hates me, thinks I'm a player. It wouldn't–"

"Right you are!"

My head snapped toward Danica's car. I'd neglected to remember that my sister couldn't drive and needed a chauffeur.

Nicole slammed the driver's side door and stormed toward us still dressed in her business attire.

"Excuse me?" I said.

She came to a stop beside Danica. "You're right, you are a player."

"You don't know a thing about me," I said and she harrumphed.

"And I don't care to either." She looked over at Danica who growled, and I did the same. The woman looked as if she was about to implode.

"Cut it out, you two! Nicole, you need the job, and bro, you need the help. You don't need to like each other, just help each other out. If you dislike it that much, Nikki, leave when you find something else. And as for you, playboy…" She pointed an index in my direction.

"I'm not–" I protested.

"Maybe not, but you have to admit that you've been…um…Anyway, it doesn't matter. You're a good man and you know that you're not cut out for that shit." My sister turned to her best friend. "And you need to cut him some slack. Now, get me home. I'm tired, I'm cranky, and my feet feel like they're about to burst."

With that, Danica marched to the passenger side of her car and got in while the two of us watched on.

A moment later, Nicole's gaze went from the car to me. "Fine, I'll take it, but I'm out of there the minute I find something else."

"I wouldn't expect anything less. Thank you."

She nodded. "Keep your dick in your pants, stay away from me, and we'll be fine."

When she turned heel and made to leave I said, "What makes you think that I can't keep business separate from pleasure?"

She paused by the driver's side door. "Because," she smirked at me after a slow assessing gaze that had warmth pooling in my belly, "once a player, always a player."

Nicole's last words reverberated in my head long after her and Danica had left. It wasn't true, but she refused to see the proverbial light of day. Something about that fact niggled at me.

I've never agreed with men who saw their bachelorhood as a means to debauch as many partners as they could. So I went home with my fair share of women. It didn't mean I'd slept with all of them. Sometimes it was nice to have an intellectual conversation, or simply hang out, cuddling while watching a movie. Regardless of my activities with my suitors, I was always up front with them about what I was looking for.

Despite my trying to impart this knowledge on Nicole, whenever she'd give me two seconds to get a few words in edgewise, she still managed to make me feel like a complete jackass.

Why do you even care what she thinks, when you've never given a damn about what anyone else thought before?

As much as I'd probably like to deny the why, there was something about the tiny spitfire that set me off. To put it simply, I liked her. Always have. The woman was an enigma, a complex puzzle that was wrapped in riddles that held no answer. For the moment.

My head was pounding by the time I gave into exhaustion and went to bed. Having taken inventory of my life, I found myself grossly disgusted with the man I had become.

For the second night running, I surmised that a change could be good. That macho guy I'd allowed myself to become wasn't me, but how the hell could I let down my guard again?

I drifted into sleep, confused and hating part of myself.

CHAPTER 5

The next morning, I arrived at the office and wondered if Nicole would show up like she said she would. Not having discussed a time, salary, benefits…anything, I'd made sure that my schedule for this morning had been cleared of meetings.

I was drafting up a PR pitch to win a large account when a knock came on my open door.

"Yes?"

"I'm here."

Looking up, I hurried to push most of my paperwork to the side.

"Please shut the door behind you, Nicole." She nodded. "I guess you stuck to your decision. Thanks for coming." I took in her attire. Black pin-striped pencil skirt, up to her mid-thigh…*Nice*; crème satin blouse, unbuttoned enough to see the tops of her peaks…*Gorgeous*; natural make-up, but accented with dark red lipstick…*Sexy as fuck*; and her chestnut brown hair was up in a loose chignon, showing off the length of her slender neck, the tresses begging for a man to let them loose and run his fingers through them…*Beautiful*.

The screeching of a record resounded in my head. *Hold on…What?*

"Where do you want me?"

Sexually explicit answers swam through my thoughts, but I shoved them to the side. It wouldn't do well to anger the she-devil on her first day.

I cleared my throat. "We have a few things to discuss

first." I gestured to the chair in front of my desk. "Have a seat."

I went through the motions of explaining that Nicole would have full health and dental benefits from the get-go. She was more than happy with the other perks that came with the job, but a little hesitant about the travelling that would be needed on occasion.

Her eyes bulged when I pointed out her salary, which was a bit short of six figures. "Are you sure about this?"

"About what?"

"Don't you think the salary's a bit much?"

"Are you asking me to lower it?" My brow arched. "I would have thought it obvious, with the fact that you're not my biggest fan, that some kind of compensation would be more than appropriate."

She blushed. "Well..."

The zing to my cock was potent, thanks to her reaction. Clearing my throat and trying to control my lustful reflex, I said, "So it's settled then?" *Please agree before I embarrass myself.*

She gave me a small nod and her game face returned.

"Then I'll need your signature on this stuff." I slapped a pen on top of the packet of papers and slid the entirety over to her before leaning back into my chair and crossing my arms over my chest.

She leaned forward, the white lace of her bra peeking through the gap in her blouse.

My throat constricted, my groin stirred further at the sight.

Nicole signed her life away, got up, and stuck her hand out. I took it and held her eyes, which widened. I held on to her delicate fingers, entranced by the feel of softness and warmth a moment longer than necessary, which caused her cheeks to flush, reminding me to release her.

"So...um...my desk is..." She pointed just outside my

door into the open-concept office suite with a thumb over her shoulder.

"Yes. Go ahead, make yourself at home and then we can talk about my agenda and your other duties."

"I don't have anything to settle, so why don't I grab a notepad and pen and we can cut to the chase?" she suggested.

"Sounds good to me."

The moment the woman turned around, I was quick to adjust myself.

Before we knew it, lunchtime had arrived and Nicole was at her desk with a rather extensive list of tasks to perform, eating some kind of leftover meal that didn't seem all that appetizing.

She dropped her fork in the dish and pushed it away from her with a scowl and proceeded to be engrossed in her work-station.

"I thought that you'd be out with friends, celebrating your first day. You know you're allowed to leave the building, right?" I sassed.

Her fingers halted on the keyboard. "Funny." She kept her eyes to her computer screen instead of looking at me. "I thought you said you had a lunch meeting?" She typed a few more strokes and paused.

"They cancelled," I announced. She still didn't turn to look at me, instead, typed a few more additional notes. "Listen, it doesn't seem like you're enjoying the lunch you brought with you. I'm heading out to the deli across the street if you'd like to join me—my treat."

"Thanks, but I think I'll pass."

This time, when her fingers hit the keyboard again, it felt like I'd been dismissed.

"Fine."

During the hour I was out, my phone's alert system was getting some serious mileage. As I checked the source of the chime, appointment after appointment filled my calendar and I smiled.

Quick and efficient, the woman was turning out to be. I made a mental note to thank Danica for her recommendation. Nicole sure knew how to handle an office she was unfamiliar with. I wondered how smooth things would run once she felt comfortable.

When I got back, stacks of paper that had seen far too much of the light of day had been removed and I could only assume that Nicole had filed them away during my absence, seeing as they were nowhere to be found.

I walked into my office and noticed that even my desk looked tidier. The pile of files on the edge of it had disappeared, as well as those others that had been littering the small work table in the far corner.

I turned to say something to Nicole, but found her on the phone.

"I'll be sure to let him know," she said and giggled into the phone. "Sure. Will do, sir." She hung up, closed a file folder and got up in a rush, almost crashing into me. "Uh…here." She pushed the file at me. "Mr. Winthrow called and he's on for Monday at noon. I guess you're flying out to Austin. Did you need me to coordinate your travel arrangements?"

"That would be wonderful, thank you."

"You're welcome." She dropped to her seat, pulled up my agenda and started tapping away at the keyboard again.

Damn! The woman was like my last three assistants combined and on steroids!

The rest of the afternoon flew by, with Nicole walking in and out of my office with various files, removing those I was done with, and everything kind of flowed. Before I knew it, I heard a knock on my door.

"I'm heading out. Is there anything you need before I go?" Nicole asked.

I glanced at the clock on the bottom right of my computer screen. "No." I gave her a warm smile. She gave me an awkward look. "Thanks for today. You were great."

"It's what I do." She shrugged her shoulders. "See you tomorrow."

"Yeah."

When she took her leave, I took inventory of my workload and realized that for the first time in months I was able to leave work at a decent time. Before dinner.

I locked my office, pocketed my keys, and headed out, waving to the few of my employees that remained. The look of surprise at my early departure on their faces was comical.

I drove toward my house and then decided to take a detour. I wasn't in the mood to eat alone.

Circling the block a few times before deciding to stop and park, I walked up the front steps and rang.

Jordan answered. "Uncle Mike, what are you doing here?"

"Hello to you too." I fist-bumped my nephew and walked in. "Any room for an extra person at the dinner table?" I walked into the kitchen and watched Jake in action.

"You're not at work!"

Danica's shock had me laughing. "Thanks for that. Nicole might not be my biggest fan, but the woman looks good and knows how to work."

"Sounds like someone's got a crush," Jordan singsonged.

"Pipe down kid!" I told him.

"I think he might be right," Jake said with a smile.

"Guys!" Danica's warning tone came out. "There's nothing going on with those two, they're all kinds of wrong for each other."

"Some people would have said the same thing about us." Jake wrapped himself around her back and rubbed her humongous belly. "Look at us now." She turned her head sideways to meet her husband's lips.

"Damn you guys make it look easy." I took a seat at the table, pouring myself a glass of iced water and downing half of it in two gulps.

"Do I sense a change of heart?" Danica asked with a smirk, her arms folded over her husband's.

My thoughts about needing a change from the last two nights came to mind. "Maybe."

"Told you, man, it gets old quick…and lonely."

I nodded. Oh, how right Jake was.

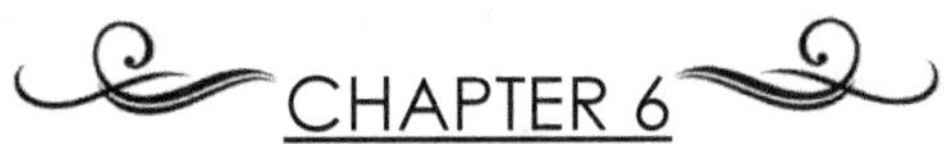

CHAPTER 6

It was early—only ten—but I found myself at home, in front of the TV, hearing my phone buzzing incessantly on the table next to me. My phone never buzzed at night.

Picking the device up to check things out, I saw more updates to my itinerary. Why the hell was Nicole working at ten o'clock at night?

I opened up my email and began to type away.

> *Nicole,*
> *Just because you're the CEO's assistant and getting paid the big bucks doesn't mean you need to be working around the clock.*
> *Relax.*
> *See you in the morning,*
> *Jackass Boss*

Despite my message, the buzzing of my phone continued and was now keeping me awake regardless of my dedication to an early bedtime. I turned the thing off, left it on my bedside table, and resolved to have a chat with my over-productive personal assistant come morning.

When my eyes closed for the final time, Nicole was all I saw. And it wasn't the bitchy, turn-her-nose-up-at-me woman, but the sweet, demure, and shy one I knew while growing up.

Friday had finally arrived and I got to the office, expecting to be alone as always, but to my surprise, Nicole was already sitting at her desk.

"Morning!" I said. "You're early, did you sleep at all last night?"

"Of course!" she snapped.

"Nicole?" I waited until she looked up at me. "Can we have a chat in my office for a moment?"

She averted her gaze to her desk, the worried look she wore was nothing less than adorable.

Don't kid yourself…she'll claw your eyes out if given the chance. I snorted at the thought as I headed toward my desk.

She shut the door behind her before taking a seat across from me. "Is something wrong? I'm sorry for snapping. It's been…a rough night, I guess."

"Don't worry about it," I said. "I couldn't help but notice that you seem to be…uh…a little overly productive."

"What do you mean? You said to keep you up to date and that's what I've been doing. I don't have my work phone yet, so I got your appointments to call my personal cell, so we could get them all in the books, and the rest I tackled from my remote connection."

"Yeah…during work hours. Your time off is your time off, didn't you get my email?"

"I did. I'm sorry." She looked away for a moment and then back at me. "I just thought that since you're so far behind that I'd put a dent into things. Plus–"

"It's fine. Really." She released the breath she was holding. "You look tired. Is everything all right?"

"Of course!" She avoided my gaze. "I just couldn't sleep so I figured I'd work."

"Hmm." I eyed her.

The room filled with awkward silence.

"Is that all?"

"Oh…uh…yeah." She got up and left my office as if her hair was on fire.

That night, there were no notifications. Funny how after months of not hearing my phone go off that I suddenly missed the disturbance that only last night had brought.

CHAPTER 7

I showed up for Sunday dinner at Danica and Jake's as per usual. What I hadn't expected was to run into an unsuspecting Nicole who seemed to be in a rush to get out the door.

"Whoa! Slow down!" I grabbed onto her shoulders. Running head-on into each other had become somewhat of a usual occurrence for us. I smiled at that, but it didn't last when I took in her tear-stained face. "Hey, what's wrong?"

She shook her head and when I tried to slide my hands off her shoulders and onto her upper arms in what I hoped to be a comforting gesture, she ripped herself from my grip. "Fuck off!" Then she ran to her car, got in it and drove off.

What the hell?

I walked into the house and slammed the door.

"What the–? Oh, it's you." Danica looked irritated.

I pointed my thumb over my shoulder. "You mind telling me what her problem is?"

"It's nothing."

"Didn't look like it."

"It's none of your business," Danica snapped.

At that moment, I saw Jake poke his head through the patio door. "Hey, Mike, we're out back."

"Be right there. Are you okay?" I asked my sister.

She nodded. "I'm fine. Just worried about her, that's all." She sniffled.

"Hey," I pulled her in for a hug, "it'll be all right, whatever it is." I rubbed her back as she cuddled into me.

"But–"

"You told him?" We jumped at Nicole's voice, coming from the doorway.

Where the hell had she come from?

"No!" Danica said.

"Oh! I'm just back for my purse." She reached for the item on the table by the door, "I'll go."

"Can I have a word with you?" I asked her.

"I can't. I have to go." The fact that her eyes aimed themselves everywhere but on me hinted how uncomfortable she was.

"It's only for a minute."

With a huff, she said, "Fine." The woman walked up to Danica and I heard her whisper something in my sister's ear. They looked at each other and Nicole walked out. I followed.

"Listen, if you need–"

"I'm fine, all right?" Then, she mumbled something indiscernible under her breath and looked at me. "Look, I'm sorry for telling you where to go earlier. You caught me by surprise and at a really bad time. Have a safe flight out and I'll see you on Wednesday."

"Sure."

With that, she got in her car and drove off.

I walked into the house to find Jordan, Danica and Jake, in that order, standing before me, each of them sporting a smirk.

"What?" I asked. "I was just making sure she's okay."

"Yeah, yeah." Jordan rolled his eyes.

"Uh…huh!" Jake added.

"What the hell?" was what came out of Danica's mouth before her eyes shot to the floor. "Oh my God!" She looked up at all of us and Jake's eyes grew with realization.

"It's time!" he shouted and darted for the stairs. "Jordan, turn off the grill. Mike, get her in the car. I'll go get the bags."

Jake in panic mode was a great source of entertainment. I

knew there'd be enough time to razz him later, so I did as he instructed, and so did Jordan.

Five minutes later, Jake had yet to join us. Leaving my sister and nephew in the car, I went in search of the man in question to see what was taking him so long.

As I stepped through the threshold, I found him sitting on the stair landing with his wife's and their babies' hospital bags between his legs, his head in his hands. He looked up at me and I saw sheer terror mirrored in his eyes.

"What if something goes wrong? What if she has the babies on the way? What if–"

"Brother, she'll have them on the way if we don't hurry up. Your wife needs you to have a straight head right now, so get your shit together and let's go Daddy." I patted him on the back.

That seemed to have done the trick. Jake snapped out of it and gave me a beaming smile as he got to his feet. "I'm going to be a Daddy!" He grinned, emanating with pride.

I harrumphed. "Reality check, you already are."

"Yeah, but this is from the get-go," he said. "Fuck! Let's go!" He ran out to the driver's side.

"Oh no you don't!" I grabbed his shoulder and pushed him toward the back seat. "I'm driving. I won't have a loopy father-to-be getting us into an accident on the way there, I value my life too much. Take care of your wife."

I sat with Jordan in the waiting area, no word on what was going on. The last bit of news was given to us nearly two hours before, and Danica had been fully dilated and about to begin to push by then. I worried about my sister, the twins, Jordan, and Jake too.

Footsteps came barreling down the hallway and Jake's parents came into the room with a panicked looking Nicole on their heels.

"How is she? Did she have them? How do they look?" Jake's mother fired.

I shook my head. "No news since I called."

Nicole leaned back against a wall as Jake's mother took a seat beside Jordan.

"Are you okay, sweetie?" she asked my nephew. The kid nodded, but I could tell he was just as worried as I was. The woman cradled his head in her chest and hugged him tight, while Jake's dad stood beside her, his hand on her shoulders. Nicole remained a silent observer.

Knowing that Jordan was taken care of, I began to pace the hallway, left to deal with my own apprehension.

A hand on my arm had me stopping.

"Coffee?" Nicole asked.

"I could use it."

"You know it'll be fine, right?" she said when we were far enough away from the others.

My hand brushed down my face and rubbed at the scruff on my cheek. "God, I hope so."

"Just so you know, I cancelled your trip." She smiled at me. "Winthrow sends his congratulations and expects pictures."

I chuckled. "You're an angel sent from God."

"God wasn't the one who sent me, your sister was." She winked.

I smirked. "Smartass!"

"Jackass!" She chortled.

"Be nice," I warned. "I'm your boss."

"Not outside of work you're not." The light danced in her eyes.

"You seem happier than earlier."

"It's not hard when your best friend's–"

A man stopped right behind her and interrupted before she could finish. "Nicole, what are you doing here?"

Nicole's body stiffened and my brow arched at her reaction.

"Landen-Withers family?" I heard from behind me, and I pulled Nicole with me, but she didn't budge.

I turned to see what the hold-up was and the mystery man had latched on to her other arm.

"Can we talk? Please?"

"I have nothing to say to you." She attempted to pull her arm from him, but his grip stayed firm.

"Come on." He looked determined. "Don't be like that."

"The lady said she has nothing to say to you," I said, taking notice of the glistening of her eyes. "Let go of her."

"Who's he?" Mystery Man asked.

"Uh…my…" She cleared her throat.

"Her boyfriend. Come on, baby." Again, I attempted to pull her along. When she didn't budge, I turned back to Mystery Man, but it wasn't him holding her back this time, it was she who had halted. I positioned myself in front of her and cradled her face between my palms. I bent forward to gaze into her eyes. "Honey, we have to go, they're calling for us."

She gave me a curt nod.

"Your boyfriend, huh?" The man smirked. "Listen, Lisa's out of town for the weekend and since you're here…"

Who the hell was this guy and why wasn't he giving up? My arms dropped to my side and my fists clenched. "Seriously! You're propositioning my girl in front of me?"

"She's not your girl."

"Really?" I smirked and a wicked idea came to mind. I hoped that Nicole would play along, and that I didn't pay for it later. Then again, I'd rather see her mad than on the verge of tears like she was right now.

I kept hold of the sides of Nicole's face and leaned in, brushing her lips with mine and pulled away to look her in the eyes before leaning into her again. She responded upon contact this time. To any onlooker, the kiss looked sweet. Her hands landed on my chest and I hoped that the shiver I felt coming from her was one of enjoyment, and not of revulsion.

When I pulled away, she gave me a look that I couldn't quite read. Her lips had tasted of coffee and something sweet mixed with cinnamon and I found that I wanted to kiss her again.

"I get it," the man said. "Sorry, man. I just thought that you were like all the others."

The others?

"Get lost, Dean." Nicole's eyes blinked and fury appeared in those emerald orbs. "Come on!" She grabbed my shirt and tugged me toward Jordan and the rest of the family. "You and I are going to talk later," she whispered as we got further away from the man named Dean, and I didn't need to look behind me to know that the guy was still watching us. I felt the man's frustrated gaze burning into my back.

She dropped her hand from my shirtfront and I threw an arm around her shoulders, pulling her into my side. "He's still watching," I whispered in her ear and felt her shudder.

She grumbled. "Cut it out!"

Danica and the babies were doing well, despite the labor having been difficult. The doctor informed us that we'd be able to go in once they brought her to a private room.

Relieved, my ass fell to the nearest free chair, nearly missing its edge. I cradled my head in my hands.

A pair of shoes made their way into my field of vision and I looked up into fiery green eyes. My fatigue was potent, but I was glad that I could feel something other than worry at this point—mainly apprehension at incurring Nicole's wrath from that earlier display. She blinked and then her features softened. "Are you okay?"

"Funny…I thought I should be asking you the same thing," My voice was void of humor. "Who was that asshole anyway?"

"Who…Dean?" I gave her a *duh* look. She looked at the wall, just past my shoulder. "Just an ex."

"Just an ex, huh?"

"About that…um…" she whispered, looking around for prying ears.

I smirked. "Kiss?"

Her shiftiness came back, accompanied by a blush. She nodded, swallowed hard. "It can't happen again."

"Don't worry about it. You needed help and I knew what would work."

"Thanks…I think." She met my eyes for a brief moment and then took the seat next to mine.

"You're welcome." I leaned my head back onto the wall and closed my eyes. "For the record," I turned my head to look at her, "you deserve much better than that prick."

She nodded, looking down at her hands for a long moment before she shot back to her feet. "I should go. Get some sleep before work."

"I think your boss will be fine if you took a day off."

"Yeah, but it won't pay the bills will it?"

"Don't worry so much. If you need an advance, all you have to do is ask," I said. "Stay. She's your best friend, you're like family to her."

"But what'll everyone at work think when we're both not there?" she asked. "I'm not getting sucked into some forbidden office romance rumor."

I laughed. "They can talk all they want. I'll just fire their asses."

She giggled. "Well that's a bit much, don't you think?"

"Fine. You can pretend to dislike me around the office," I joked. "So long as you're ready to take what I dish out right back."

"Just don't make me cry like you used to," she said.

My heart sunk at her revelation. "I made you cry?"

"It was a long time ago, Mike," she said as if it was nothing. "I was an over-emotional teenager. It's nothing."

"No, it's not." I felt like a class-A jerk. "For what it's worth, I'm sorry."

"Like I said, it's in the past. I'm fine." She gave me a brief look before looking down.

Fine. Yeah right!

If there's one thing I've learned in my thirty-six years, it was that a woman was never fine when she said she was.

CHAPTER 9

A week had gone by and my rescheduled trip to Austin was approaching. Since the restructure, things had gotten out of control and Winthrow, the Vice-President of that particular location, had requested that I hang around for a few days to sort out additional things. Needless to say, with all the board meetings, I needed some assistance, and I was sure that Winthrow had a hidden agenda somewhere in there, as was the custom.

"Nicole, can you come in here?" She waltzed in within seconds. "I'm going to need you with me in Austin," I said without lifting my head from the paperwork before me.

She fidgeted. "I can't!"

"I need you there, Nikki." I didn't hear confirmation or defiance, so I looked up at her. She looked nervous. "What is it?"

"Nothing…it's nothing." She took a deep breath. "Fine, I'll go."

"Good. I'll have a car pick you up and meet me at the airport by seven on Monday morning."

"Yes, sir," she said, and then I could have sworn I heard her mumble *jackass* as she walked away. The moniker made me smile.

"And Nikki?" She popped her head through the doorway. "Bring something nice for an evening out while we're there. I wouldn't be surprised if Winthrow took us out somewhere fancy during our stay."

"Sure." She looked far from enthused.

I sat back and watched Nicole return to her desk. She

looked troubled and for some reason, despite my asking her, I knew it was useless to inquire further about her sudden discomfort.

For a week now, since that kiss in the hospital hallway, I had imagined kissing Nicole again. The taste of her, the feel…it hadn't been enough. I wanted to bump into that Dean character all over just so I could have a repeat.

Maybe she'd give in just a little bit more.

Maybe it would be enough to quench my sudden thirst for the complex woman.

To be honest, I was shocked that she hadn't tried to tear me a new one for the stunt at the hospital. Hell, I was curious as to why she hadn't pulled away or denied our fictitious involvement since I repulsed her so much.

Maybe it's because you don't?

I walked out of my office and stopped by her desk on my way out for a late lunch. "Why don't you take off early today?"

"What?" She looked at me perplexed. "Do you not want me here? Am I not performing to your satisfaction?"

Heat suffused my face. "Excuse me?" My blood simmered. I grabbed her arm and pulled her toward my office.

"What are you doing?"

Door closed, I got in her face. "I was giving you the afternoon off because you look like something was on your mind. You don't want to talk about it, that's fine. All of your work is done for the day, and it's Friday. People generally enjoy getting an early start to their weekend. I thought that you'd appreciate the gesture, what with all of the great work you've done. And as for your decreased perception of me, I'd appreciate it if you left that outside of work. For the record, I'm not who you've made me out to be in that thick head of yours. Get out of my office!" I sat down at my desk with my head tilted back against the headrest, eyes closed and my hands pulling at my hair.

The door opened and closed with a slam.

I groaned, rubbing my hands down my face in exasperation.

Damn woman!

CHAPTER 10

By Monday, I hadn't had a decent night's sleep in three days; haunted by dreams of a certain PA that indulged me in a few provocative scenarios. To my chagrin, when the woman met up with me at our terminal gate, she was far from the accommodating woman of my dreams.

Nicole acknowledged me, filled me in on a few changes in my itinerary, and answered with yes's and no's unless she had to elaborate on something. It was clear she was disgruntled.

When she boarded the plane ahead of me, Nicole tensed, making me wonder.

"Have you not flown before?" She shook her head to indicate the negative. "Never?" I had the urge to laugh, but one glimpse at her petrified face as she took her seat had my humor dissipating. She was sitting by the window and instead of being positioned to look out, she'd shut the partition and turned her body toward the aisle. "The view on a clear day like today is breathtaking, and here you are looking freaked out. Do you want to switch seats?"

"I'm fine." Her voice croaked. Despite knowing that she'd have to travel, it was clear to me that she'd forgone the conclusion that travelling would encompass flying to some of our destinations. To be honest, I didn't drive anywhere for business; the distances being too great and time was of the essence in my business.

"You know it's the safest way to travel, right?" I pointed out in an attempt to reassure her.

"Can you just stop talking?"

After a few minutes, the plane started taxiing the runway. Despite her snappy persona, I kept a close eye on my travel companion. She had gone from tense and uncomfortable to full on panicked.

Nicole's eyes were a stormy sea green, and her tanned face had shifted to the color of a pale white sheet. She wasn't faring well. So I grabbed her hand and held it. That got her attention. I turned to look forward so that she didn't know that I was watching her.

"Relax," I whispered.

She tried to pull her hand out, but when the plane jutted forward, gathering speed for take-off, her grip tightened, her manicured nails digging into my palm painfully. "Oh-my-god-oh-my-god-oh-my-god!"

"Breathe, you'll be fine."

"That's what they said about all of those flights that have fallen out of the sky." Her sarcasm was potent.

The cabin began to shake as we encountered a bit of turbulence while the plane gained altitude.

When her other hand clasped the top of our already joined ones, I was quick to reassure her. "It's normal." Next thing I knew, her eyes were shut tight and tears began to fall. "Hey, we're fine. You'll be fine. Just breathe." She was practically hyperventilating and the last thing I was looking for was a scene that would freak the passengers out. "Nikki, look at me." She shook her head despite my soft approach. "Nicole, look at me now!" I demanded on a quiet tone that brokered no argument. She did it with reluctance. "Good…you're okay." I cupped her cheek with my free hand. "Just keep looking at me and breathe. Don't you pass out on me!" I warned, crooking my lip up on one side, but her eyes found no humor in the moment at all.

When the turbulence subsided and we reached maximum altitude, the flight smoothed out.

I got Nicole a few drinks, limiting her to two. She could use them. The flight attendant commented that it was early, then relented when she took one assessing look at Nicole's demeanor.

"Are you okay?" My assistant's left hand still clutched my right, but had relaxed some.

"Yeah." She lifted the window partition and took a quick glance, her face, which had gained some color, ashened.

I patted her hand. "We'll get you something for the way back."

She whimpered. "I think I might rent a car and drive." Her comment lacked her usual sarcasm.

"That would take too long. It's a day and a half drive, Nicole."

She muttered a curse. "I don't know if I can do this again."

"You can." My thumb traced soothing circles on the top of her hand. She pulled it away and put it in her lap. "You'll get used to it. The trick is to do it regularly."

She snorted. "I'll take your word for it."

I turned to face the front and smiled to myself.

She'll see.

Hands clawing at my sleeve, grabbing—pain is what woke me.

"Something's wrong! I feel like we're falling!" When I looked down, Nicole's face was pressed into the side of my arm, one hand clutching my hand again and the other, wrapped around my bicep, digging its nails in. At that point, I was thankful for my suit jacket, because it was the sole

barrier that kept her from breaking skin as she dug her claws into me.

"We're making our descent," I explained. "It means we're getting closer to landing."

"You mean crashing!" came muffled into my sleeve. I

chuckled. "It's not funny!" she whisper-yelled at me. "We're going down too fast!"

"This is normal, Nikki." I felt her body quiver against my arm.

With the bit of turbulence we experienced on our final approach, Nicole was glued to me, and had she been able to be unbuckled, I was sure she'd have been on my lap. Her face was in my neck and the arm she had been holding on to was now wrapped around her shoulders. Her entire body shook against me, but it was her whimpers that broke my heart.

When the plane had stopped moving, Nicole wasn't making signs of letting go.

"Nicole," I said in her ear, "we're here."

No response.

"Nikki?"

Nothing.

"Honey, it's time to get off the plane." I ran my hand in the hair at the back of her head.

I felt her take a deep breath and pull away. "I'm sorry." She blushed and the seatbelt sign flickered off. Her demeanor changed from one of embarrassment to one of anger or frustration, it was hard to tell. "Next time, you can have the window seat. I'm out of here!" She stood up, almost bumping her head on the overhead storage compartment, and stepped over my legs to make her way down the aisle, leaving her carry-on behind. I shook my head at her, a smile present on my face.

"You're welcome!" I called out to her, taking both our bags out of the overhead storage compartment.

"Jackass!" she cursed, and I ignored the dirty looks that were aimed my way.

"You have to love that love-hate thing she's got for me. I'm cute enough to cuddle with on a plane when she's freaked out, but I'm not good enough for the real world," I said to my audience. I got a few nods and chuckles from some of the men surrounding me, along with sympathetic expressions from other passengers.

We arrived at WI's Austin office by hired car, and Nicole had yet to say a word to me since we'd vacated the plane. She was busy checking email on her phone and I could tell that my itinerary would be filled for the next few weeks, just by the way the damn thing was buzzing in my jacket pocket.

When the doors opened, she was quick to step out and walk through the building's front doors, leaving me behind with her bags yet again.

Inside, she stopped at the business boards to check which floor the office was located on and I passed by her saying, "Follow me." Soon enough, I heard the clicking of her heels fall in stride beside me.

We came to a stop at the bank of elevators and I motioned for her to precede me when the doors opened. Up to the top floor we went, and when the doors cleared, we were met with a posh and quiet reception area.

"Mike!" Damien, my head of communications greeted us. "Winthrow is waiting for us in his office. Who's this?" He swept past me and captured Nicole's hand.

"Nicole Baxter. I'm Mike's PA." Her tone held a sharp edge as my name escaped her lips.

"Damien." He tried to woo her with a kiss on the top of her hand, but she pulled it out of his grasp before his lips could make contact.

Smile forced, posture stiff, she said, "Nice to meet you."

Damien looked at me with a questioning look, and I knew he was asking if we were involved. I shook my head.

"You ready for this?" he asked me.

"Am I ever ready for one of Winthrow's pitches?" I sighed. "Let's see what he's got for us this time."

CHAPTER 11

"No!" I said with finality. "I'm not risking it, George. We've been over this before. If it doesn't work, I stand to lose half the damn company. I doubt you're prepared to answer for the loss of livelihood for most of the people in this office, because I'm sure as hell not going to be closing down the Jacksonville location. We're still not remotely close to being in the clear from the stunt Dad pulled."

"Listen, I know it's a huge risk, but it could pay off, Mike. You haven't even taken a look at the research yet. The numbers prove that if we run this crisis management pitch for Fleishman, the way I know we can, it'll be the thing to set us back on top." Winthrow handed me the bound booklet he'd prepared and I handed it to Nicole without giving it a glance.

"I can't, George," I said.

"Wait!" Our heads snapped in Nicole's direction. Her head was bent, her nose buried in the opened booklet I had handed her. "This could work!" Her gaze met mine.

"Nicole." I sent her a non-verbal cut-it-out message with my glare.

"No!" She shocked me with her adamancy. "I think that George might be right on this. It might be what we need to propel us further in the industry. Just look at these graphs. There's nothing here that suggests that Fleishman is carrying a trend that'll sink us. If you look closer, it's quite the opposite." She tried to show me, but I ignored them. "I think Danica should take a look at this and give us her opinion on overall cost and profit, don't you?"

She was challenging my authority, but she did have a point. As annoying as it was, she was still not going to get me to concede.

"My answer isn't going to change." I stood up and ran my hands through my hair. "I'm done discussing this. We've been at this all day, and we haven't even tackled half the issues on the docket that's brought me here. I'm heading to the hotel and expect tomorrow to go as planned. No more surprises, George." I walked to the door and paused. "Nicole, are you coming?"

I caught her whispering to George, and Damian was stifling a laugh when he noticed the irritation on my face as I overheard the last she'd said.

"Work on me?" I chortled. "I'd like to see that."

"Pipe down, you baby." She walked past me, smirking as she patted my cheek.

George chuckled. "I like this new assistant of yours, Withers."

"You like her now because she's siding with you. Be ready for tomorrow's meet with the board. Goodnight."

I shut George's office door and marched toward the elevators. Nicole had her bag and seemed pleased with herself. That just served to annoy me further.

"What?" I asked as I noticed her watching me on our ride down.

"Are you always like this?"

"Like what?"

"Like a five-year-old pulling a tantrum whenever something doesn't go your way." She laughed. "Look at you!"

"You shouldn't have said anything back there."

"Why not? I'm a business major! I may have never run a large corporation, but I sure as hell did well for myself back when I had my business." She crossed her arms over her chest with smugness.

"You're new to Withers International and I don't expect you to know the ins and outs of my company right off the bat. You have no idea how many times Winthrow's suggested something similar to this before, and how many times my father took him up on his ideas, only to lose millions on dead-end deals!" I ended my rant on a growl. "It's just like you to judge before knowing all the facts."

"I don't need to know all the facts about what Winthrow did or didn't do before now. I took a look at a proposal and thought it would be good business. The facts that were presented were all the facts I needed to give my professional opinion on," she defended. "I know what I'm talking about, and Danica will more than agree with my opinion and support George with this Fleishman project. There are always risks, but you can't thrive if you're not willing to take chances, Mike. You should know that better than anyone."

"I don't need your professional opinion." It clicked that she mentioned she'd had a business, so I played into that. "And what happened to that little business of yours, Nikki?" I towered over her. She backed away, landing herself in the corner, looking trapped.

"Well…I-I gave it up."

I smirked knowingly. "You flopped."

"No." She couldn't meet my eyes.

"Really, then why?"

"Because I was tired of it, okay?" She tried to push me away. "Back off!"

I didn't. I stayed put, staring her down. There was a lot more to that story of hers, and I was bound and determined to get to the bottom of it.

My tone softened as I leaned closer. "Why?" I could see that giving her business up hadn't been a positive move for her.

"I had my reasons. I don't want to talk about it." Her voice shook. "Now will you please back off?"

This time I did.

But the conversation was far from over. If she hadn't run her business into the ground and she loved it so much, why the hell wasn't she still running it? And what had it been?

Don't kid yourself, you want to know a hell of a lot more than that.

Arriving at the hotel, I helped Nicole with her bag and checked us both in. We had rooms down the hall from one another so I escorted her to her door.

"Have dinner with me tonight," I blurted out when we stopped at her room.

She got her door open and held it ajar, turning to me. "I don't think so. Office hours are up. I'm done with you for one day."

"A simple no would have sufficed." I walked away adding a mumbled, "Ice queen."

"What was that?"

I turned and marched back to her.

She'd let her door close against her suitcase and there she stood with her hands on her hips, fire brewing in her eyes.

"I called you a fucking ice queen," I said. "For someone who's so smart with business, it amazes me that you can be so damn stupid in your personal life. You might want to practice what you preach on taking chances. It applies to everyday life too, honey."

She stood there like a fish out of water; her mouth opening and closing as if trying to come up with something.

"Don't call me that!"

"You're right, honey doesn't suit you. You're more sour and tart than anything sweet. Other than that, you're frigid and blind to everyone around you."

She stood there, looking as if someone had gutted her for a moment. I felt awful and was on the verge of apologizing for running off at the mouth, when she decided to read me the riot act.

"Don't you dare stand there and pretend you know me!" We stood toe-to-toe. "We may have grown up together, but you have no clue who I am or what I've been through since you left."

"It goes both ways."

Somehow, in the middle of our argument, I realized how much fun it was to spar with her. She gave as good as she got, and there was something sexy about the blaze in her eyes and the presence this tiny spitfire could project.

"I suppose you might be right, but I still maintain my initial opinion about you."

"Why are you so bitter about that anyway?" I guessed aloud. "Bad experience?"

Bingo!

She didn't answer with words, but the stricken look on her face told me everything I needed to know. She'd been crossed before, and if I took a guess, her ex was the culprit.

"Something tells me that Dean might have played a part in that." Her face darkened and hurt flashed through her eyes. I took a step toward her and grabbed her chin gently so I could tilt her face up, read her expression in its entirety. "I've got it pegged, don't I?"

She pulled her face out of my grasp and stepped back. "You know nothing!"

"No!" I shook my head. "You know nothing. Just because you've made some poor choices with men in the past and they turned out to be total jackasses, doesn't mean that we're all the same. Is it so hard to believe that just because we're not committed, that we're capable of being good men?" Guilt crossed her face and I continued in a gentler fashion. "Open your eyes, Nikki, there's a whole world out there!"

"And I suppose that you're out to sample every last tasty morsel there is?"

The smidgeon of empathy I felt for her dissipated and anger took over. "If that's what you're determined to think, then go ahead," I said. "I can see it's pointless to convince you otherwise and I'm done justifying myself to you. It wouldn't matter if I told you I hadn't been with anyone in a month...two...or three, you still wouldn't believe me."

"You're right." She huffed, "I don't! And newsflash,

that's not a miraculous feat, Michael." The click of the locks was heard and next thing I knew, I was face-to-face with her door and a muffled, "Goodnight!" followed.

CHAPTER 12

Part of me was relieved that Nicole had retreated and shut herself in her room. The tension between us had grown so thick that I was on the verge of doing something stupid. Like kissing her.

She's trouble, I reminded myself, plus, you gave her your word you wouldn't make a move.

After dropping my luggage off and ordering a room service dinner I'd only picked at, I headed down to the hotel's bar and found a stool.

"Two shots of whiskey and a beer chaser," I told the bartender. With a nod, the man went to work.

Most of the next hour was spent watching football, which was interrupted in the third quarter by a familiar giggle. I turned to find the source of said giggle, and promptly jumped to my feet, heading toward the exit, hoping to all hell that I wasn't spotted when my escape entailed walking past her.

Thinking I was in the clear, I was proven wrong when my name was called out.

"It is you!" The woman got up and launched herself at me after I'd turned to face the music.

"Tracey," I said, less than charmed.

"You're back?"

I pulled her arms from around my neck and set her back. "Just for business. Listen–"

"Oh, Mikey!" I welcomed the interruption and turned to

find Nicole heading in our direction with what I can only describe as a strut meant to seduce. "I've been looking all over for you, baby." When she reached us, she subtly wedged herself between me and my ex, pressing her front into my arm.

I detected a slight scent of wine and chocolate on her breath as I peered down at her. Was she drunk? "Nicole?" was all I could manage, too shocked at the turn of events.

"Who's this?" Tracey asked, arms crossed at her chest and stiletto tapping on the floor.

"My…" But the words evaded me.

"His girlfriend," she said and looked proud of it, extending her hand, "and you are?"

"His fiancée!" she stated on a dry tone.

Nicole turned to me. "I thought you said she was your ex-fiancée?"

I have to admit, Nicole was convincing.

My gaze left Nicole's and set itself on Tracey. "She is."

By then, I'd gotten over my shock. I wrapped my arm around Nicole's shoulders and pulled her into me.

"Babe, you remember what we talked about earlier?" Nicole went on and I nodded, choosing to keep playing her game. At least it got Tracey to back off. My savior got closer, crooking her finger so my face lowered to her height. "I want more." She pressed her tits into my chest and gave me a peck on the lips. Just as quick as her lips touched mine, they disappeared and she stepped back.

"I'll be right behind you," I told Nicole.

"See you up there, sexy." She winked at me and sent Tracey a nasty look before retreating from the bar.

"Tracey, I wish I could say it was good to see you, but we both know it's not. Go back to your date, I've got to go!"

Taking my leave, I high-tailed it out of there, and caught up with Nicole who was waiting at the bank of elevators.

"Glad to see she stayed behind." Nicole's sarcasm was potent.

"Yeah, about that..." I motioned behind me with my head.

"I figured I owed you for how you helped me with Dean," she said. "When I saw you standing there, stiff as a board, I looked around you and realized who she was."

The elevator arrived and I motioned for her to go ahead of me.

"How do you know about her?"

"Danica showed me a few pictures of you two after she moved back," she explained. "I don't know what happened between you two, only that you were together and getting married one minute, and then you weren't."

"Oh."

I walked Nicole to her door. "Nice delivery on that scene by the way."

"I'll take that as a thank you," she blushed, "but it doesn't mean anything."

"What were you doing down there anyway?"

"Having a drink."

"Alone?"

She shook her head. "Damian joined me. I saw him off and noticed you."

"You had drinks with Damian?" Jealousy was an ugly sentiment, but I recognized it for what it was. "Was it a date?"

"Oh, hell no! He's not my type."

"Good," I said and felt myself calm, "because he's a player in every sense of the word."

"Takes one to know one."

"And there you go ruining a nice conversation." I sighed. "Goodnight, Nic."

"What, no more fight left?" She was goading me?

I paused and shook my head. "Goodnight."

"Mr. Player is out of words!" I could hear the smile in her voice. "Wow!"

Enough! I turned and ended up with her backed against her door. She gulped and looked up at me.

"Honey, if you're going to play the game, play it right." My voice had gone husky.

"Are you insinuating that I'm playing you?"

"You couldn't play me even if you tried," I told her with an air of smugness, smirking for effect. "It's not like you."

"Really?"

"Really." My eyes paused on her parted lips before they moved to her eyes.

"I bet I could give you a run for your money." She ran a fingertip down my cheek. "You see, I know how you guys work." My head bent toward hers. "So I know what it takes to…"

I licked my dry lips. "To what, Nic?"

I felt her breath on my face. "To…um…"

My lips crashed onto hers and there was no doubt that she was interested in what I had to offer at the moment. Her arms wound around my neck, pulling me in, and when I traced the seam of her lips with my tongue, she moaned, opening to let me invade her mouth.

For a quick moment, it felt like a current flowed between us, and then the moment broke like a slap in the face…

Wait a minute!

Hand to cheek, the sting radiated heat under my palm as I realized I had indeed been slapped.

I backed up a few steps, letting my arms fall at my sides, and looked at a shocked Nicole who held a hand over her mouth, shock at her actions all too evident.

"Mike–"

"Like I said…you couldn't play me if you tried." I smirked at her and started for my own room. "You're not capable of that," I added over my shoulder.

I felt her gaze on my back the entire way to my room. The door shut behind me and a few seconds passed before I heard the discernible click of hers.

Heart racing, I cursed at the effects this latest altercation had brought. Nicole was getting under my skin and I wasn't sure if there was anything I could do to stop it.

CHAPTER 13

I tossed.

I turned.

I couldn't sleep.

I paced my suite so many damn times that it was surprising that my feet hadn't worn through the plush Berber carpeting.

What seemed like hours later, I found myself down at the hotel's gym, trying to work out my frustrations. No matter how much I did, I couldn't get rid of the feel of Nicole's lips pressed against mine, her tiny frame wrapped around my body, her taste, her smell…

Fuck!

Walking away from the gym, I knew I wouldn't be able to find sleep despite the physical exhaustion I had subjected myself to. Pausing at Nicole's room's door, I heard the television's low chatter. Somehow, knowing that she too seemed to be having issues with insomnia satisfied me. I kept moving toward my room, my foot catching on something when I walked over the threshold.

A note.

Jackass,

If it's a game you want to play, I'll play it to your little heart's content. Fair warning though…I NEVER LOSE.

Yours truly,

Ice Queen

And here I had been debating an apology for my earlier words and actions.

I shook my head, letting my ass drop to bed's edge before picking up my phone to dial Nicole's room's number.

She picked up on the first ring.

"Are you sure you want to do this?"

"You scared?"

*No. Nervous...crazy...*I chortled. "Hardly! Game's on!" I declared and hung up.

At some point in the wee hours of the morning, I managed to fall asleep.

It was the pounding on my door that had me jumping three feet off the bed and rushing to answer it the next day.

Where the fuck is the fire?

"Why hello, handsome!" Nicole stood there smirking at me, looking like she'd had a full night's sleep, and then I realized I was in nothing more than my boxers. The wicked gleam in her eyes couldn't be missed. "Maybe I should have brought up this little game of ours sooner. Working for you does have its perks." My jaw dropped at her words. When she made to walk in, I backed away from her. "You should be dressed and ready to go by now, Mr. Withers. I guess I'll meet you at the office."

She made for the door, but I caught up to her, wrapping my arm around her waist and pressing my front into her back.

"I think you can wait," I rasped in her ear.

"This isn't a good time to show you how it's done." Her words held humor.

"I'm sure you'd love that." I nipped her ear. A whoosh of air left her lungs. "I bet I could show you a thing or two myself." My words were laced with promise and my erection proved my utmost capability. I rubbed it on her skirted backside.

"Mike." Her voice had gone a few octaves lower, raw and

sexy. She turned in my arms and set her palms down on my bare chest. She whispered, "We're going to be late," against my lips.

Before I could lay one on her, she backed away. "Tease!" I growled.

She smirked. "You asked for it, stud. Now, get dressed so we can go, please. I have no urge to have to explain our tardiness when, only yesterday, you were the one to complain about wasting time. Do you?"

She was right, this game of ours would simply have to wait.

CHAPTER 14

On the way up to the Austin office, Nicole filled me in on the day's preparations. "I made sure that refreshments and everything else you requested were provided for today." Her businesslike tone was back. "We've got the phone system, projector, laser pointer–"

"Thank you. I'll need you to take today's minutes. I suspect that we might see fireworks before the day's end."

"I'm hoping!" Her double-entendre hadn't gone unnoticed, and I wondered what she was playing at. A few seconds later, she moved closer to my side. Next thing I knew, a gentle hand glided over my crotch. My breath caught.

As quick as it had happened, it was over.

I looked down at Nicole whose shoulders were bobbing up and down in silent laughter, her eyes trained forward.

I groaned. "I hope you're having fun."

"I'm enjoying myself…um…immensely." She looked down at my crotch and the ding of our lift was followed with its doors opening. The woman hurried off with a seductive sway to her hips.

Taking a cleansing breath, I followed.

"Good morning everyone!" Nicole proceeded to introduce herself with a handshake.

Men stood and shook my hand, nodding their approval of my new assistant.

If they only knew how much trouble she could be…

The day had gone great, with the exception of a few minor glitches. By glitches, I mean my focus being diverted on occasion by a certain someone's hand making its way onto my thigh. It wasn't so much the hand, but what the hand was doing: the gripping, stroking, it's subtle yet suggestive taunts. It was safe to say that I walked away from a day's worth of board meetings with a massive case of blue balls thanks to Nicole.

And we still had dinner to contend with.

It was six-thirty in the evening and I was knocking on Nicole's door for our anticipated dinner with Winthrow at some posh new restaurant of the man's choosing.

Nicole opened with a frantic look on her face. "Help me out, I'm stuck."

My eyes travelled the length of her body. She stood in black four-inch heels, one arm folded behind her, holding a champagne colored cocktail dress from falling off of her body.

This could be fun.

After an entire day of being at her mercy, payback could quite possibly be my own delight if I chose.

The door clicked shut behind me. "Turn around."

The minute my fingers touched the skin of her lower back to assess the situation, I saw the goosebumps spread on her skin. My lips tugged upward at her reaction. All was fair and all that jazz, right? "The zipper's snagged," I said, not putting forth much effort to get the material free. The zip slipped from my fingers with a jerk.

"What's the matter?"

"It's just more stuck than I thought it would be." I reached for the tab again and the scent of her perfume wafted toward me. Damn she smelled good. So good, I moved closer and nuzzled the tender skin behind her ear.

Her breathing had sped up and her coloring was flushed, but only slightly. "What are you doing?"

I nipped her earlobe to be greeted with the hiss of an exhale. "It would be so easy right now." My fingers freed the snagged material.

"Mike."

I zipped her up all the way. "There!" I said and patted her on the ass as I took a step away. "Let's go."

"Thanks," she muttered with an eye roll and passed me when I opened her room's door, her matching clutch in hand.

I grinned. "You're welcome, sweet cheeks."

CHAPTER 15

As always, the venue was upscale. The Mediterranean restaurant had it all: eclectic music that emitted sensuality, complementing décor, premium liquor, and a fabulous wait-staff. Winthrow had impeccable taste when it came to culinary institutions, and it sure showed by his waistline.

I found myself indulging in a drink after George had persuaded Nicole to dance with him.

Watching as the man sashayed her around, making her laugh, I felt envious of George for putting a smile so large on her face. These days, the woman radiated with glee, so long as I wasn't close to her.

"I haven't had that much fun dancing since before my wife passed," George said as they returned to their seats.

"I'm sorry for your loss." She leaned over the table's edge and put a hand over his. "I don't think I've ever danced with someone who knew how to handle a dance floor like that." She giggled. "Not for years anyway."

"Then you haven't seen this guy." George pointed toward me.

"Really?" Her eyes held a mischievous glint.

"If you think I'm good, he's Fred Astaire," he joked. "You should have seen him at last year's Christmas party."

"Is that so?" She tapped her chin with her index finger. "Interesting…"

"You don't believe him?" I asked.

The older man chuckled. "I think this girl's just invoked a challenge, Michael."

"I think you're right." I stood. With a smirk, I put my hand out for her to take. "Let's dance."

Nicole laughed and winked at George while accepting my invitation. "Show me what you've got, boss man."

The minute she put her hand in mine, I pulled her to her feet and into me. Her eyes went wide with surprise. I released my hold around her waist, twirled her and then proceeded to lead her toward the open floor.

The seductive tone of the music rendered it unsuspicious of our close proximity and so I took advantage of it. Her body molded perfectly to mine, pliable to my lead.

"Point proven!" She let out a sultry laugh. "Where did you learn all of this?"

"There are perks to dance lessons when you're prepping for a wedding." I looked past her, unwilling to let her see the resentment in my expression, although my tone was more than enough to convey it. "That was one of the things I did to keep Tracey happy."

As if she knew I didn't want to talk about my ex any more, she kept quiet until I broke in. "You don't seem too new to this sort of stuff either."

"I've been dancing since I was three."

"So those leggings and leotards weren't a new fashion trend you were trying to start?"

Nicole laughed. "I wasn't the best for clothes, but I was never that bad, Mike."

"I agree." Our eyes locked and I could swear the temperature ratcheted up a notch or two.

Nicole broke the connection first and looked in our table's direction. "We should get back. George looks lonely. Thanks for the dance." She tried to pull back, but I pulled her into me and gave her a sensuous dip. I bent forward toward her and followed her back up, our faces mere inches apart, her breath fanning over my lips with a hand on her thigh, holding her close.

I smiled. "You're welcome."

Disentangling ourselves, I wrapped her arm around mine and escorted her back to our table.

"You two looked comfortable out there," George said, "like two lovers just getting warmed up."

"Must have been the song." Nicole shrugged her shoulders and took a large sip of her wine, avoiding eye contact with me. "It's easy to make it look like that when you have a good partner."

"You two sure know how to make it look effortless," Winthrow said. "If I'd dipped a woman like that, I'd probably put my back out, or fall flat on my face, crushing my partner."

Nicole gave the man a polite smile and I chuckled. The aura of suspicion had evaporated and the three of us fell into another comfortable conversation.

When dinner was over, Winthrow got up to take his leave.

"You're off?" I asked.

He nodded. "This old fogy is in need of some sleep. I'll see you both tomorrow."

I shook his hand and he kissed Nicole on the cheek, bidding us both a good night.

"We should get going too," Nicole said when Winthrow had been gone for all of two minutes.

"Maybe you're right." I made to get up and offered her my hand.

On the ride back, the town car was silent with a ponderous Nicole. Her legs were crossed at the knee and the skirt of her dress had ridden up, exposing a generous amount of her bare thigh. My hand moved to trace dainty patterns on it.

She looked down at my hand. "W-what are you doing?"

"Having fun," I said with nonchalance.

The driver eyed us in the rearview mirror.

"Keep your hands off," she whispered. The increase in her breathing proved further that I was getting to her.

I leaned into her ear. "Why would I do that? You can't play this game according to your rules, Nic." I nipped her earlobe eliciting a shiver.

"Mike." I smiled, nuzzling the skin of her cheek and, whether she meant it or not, her head tilted toward my nose as if begging for more.

"You've caused me a lot of trouble today," I told her. "I think it's only fair that I collect."

"I thought that's what you did when you came to fetch me before dinner." She pulled away to look me in the eyes. "I'm not sleeping with you, Mike."

The car stopped at our destination. The driver exited and came around to let us out.

"We'll see," I said with confidence, turned and left the vehicle, offering her my hand. She made to take it and then decided otherwise, but too little too late. I grabbed onto her wrist and helped her anyway.

When the elevator doors closed, we found ourselves alone in our confines.

"Ready for tomorrow?" I asked casually.

Nicole's brows furrowed. "Yeah, why wouldn't I be?"

"Because we're flying back."

She grumbled. "You just had to remind me."

"Don't worry," I turned to her, "it gets easier."

"Yeah, yeah. Remind me to get drunk before boarding this time."

I harrumphed. "What's that going to help? You were worse after your two drinks the last time." I stepped toward her. "I have other ways, you know."

"I'm sure you do," she said and held out her hand, stopping me from getting closer. I applied pressure against it, setting my palms against the wall on either side of her head and leaned closer. "I'm not sleeping with you," she repeated her earlier words, but her statement didn't seem as adamant.

"So you say," I whispered and closed the gap between us with an intense kiss that made my head spin.

When our elevator reached its destination, she was plastered to my body, her legs around my waist, fingers fisting my hair and pulling me into her as I had a hand on her ass and my other on her back.

I opened my eyes and began to walk us to her room, which was closest. I pinned her against the wall beside her door and indulged in the soft skin of her neck, all the way down to the spot where the swell of her breasts began.

She arched into me like a cat in heat. I slowed my ministrations as I aimed for another taste of her mouth.

The realization that I wanted her like I wanted my next breath hit me tenfold, and I knew I had to end this. Despite my obvious attraction to Nicole, the dance we'd been doing over the course of the day wasn't a game I wanted to play. It was hers. And she deserved more than that. If I were being entirely honest with myself, so did I.

My aggression tapered off and our kisses grew softer, almost tender, as I let her slide down the wall, feeling her every curve against my body. Her moist breath hovered over my lips when I managed to find enough resolve to pull myself away from her.

Eyes shut, I pinched the bridge of my nose and took a deep breath before opening them and seeing the deep greens of her irises. She was mesmerizing when she was fired up with sexual tension.

"I…" I backed away, feeling the heat of her body desert me altogether. "Goodnight, Nic," I said with a hoarse voice before turning and walking toward my room. Not wasting time, I entered it, bolted the door, and took a deep breath as numerous thoughts careened together in my head.

Why the hell did you ever agree to this?

My competitive nature had caused me to give in to Nicole's games, not to mention my lust had been a strong player in that decision as well. The problem was that the more time I spent with my assistant, the more I wanted her. And the less of a game it was.

I had to put a stop to it.

CHAPTER 16

The day flew by, leaving me feeling restless without any further advances from Nicole.

Sure, it was what I wanted, but her lack of attention throughout the day, the drought in conversation that had been reduced to short and abrupt answers, left me thinking that my backing away from last night's heated interlude had left her insulted.

Despite Nicole's mood, or maybe because of it, I felt the need to make amends after our last meeting ended. I scrambled to get a packet of anti-anxiety medicine from the hotel's concierge.

"Here." I handed the medication over. "Take this before we take off for the airport."

Without more than a thanks, she took the meds with the help of the bottle of water she had in her purse.

By the time we arrived to check in for our flights, however, I noticed that the drug's desired effects had yet to take. Nicole's twitchy demeanor had me grabbing for her hand.

What surprised me the most was the fact that she wasn't fussing to get away. My thumb rubbed the top of her soft skin in a soothing manner and I felt her body slump toward my side as she relaxed against me, in line.

Nicole's steps halted as we reached our seats. When I finished stowing away our luggage, I noticed she had yet to sit down. One look down at my ticket had me realizing that they'd assigned her another window seat.

"Do you want to switch?"

"Do you mind?"

"Not at all." And we did just that.

"Thank you," she said with a shaky voice.

Within fifteen minutes, the plane made to taxi the runway for takeoff. Nicole stiffened and grabbed the ends of the armrests. I watched on as, with eyes closed, she took deep breaths. She mumbled something inaudible to herself which I could only presume were words of courage.

Her deathgrip on the armrests tightened as her attempt at controlling her fear was failing. When the plane sped up to take off, I grabbed her hand myself and turned her head to face me.

"Kiss me." She shook her head. "Just kiss me, Nicole."

I didn't wait for another response. I pulled her face to mine and kissed her deep and soft. She moaned in my mouth, her hands cupping my face as she gave in to my distraction.

The plane's landing gear left the pavement and the small bout of turbulence started as we gained altitude.

When the plane smoothed out, I pulled away and leaned my forehead to hers, trying to regain my breath. I could have easily kept on kissing her, instead I asked, "Better?"

She bit her bottom lip and nodded. Seeing her lean in for more, my heart swelled but I backed away regardless.

She huffed, turned to face forward and said, "Why'd you do that if you don't want to kiss me?"

"Trust me, honey," I began, "I want to do more than kiss you right now." I turned to look at her and saw the deep crimson infuse the skin of her face and neck.

She leaned into my ear and whispered, "It's too bad you can't have it all, huh?" Her teeth nipped my jaw before she pulled back.

I guess the games weren't over.

"Devil woman," I mumbled under my breath, feeling her body shake with laughter. What surprised me most was that she had yet to release my hand, despite all signs of panic having left her.

When our flight began its descent, Nicole grabbed hold of my face and pressed her forehead to mine. Her eyes were shut tight and her breath, scented of mint and coffee, fanned over my face. My mouth watered for another taste of her, but the kiss remained absent.

When the plane touched down and halted at the gate, I caved into my urge, but only slightly, as I pressed my lips to hers in a chaste peck.

"Well done." I smiled. "You'll adjust just fine."

"Yeah, with a butt load of tranquilizers and a man to hold my hand," she said, nowhere near as terrified as she'd been the first time around.

"Do this often enough and you won't be in need of either." I gave her thigh a supportive squeeze. "Come on, let's get you home."

Exiting the airport, I hailed us a cab, ordering the driver to drop her off first.

We pulled up to a large house with darkened windows and a well-lit porch. *Business must have been good.* I turned to her and said, "I'll see you tomorrow."

She nodded. "Goodnight."

"Goodnight."

Making the driver wait, I watched on until she was tucked away inside before heading home.

Exhausted and flustered as I walked through the threshold, I grabbed a beer from the fridge and collapsed on the couch

to check my messages. Scanning through all of them, I landed on one from Danica.

As I was about to dial her number, my phone rang in my hand.

"Think of the devil…" I said, smiling as I answered. "How are you, sis?"

"I just got a call from Nikki who said that there's a proposition I need to take a look at?"

I grumbled, my easy-going mood having evaporated. "Hello to you too."

"What's this about?"

"It's nothing and I've already told Winthrow we weren't going for it."

"Uh-huh! And that's why Nicole thinks that it's something worth looking into?" I didn't answer. "So how's it going with you two around the office?"

"Fine." I left it at that.

"The tension's gone?" Her voice denoted she didn't believe the possibility.

"I wouldn't say that." I recalled the events of the previous day and how she'd set me on fire. "It's fine. We're fine."

"Why do I sense that something's up?"

"Why do you think that something's up?"

"Because Nikki sounded weird when I spoke to her and, come to think of it, so do you. Did something happen in Austin?"

"You mean, aside from me having to prevent her from passing out from a panic attack on the flight there…maybe," I said without thinking.

"Mike! Wait, she freaked out?"

"Yeah." I chuckled. "She's never flown before."

"Never?"

"Nope."

"Huh! Funny, I never knew that," she said. "So what do you mean by 'maybe'?" I could see that my lack of censorship was going to cost me.

"Maybe something happened…maybe it didn't."

"What happened, Michael?" She sounded less than humored.

"A gentleman never kisses and tells." It had been a while since I'd riled up my sister.

"You didn't!" she said with shock. "She would never!"

"Why don't you ask her who came up with the latest game?" I told her. "Let me tell you one thing, Nicole sure has changed some since her high school days. She's not so innocent."

"I'm asking you, Michael," she whined. "What did you do to her?"

"Far less than she's done to me, that's for sure," I mumbled. "Now, if you don't mind, I need to get to bed. Your best friend has been wreaking havoc on my sleeping habits."

"You fucked her!" She shocked me with how crass her conclusion sounded, just as much as she accused instead of inquiring.

"What? No!" I began to ramble. "I just haven't been sleeping that well. Then there was the whole thing at the hospital, and the hotel bar…" *Why the hell am I telling her this?*

"The hospital? What happened that you needed the hospital?" she asked. "And what bar?"

"When you were in labor, we ran into one of her old friends."

"Oh no…not Dean."

"Yeah…how'd you know?"

"There's a reason why she doesn't like you," she began, "and it all boils down to him."

"I kind of figured as much. The guy's an idiot, by the way." I figured that Danica might know why, so I asked. "What happened?"

"Look, it's not my story to tell, but whatever games you two are playing, you need to stop. She's been through more than enough and I love you both too much to see either one of you getting hurt."

"I'm not playing her, Dani," I told her. "It's more than what I can say for her, though."

"She wouldn't!"

"Oh, trust me, she would, and she's got game too."

"Why do you seem bummed about that?"

"I don't know. Maybe because she shouldn't be playing around. Maybe because she deserves better than what was handed to her? She's driving me insane, sis."

"You have a thing for her?" I heard the smile in her words. I didn't answer. "You do, don't you?"

"I think this conversation is over." I sighed. The last thing I needed was Danica in the middle of whatever this thing was between Nicole and me. Changing the subject, I said, "The meetings went well, the Austin division is back on track and that proposition will be chucked in the shredding pile whenever I get my hands on it. Goodnight, Dani and kiss those new babies for their uncle will you?"

"Don't you dare hang up on me!" I heard through the phone as I hit the end button. She called me right back, but I sent her straight to voicemail and powered down with a great deal of satisfaction.

CHAPTER 17

The following morning, Nicole was at her desk by the time I came in. Sure, I was later than usual, but it was still before seven thirty.

"Good morning," I said.

"Bite me!"

I see we're back to normal. "Bad night?"

"All thanks to you!" she said. "Your sister rode my ass to get details on what happened between us in Austin. She even mentioned Dean and the hospital. You wouldn't happen to know how she knew about that, would you?"

"I might have said something about the hospital, but I told her to ask you if she wanted details about anything else. After all, isn't that what women do…gossip?"

"Maybe in high school, but what I do on my own time is my personal business, even if it does involve you."

Leaning over, I whispered in her ear. "You're the one who started this game. Go ahead, call it quits if the truth is harder to digest now that reality is setting in." My words ended on a sour note.

"Being played doesn't sit right with you now, does it?"

"Don't pretend to know what it is I'm thinking, Nicole. We've already established we don't know nearly enough about each other to pass judgment, yet here you go again." My tone had an edge to it. "And if you want to discuss this further, I suggest an office with a door attached to it." I pointed to my office and headed straight for it.

She followed. "Well, well…" She smirked as she shut the door. "Looks like the player can't handle being played."

"Oh, I can handle it, but let me tell you a bit about my ways, honey. Maybe you'll finally believe me after you have all the sordid facts, since you just love to have those, don't you?" I continued before she could say anything. "That ex-fiancée you met a few days ago…she played me." Nicole recoiled from my admission. "I'm no player, Nic. I never was. I usually find quick connections with women who know my intentions all along. I don't want a relationship with any of them and that's why…" my voice trailed off. Would she really believe me if she knew everything? Call me chicken, call me a pansy, I don't care. I quit while I was ahead. "What do you care anyway? To you, I'm talking out of my ass no matter what I say. I don't know why I bothered again."

"Mike," she started and her tone was subdued and quiet. It made me look at her. "I'm sorry."

"I don't need your pity; it's not like you had anything to do with it. But to make sure you get it, no, I don't enjoy being played. I don't mind games, but not to the point someone gets hurt. As for our little interlude, consider it over. You won. Congratulations! It was fun while it lasted, but Dani was right, someone's going to get hurt, and I'm not willing to bet on either one of us being the victim."

"I'm sorry, I didn't–"

"Don't!" I waved her off and then looked at her. "Don't apologize. It was nice." I smiled, but it was forced. "You can go now."

She didn't budge.

Ignoring her presence, I sat at my desk and began to sort through some of my mail, but she failed to take the hint and kept staring at me. "What?" I lifted my eyes to meet hers.

"Nothing." She shrugged. "It's just…truce?"

Truce? She wants to call a truce now?

"Yeah…fine." I stuck out my hand. She came around to my side of the desk and took it, but went one step further and sat herself sideways on my lap, pulling my held hand and wrapping it around her waist. "What are you doing?"

"Giving you a hug." She smiled and wrapped her arms around my shoulders loosely. "Friends?"

"That works for me." I smiled to myself, tightening my hold on her as I wondered where this sweet woman had come from. My eyes closed as I took in the scent of her hair. It was one of my favorites, triggering memories of my mother's gardenias. But now, Nicole would forever be embedded in my memory with that smell too.

When she pulled away from me, the sliding of her hands down my arms sent a shiver down my spine, to my groin. She was quick to get up, and I was thankful because my dick was beginning to swell, and as a friend, she didn't need to be privy to the effects she had on certain parts of my anatomy. Effects I was afraid wouldn't fade—nor was I sure I wanted them to.

"I think I might have misjudged you just a little," she said, turning to face me from the door to my office.

I chuckled. "A little?"

"Just a little." She made a gesture, using her thumb and index finger, keeping them close together, and winked before turning to go back to her desk. I couldn't help the laugh that bubbled up.

By mid-morning, a rather incensed Danica came storming in with a baby in her arms, followed by Jake, who was holding the other twin.

"Good," she paused to look between Nicole's and my desks, "I have both of you here, get in there, Nikki," she whisper-yelled so as not to wake the babies and pointed toward me. Nicole obliged her friend, seeing as a few heads had lifted to peer over their cubicle walls. Jake appeared aloof as to what was transpiring. "Sit down!" she demanded, but we remained standing.

"What's the matter?" I asked.

"For starters, how about you two come clean?" she said.

"Come clean?" Jake asked aloud.

"Yeah!" Danica said. "These two have been frolicking."

I snorted. "Frolicking, Dani?"

"We're friends!" Nicole said.

"That's not what I heard," Danica said, "but you hung up on me before answering those questions last night, didn't you, Nikki?" I looked at Nicole who turned to look at me and shrugged her shoulders.

"You too?" I laughed when she nodded in response. "It explains why she's here."

"You're damn right it's why I'm here! Now explain. I'm not buying this 'friend' business one bit. You two have been at each other's throats for the last year and before then, you," she looked at me, "tormented my friend in high school and you," she looked from me to Nicole, "were smitten with him despite his jackass ways."

"Smitten?" I turned and found a blushing Nicole. One glimpse in my brother-in-law's direction and we both cracked up at her reaction.

"A simple schoolgirl crush is all it was, so check your ego at the door, jackass."

"So we're back to that again? I thought we were friends as of," I looked down at my watch, "oh…about an hour ago. Your words pain me." I clutched at my chest in a dramatic fashion.

"And what were you two before an hour ago?" Jake asked in obvious amusement.

"Uh…" I turned to look at Nicole whose blush had returned. *Fuck!*

"What was that?" Danica asked. "Nikki, you've got some serious explaining to do!"

"It was harmless," she told my sister.

"Nothing is harmless!" Danica said. "If you two were serious about starting something, then I'd be fine with it, but I know you both. There's no way you'd put aside your stubbornness, not to mention your hang-ups, long enough to make something happen."

"I think it's time for you to leave, Dani." My sister was

treading too close to divulging my interest in her best friend.

"Hold on a sec." Nicole held up her hand and turned to look at me. "Why are you so uncomfortable all of a sudden when my dirty laundry was the one being aired out?" She took the few steps to stand in front of me, her gaze assessing. "Mike?" She put a hand palm down on my chest. My eyes were fused to hers and I heard Jake let out a laugh followed by an "ouch" which meant that my sister must have smacked him. Her eyes widened as she seemed to have concluded something. "You like me?" My eyes averted themselves from hers, but landed where it made it all look the more incriminating. Her lips. Those lips turned into a smile. "Yeah, didn't think so." She moved away from me and turned to my sister and her husband. "See? There's nothing here!"

"Holy shit you're blind, woman!" Jake said.

"I think they're definitely interested in one another." Danica was grinning from ear to ear. "They're just too busy playing stupid to accept it."

Jake nodded his agreement with his wife.

"Yeah, for a good fuck, maybe!" Nicole said.

"Hey!" I said, insulted.

"Nikki!" Danica looked shocked at her friend's choice of words.

"What?" Nicole looked at me.

My brows furrowed. This woman was confusing. "What happened to…"

"The player stuff?" I nodded. "I admit, it did hold its appeal but…"

"But?" It was my turn to approach her. We stood toe-to-toe.

"But like I said earlier, I was wrong about you." She looked away from me before meeting my gaze again.

"Thank you." I smiled down at her and she smiled back. "It must have been hard for you to admit that to more than just me." She shrugged her shoulders. "For a woman who doesn't play around, I do have to say that you have it down to a science."

When I started to move closer, she said, "Not alone."

I halted. "Huh?"

"You're not alone," Danica interrupted, "and you two are so busted! Friends, my ass!"

Fuck! Thanks to those emerald eyes of Nicole's, I'd forgotten we had an audience.

In the span of half an hour we had managed to impress my brother-in-law, piss off my sister, and learn a few things about one another. Upon Danica and Jake's departure, Nicole and I were beside ourselves with mirth.

"I suppose we should get back to work," she said, trying hard to regain her composure. She made a start for the door.

"Hey, Nic?"

She turned to face me. "Why do you call me that?"

I shrugged my shoulders in response. "I like it, or do you prefer Ice Queen?" I grinned.

"I have to admit, it was growing on me." She laughed. "I like Nic too. No one else calls me that. What was it you were going to ask?"

"Do you really think I'd be a good fuck?" I bit my lip to stifle another bout of laughter.

She shook her head smiling. "You're unbelievable!" she added as she dropped into her desk chair.

"So I've been told!"

CHAPTER 18

All hell broke loose in the office by early afternoon, the next day, and emergency team meetings took place to smooth things over for an irate client.

I ended up having to take over the project, which required Nicole and I to stay behind to work on a presentation the client had demanded for first thing tomorrow morning, or else they'd pull out of their contract.

It was near eight at night and my focus was far from sound, thanks to the brainstorming we'd done to resolve the issues at hand. We had about an hour left of work to fine-tune things.

Thank God Nicole majored in business. She'd picked up on discrepancies and oversights where I hadn't—proof that two pairs of eyes were sometimes better than one—and had made recommendations that I knew the client would be pleased with. To be honest, I was impressed and even a little bit jealous that she'd come up with those resolutions.

I ran my hands through my hair and sighed.

"Why don't we take a break?" Nicole suggested, looking up from the latest printout of the presentation, holding a red pen. "We can step out for dinner and then come back with a fresh mind."

"Maybe you're right." I got up and stretched. "Where to?"

"How about the bistro across the street?"

"Perfect!" I grabbed my jacket, my stomach rumbling with hunger.

"Sounds like great timing." She giggled, then proceeded toward the office door. "Come on, Mr. Withers."

I groaned. "I hate it when people call me that, it makes me feel old."

"You are old," she said as she pushed the down button.

"I'm a year older than you."

"Nearly two," she stated. "I was bumped up a grade after first."

"Full of surprises aren't you?" I nudged her with my elbow as the elevator arrived.

"Not my fault you never took the time to get to know me while we were growing up."

"I guess we're both at fault there, aren't we? You're pretty good at hiding things."

She shrugged. "I suppose."

I was following a fast-walking Nicole into the bistro when she slammed on the breaks and I wound up plowing into her back. In an effort to prevent her small frame from toppling over, I wrapped my arm around her waist, bringing her flush with my chest.

"What the hell, Nic!"

"Dean," she whispered which made me look up.

"Fancy seeing you here." The man smirked as he approached us.

"How's Lisa?" Nicole's tone was hostile.

"She's out of town. You up for me dropping by later?"

What the hell was this guy on about? My blood simmered and my mouth ran away from me. "Seriously!" I kept my arm around Nicole.

"Come on! You don't expect me to believe that you two are really together?" he said. "I've seen you around, she's too frigid for a guy like you."

Nicole flinched and it reminded me of the time I'd called her just that in Austin. Boy did I know different now.

"Excuse me?" I gave him an incredulous look.

"Come on, Mike." Nicole tried to pull me away by the hand. "Let's just go somewhere else."

"No!" My eyes never left the man. "This guy owes you an apology."

She put a hand on my arm. "It's fine."

"Trust me, it's not." I held her eyes momentarily and then narrowed my gaze on Dean. "He's out of line."

"Out of line? Let me guess…she hasn't–?"

"Dean, that's enough!" Nicole told him.

"Is it really?" He looked at her. "So you trade me in for him or is he like the others, temporary replacements until you realize you can't get better and come begging for me all over again? What's this guy got that makes it so different this time?"

"Well," she toiled with finding some semblance of her legs, and must have, because she kept going, "for starters, he's single, he respects me, appreciates me, praises what I do, and he's sexy as hell." She took it one step further and turned to face me. When I saw a lascivious smile grace her face, I knew she was up to no good. "And he's got one hell of a package that dwarfs yours in comparison. I guess it just took the right man to make me forget you." Her hands rubbed up my chest and both my arms wrapped themselves around her and pulled her in. It may have been an act, but I couldn't help but react to her words. She had to have been either one hell of an actress who'd missed her calling, or she was genuine about most of what she'd just said.

"Does he know how much you like to get around?" Her eyes flashed with panic and my arms dropped to my sides with his revelation. "Hear this–"

"You know what…I've heard just about enough." Stepping back from Nicole and closer to Dean, I pulled my arm

back and let one fly into the idiot's jaw. I gave Nicole a fleeting look. "I'm out of here."

"Mike?"

I turned my back to both of them. "Go home, Nicole. I'm going back to the office."

"Mike!"

"I'll see you tomorrow. Just…go home."

I left before any of them could say or do anything to stop me. The fucker had one hard jaw. Shaking my fist, I was convinced it would be bruised and sore come morning.

The bistro's door chimed as I pushed it open. I registered the sound of a slap and a rather heated dialect from Nicole, followed by heels clicking behind me.

CHAPTER 19

I made it back to the office by myself. As to where Nicole had headed after she left the bistro, I had no clue. One thing was for sure, she never chased me.

Part of me was glad that she'd done what I'd asked of her, and the other felt upset that she hadn't followed me to discuss what had happened.

My mind was reeling with Dean's insinuations.

Was Nicole promiscuous in nature? I highly doubted it.

Had she been with as many guys as Dean had alluded to? Her reaction to the man's words told me that she wasn't as innocent as I'd presumed her to be.

But that doesn't make her a slut.

The more I deliberated things, the less I believed Dean's claims.

Nicole and I weren't all that different really. If anyone understood how weak a person could make another, I could. Part of my leaving Austin was so I could make sure I wouldn't fall prey to Tracey's clutches.

Like me, maybe she sought out men to quench certain urges, not always sexual, without forming attachments.

As I sat at my desk, I saved the final version of Nicole's and my presentation and sat back, my mind still muddled with so many questions.

With a hand scrubbing down my face, I wondered why Nicole hadn't tried to defend herself against Dean's words. I felt like a heel for coming to her rescue, yet not being man enough to stick around to hear her side of things.

Then there was the fact that she hadn't even tried to disprove anything.

Maybe she was embarrassed?

Was her attraction genuine? Maybe she was out for a good time, and because Dean had called her out on it, she'd given up because she knew I didn't like games? I doubted the latter, but then again, I'd been wrong where women were concerned before.

One thing was certain. We needed to talk it out.

I reached for my phone and dialed. Nicole's voicemail kicked on and I ended the call without leaving a message.

Finding my resolve, I gathered my briefcase and headed down to the parking garage, peeling out onto the road.

Fifteen minutes later, I was parked in front of Nicole's house. Her car was there, but the lights were off. My stomach sank and then I caught the flickering of what seemed like candlelight from the picture window.

Hope restored, I stepped out of my car, locked up and walked to her front door. That's when I heard the sultry sound of a voice I hadn't heard in years. The words, the guitar, the song…

It's her?

I knocked, but the answer never came, only the continuous playing. I tried the doorknob and it turned, granting me access to her home. I let myself in and followed the melody.

She was in the front room which looked like some kind of library-den turned into a very comfortable music-slash-sitting room of sorts with a desk, laptop and some other equipment I couldn't discern.

Nicole's back was to me as she sat on a piano bench, facing her wall of floor to ceiling library shelves, her singing flawless in accompaniment to her strumming tune. She transported me to the past…

"Tracey, I was thinking about our wedding song."

"I thought we'd decided on Tony Bennett's The Way You Look Tonight?"

"I know, but I stumbled onto this today." I waved the CD. "I forgot that I had it."

"What song? Who sings it?"

"You wouldn't know her. I don't even know who it is, but the song is perfect." I walked to the stereo and popped the disc in. Maybe she'd think it was foolish, but I pressed the play button anyway. "Listen."

"Where'd you get this?" she asked after I'd powered down the stereo.

"Back in high school. Ben and I used to play pranks on my sister. I found it under her bed and thought she'd taken off with one of my mixes like always, so I took it back."

The CD, as it turned out, wasn't mine, but something about that voice, the emotion and the combination of honesty and hope in the words had me keeping it for myself. Days, weeks, months went by, and the disc was left unclaimed, and I continued to enjoy it.

"I didn't peg you as someone to barge into people's houses without permission," Nicole said.

I hadn't heard her stop playing, caught up in my daydream. "How'd you know I was in here?" Her back was still turned to me.

"I heard the knock. What do you want?"

"The way you play…" *It's better than your CD.* "That was beautiful, Nic."

She bowed her head and sighed. "What do you want, Michael?"

"I wanted to apologize for earlier."

"Don't you mean you wanted to hear an apology from me?" She sounded hurt and bitter.

"No. Like I said, I came to apologize."

I heard her knuckles rap on the laminated wood of her guitar and then watched as she got up and set the instrument down beside five others that were lined up against the wall on their stands.

"Whatever it is, your apology is accepted." She moved to lean against the wall and stared out the window. "You can go now."

"Can we talk?"

"I think enough was said tonight."

"I rather hear your side than that jackass'."

Her short laugh held no humor, but at least she looked at me when she spoke next. "What's it matter?"

My eyes refused to let hers go. "It matters."

"You want to hear the whole sordid story?" I didn't answer. "You want to know about the part that Dean and I used to be engaged? How about the part that he was fucking his PA, Lisa, behind my back? How about the other women I suspected him of being with, but chose to forgive? Oh…but I never forgot, Mike. Do you want to hear about me turning into one of those women after we broke it off and he was seeing Lisa?"

She turned her entire body to face me and assessed my reaction, but I gave her nothing. "Do you really want to hear about how weak I was? That no matter how many men I ended up with, that I always went crawling back to him?" She wiped at the tears, furiously. "I bet you're pretty proud of yourself aren't you? Finding out that Little Nikki was no better than you with getting around. It doesn't matter that I didn't like it, but for however long the connection lasted, the dark thoughts of the past would disappear and I was convinced that I had moved on to something better."

"Nic–"

She held up her hand to stop me. "I'm a hypocrite, a slut, a weakling…" she listed.

Her self-deprecation was too much for me.

I walked up to her and stopped to stand about a foot away. "I don't think that," I pulled her into my chest, "but what I do think is that you need a hug."

She released a sobbing laugh into my chest and with the

way my shirt was getting soaked, I gathered that she had more tears than laughs needing to be let out. This woman was hurt beyond measure, just like me, but she had never been able to get away. No wonder she'd despised me before knowing my story.

"I stopped…a month ago, I stopped. I came close to breaking down a few weeks back. And then I found out he was engaged to her. I can't do it anymore. I turned into someone I hate and I can't do that to Lisa, despite all that she's done to me."

"Is that when…" I began, but she knew where I was going with my words.

I felt her head bob in a nod. "When I ran into you at Dani's, yeah."

"I'm sorry."

"Please don't say that. You make me feel like I'm being pitied. I don't deserve anything from anyone, least of all you."

"You deserve better than what you got with Dean, Nic, that's for sure," I whispered into her hair.

"But I was unfair."

"You had your reasons." I buffed my cheek on her tresses. "Now, answer me this…since when do you play guitar?" That gained me a laugh, then, she looked up and gave me a crooked smile that had me smiling right back. "I figured a subject change was in order."

"I've been playing for as long as I can remember. My dad used to play, he taught me."

"How come I've never heard you play before? I mean, I know I wasn't around unless it was to annoy you and Dani, but she never mentioned that you played either."

"I never told her much until I took Dad's and my dream and turned it into something we'd always wanted."

"Ah, that elusive business." She nodded. "What was it?"

"A music store. I sold instruments, taught lessons, and even ran a small recording studio in the back for people who wanted to record. It was a lot of fun." Her smile was infectious.

"You loved it."

"I did." Her face darkened.

"Should I ask you what happened?"

"No, but it comes with the whole story, so I'll tell you." She sighed and led me to the couch where we sat. "Dean took me for one hell of a loop when he left me. What was worse was that Mom got sick around the same time. It took a long time for the doctors to figure out what was going on with her. After a while, we'd run through all of hers and my father's savings, Dad's life insurance, everything."

I listened on.

"It wasn't a good time in my life. Because music made me feel, the combination of my failed relationship with Dean and my mother's failing health was too much. I couldn't be around music, I wasn't able to concentrate on the business like I should have been, and things just fell apart."

"Oh, honey." I squeezed her hand.

"I'd still have the shop had Mom not needed so many treatments. I had no choice but to end my lease and liquidate everything.

"Mom wasn't happy with my decision. As retaliation, she deeded me this house and made me promise that I keep some of the money I made from my liquidating the store's assets for myself. So I paid off the mortgage with my chunk, and all of her various treatments with the other. I saved the rest for a rainy day."

I nodded in understanding. "Is your mom okay?"

"No." She looked down. "The cancer caused a clot to form and she had a stroke right before Danica moved back here. She died."

"I'm so sorry."

"Needless to say, I've taken up odd administrative jobs, thinking that the monotonous busy work would keep my mind busy enough from all things Dean, and Mom, and where I wanted to be, and no longer could be." She let out a long breath. "It worked, and Business Administration is something I'm good at. At least I think I am. I haven't heard a word about my work ethics being less than stellar yet."

"But it's not who you are." Her lips tightened in a flat line in response. "You deserve a lot more. You deserve to be happy, to have your shop again, and give those lessons you love giving."

"And I'll have that again…someday." She smiled up at me as if knowing a secret I had yet to discover. "The salary you're giving me at Withers is so much that if my projections are right, I'll be able to get started on building my stock in the next six months."

"Are you saying that you're leaving?" I felt bereft despite knowing where her heart lay.

She smirked. "You knew I would all along."

I groaned. "I know, but how in the hell am I going to replace you?"

She giggled. "I'm not that good."

"No, you're better."

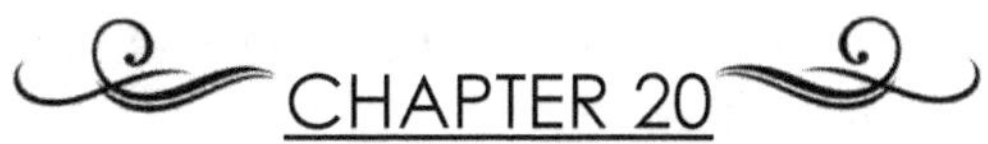

CHAPTER 20

When my head hit the pillow tonight, something felt as if it was missing.

I tossed and turned, paced, and sat in the dark.

I even tested out the heated milk trick. I spat that shit straight out, and wished I had an espresso maker so as to turn it into a macchiato or something of that sort. As girly as the drink was, it would have tasted better.

Morning came and I found myself at work, tired and on the verge of falling asleep on my feet. I had ended up using an old trick, but remembered it only too late—Nicole's CD.

Yeah, I still had it. Her melodic voice soothed me, her words lulled me into a fitful sleep that lasted an hour before it was time to get up and go, thanks to my trusty alarm clock.

By lunchtime, our disgruntled client was more than ecstatic with our new look for their campaign and the numbers we'd projected. Suffice to say, the account was secure.

Nicole had been quiet and kept to herself throughout the morning. She looked about as tired as I felt, which was saying something, since I'd left her place before midnight.

Getting up, I went to her. "What do you say we get out of here?"

She did a double-take. "What?"

"Let's get out of here. I'm eager to start the weekend and

I can use some sleep and it looks like I'm not the only one."

She smirked. "Stud, are you trying to get me to go home with you?"

"That's an idea." I grinned. "Let's discuss this in my office, away from prying ears."

"Should I be afraid?"

I gave her a mock mischievous laugh. "Very."

"About me going home with you," she began after my office door closed behind us, "I thought we were done playing games?"

"Yeah, we are, but I get a kick out of your reactions." What can I say? Some games are fun to play, and flirting doesn't hurt anyone.

"I know what you mean." She smiled and leaned against my desk, her legs looking fabulous in another one of her pencil skirts.

Did I mention how much I loved her skirts?

I stood, mere feet from her.

"I especially like it when your eyes go wide," she said, running a finger over her collarbone and down between her breasts. My jaw went slack. "Yeah, just like that."

I cleared my throat. "You've got a mean streak in you, Nic." I got up and faced off with her. "So, what do you say, you up for an afternoon veg-fest?"

"I don't know if it's wise." There was no doubt she was flirting as she looked up through her lashes, "my boss might have something against me with spending time with a colleague outside of work."

"Fuck your boss!" I said, carrying on with our play on words. Seeing how far she would take it was too much fun.

"That's an idea." Mischief shone in her eyes. She wrapped her fingers around my belt loops and pulled my torso into hers.

I groaned. Okay, so maybe we were taking this too far now. "Nic, this isn't smart."

"I know, yet, it's brilliant at the same time." I knew where she was coming from with that statement. No matter how much I'd been resisting her, there was always that unseen force that pulled me back in. "Tell me something, Mike, why is it that every time we've kissed, that I can barely stay under control? Why is it that even though we've called it quits on our game, that I still feel the need to tease you?" She continued. "How is it that I can't seem to sleep at night without waking up…" she leaned up, pressing her chest into mine as my head inched down toward hers, "wet?"

God, help me!

Her lips met mine in a brief kiss—a teaser.

"Nicole…" My voice croaked.

"The way you say my name," she purred, "it makes me want to make you say it again."

"Fuck!" I felt what was left of my resolve break.

Grabbing the back of her head, I crashed my mouth to hers. I pulled away and watched her face, her eyes, and looked down at her lips.

"I hope you're ready for this, because once I start, I don't think I'll be able to stop."

She gave me a vigorous nod and pulled me back down to her lips. I picked her up, sat her on my desk and ran my hands up her legs, pushing her skirt up inch by inch.

Her hands slid from my nape and I felt her fussing with my tie while I cradled and supported her back, our mouths fused to each other.

Her fingers were popping the buttons of my shirt out of their eyelets, her lips found the skin of my chest, and then she pulled back enough to look up at me.

I took her mouth.

A trail of fiery kisses was passed down from her mouth, over her cheek and jaw. She arched her neck, pushing her body into mine as I moved further down and nipped her collarbone. Her tiny hands were busy undoing my belt, and I ached to be freed from the confines of my slacks.

"Oh God!" she whispered when she pulled me out of my underwear, my pants down by my ankles, yet my skivvies were still wrapped around my thighs. Smirking up at me, she licked her lips. "I hope my boss will be holding it against me for inter-office relations."

"Honey," I smirked at her slyness, "I'll do more than hold it against you."

Her hand pumped me once. "Promise?" she asked, and a moan pushed past my lips when her thumb traced the slit of my cock.

I gripped her hand to stop her actions and her eyes came up to meet mine as if expecting an answer. I delivered it without words.

With the lacy barrier of her underwear pushed off to the side, Nicole guided me to her heated folds. The moment our sexes met, it took everything in me not to thrust into her with the urgency that consumed me.

I groaned into her neck. "Condom."

Giving her a sheepish look as I leaned over the desk and reached into the top drawer, I pulled out the foil packet.

Nicole snapped the package from me, tore into it with her teeth and proceeded to roll the rubber on.

"I'll die if you don't hurry this up."

She nipped my ear, her cheek nuzzling against mine and its scruff. "I need you inside me," she whispered before leaning back.

Lifting her hips, I thrust myself to the hilt, Nicole's cry muffled by my shoulder.

Damn, she was tight. I lowered her ass onto my desk, scattering the few items that were in the way. She wrapped her thighs around my hips and my hands rubbed up her legs, luxuriating in the feel of her. "I've dreamt about how you'd feel wrapped around me like this." I pulled out, leaving the tip, and pushed in fast and hard, feeling her cervix as I bottomed out, loving the sight of me disappearing into her slick pussy. "You feel amazing."

"Mmm…"

I found a rhythm that seemed to satisfy us both, but I needed more. I craved her closeness.

Leaning over her, I picked her up and sat in one of the

visitor's chairs that faced my desk. She straddled my thighs. The grinding of her pelvis against mine sent spots flittering across my vision and her rhythmic clenching threatened to throw me over the edge.

When her internal spasms began to take over and her body shook, I clamped my mouth over hers to muffle her erotic sounds. The inappropriateness of our act combined with the possibility of getting caught was a surefire thrill.

When her hips bucked over mine, her body seized. I gave her an upward thrust and slammed her hips down over mine. Heat sizzled up from my balls as I came hard and fast, crying my release in Nicole's mouth as she had with me. Fuck, I had never come like that before.

"Wow!" I said against her mouth.

"Uh-huh." She started to giggle. "Mike?" She pulled back to see my face.

"Yeah?"

"Do you think that my boss will forgive me for this indiscretion?" She smirked.

"Only if you promise to do it again." I laughed.

She looked at me with a confused look. "You mean not to do it again, right?"

"No." I pecked her lips. "I meant what I said, exactly as I said it." I tucked the hair from her face behind her ear and kept my hand on her cheek. "Now that I've had you once, I'm going to need you again, Nicole."

"But we're not playing."

"No, we're not." I was serious. Her body stiffened. She tried to back off of me, but I kept her right where she was. "And never do I intend on playing you." My words were firm, my intentions honest.

"I should go." She gave me a chaste kiss. "Thanks for the early weekend." She got up and began straightening her appearance.

"Nicole," I started, confused at her sudden distant behavior, "you never answered about spending the rest of the day with me."

She stopped dead in her tracks but didn't look at me. "You got what you wanted out of it, so is the rest really necessary?"

I finished buckling my belt, seeing that she was vexed.

Before she could run off, I grabbed her arm and pulled her into my chest. "The rest is necessary." I looked down at her. "A player would fuck and run, Nicole. Is that what you are? Because it's not what I am, or what I do after I've been with a woman."

I released her and gave her the opportunity to decide. She looked conflicted. For what felt like an eternity, I knew fear prevented her from saying anything, but my anger got the better of me, and so did my mouth. "I guess I have my answer." I grabbed my briefcase and headed for the hallway. "Have a good weekend. See you Monday and don't forget to lock my office door on your way out."

I was watching the elevator doors close when a tiny hand stopped their progress, their sensors being prompted to open once again.

"So where are we heading?" She gave me a shy smile as she walked into the elevator, her purse in hand.

"I'm heading home," I told her, "as for you, I don't know."

"I'm sorry. It's just…I'm scared."

Me too.

CHAPTER 21

Despite Nicole's admission of her fear, the moment had passed. I headed home alone, but not without leaving her by her car with a kiss of reassurance that what had happened in my office hadn't been a quickie to satiate physical needs. I understood her behavior, even though it frustrated me.

Once home, I shut the front door, made my way to the couch, and let myself drop. Whatever energy I had left had been zapped by Nicole and our carnal activities.

I could still feel her on me.

It amazed me that a woman from my past was able to affect me so much. A girl I had spent countless times pulling at her pigtails, teasing about her braces, making her blush with flirtatious connotations. I'd had an inkling that she'd had a crush on me back then, but I never knew for certain until yesterday, and it was clear to me that I had never bothered to get to know much about her either.

And now…now I loved the look she got when I got her riled up during our sparring. Seeing her stumped and not knowing what to say next was even better.

For the first time in a long time, I wasn't satiated with a single dose of sex like I would have been with the other women before her. With one all too short taste of Nicole Baxter, she succeeded at making me need more. Hell, I was already sporting an erection that could pound nails at the thought of being with her again.

Like that'll happen.

I draped an arm over my eyes and prayed that sleep took me because my mind was reeling with all things Nicole. The words she uttered to Dean when we were in the bistro came to mind again and mixed with what had transpired between us earlier today. Those memories intermingled with the ones of a painfully shy and easily embarrassed teenage girl who had written and performed the songs I had carried with me all of these years, not knowing that those thoughts, those words and feelings, were all hers. With my thoughts consuming me, I never realized that I had fallen asleep as I'd aimed to do.

My cell rang beside me and when I went to roll over to grab it, I found myself weighed down and unable to move.

Looking down, I saw a beautiful head of chestnut hair. Nicole's.

Confused at her presence, I was careful not to roll her off of me and onto the floor when I stretched for the ringing device.

Without looking, I answered, not wanting to wake the woman cuddled into my side.

"Hello?" I croaked.

"Are you sleeping?"

"Dani, what's up?"

"I was wondering if–"

"Who is it?" Nicole asked, her voice sleepy. She nuzzled my chin with the bridge of her nose and sighed.

"Shh…it's okay," I said with the phone pulled away from us and winced because I knew what was coming next.

"Michael, who was that?" Danica asked as I replaced the phone next to my ear.

"What's the matter?"

"Was that Nikki?" I didn't answer. "Mike, answer me right now, dammit!"

"And if I said it was?" I groaned when Nicole's knee came up to drape over my leg and nudged my crotch.

"We need to talk."

"I know. How about tomorrow?"

"I think you better be here for breakfast or I'm hunting your ass down. If you hurt her, I'll kill you."

"Don't worry, sis, I don't plan on it." *If anyone gets hurt in this, it'll be me.* I needed to figure it all out and quick for both our sakes.

"Tomorrow then. And don't think Nicole won't be getting a similar talk."

I smiled. The damn woman was like my mother. "Yeah, later, sis."

"Bye."

I shook Nicole awake the minute I hung up with Danica. Well, at least I tried to.

"Mmm…" She snuggled into me more, her knee nudging my crotch again, making it difficult for me to focus with the increased blood flow to my groin.

"Nic," I whispered, humored by how deep the woman slept, "it's time to wake up, honey."

"Do we have to? This is…nice," she whispered and her hand snuck past my few undone shirt buttons and rubbed my chest.

"As nice as this is, how'd you get in?"

"Your door…unlocked. You…upset," she mumbled and I knew that she was fading out on me, "check on…make sure…okay."

"I'm fine."

I was going to tell her that she shouldn't be here, but my body was humming with how close we were and sleep beckoned me because quite frankly, I was comfortable, not to mention, still exhausted. I closed my eyes and next thing I knew, I felt her lips against my jaw and my head lulled to the side, resting on the top of hers as I fell into slumber once more.

When I woke up, the moon was high in the sky, my lights were off except for a lamp on the end table and I was covered by a blanket. The house was quiet and Nicole was gone.

I pushed the blanket to the side and when I sat up, my foot nudged something on the floor. My phone. I picked it up and noticed I had a few messages.

Scrolling through, I found one from my enigma.

> *Handsome,*
> *Thanks for the cuddles, the warmth, and the relaxing afternoon. I didn't want to overstay my welcome and would have woken you up, but you looked too peaceful so I let you sleep.*
> *Enjoy your weekend,*
> *Your Ice Queen (with confusing tendencies)*

A smile spread onto my face. She knew that I had been upset with her, but despite that and her fears, she had been concerned enough to check up on me.

Tracey would have never done that.

I brushed that thought away and sent Nicole a reply.

> *Beautiful,*
> *Thanks for the cuddles, but I wish you'd woken me up. I'm now feeling the chill from the pool of water you left behind when you shed that layer of ice. The blanket was a nice touch but I can't help but wonder what you would have done if there wasn't one around.*
> *Your Jackass*

Within minutes, I had a reply.

> *I would have stayed to keep you warm.*

Texting was a nuisance to me, so I hit the call button.

"Hello?"

"I hate blankets." I smiled into the phone. She laughed. "I wish you would have stayed."

"And then what?"

"I don't know, but do we really need to figure it all out right now?"

"I suppose not."

"What are you doing?"

"Hanging out with my guitars and a glass of wine while sporting some rather pitiful looking pajamas." Her voice sounded relaxed, peaceful, happy. "You?"

"I'm right where you left me," I told her. "So about those pajamas…are they as bad as those penguin ones you used to wear when you slept over back in high school?"

"Oh God!" I could just imagine the mortified look on her face. "Those were nasty!"

I laughed. "They were cute."

"These ones aren't that much better."

I have to see for myself.

CHAPTER 22

I grabbed my keys, slid on my shoes, locked my front door and jumped in the car. Our banter continued as I teased her about what I thought she was wearing.

"Take a picture and send it to me," I told her with a smile as I reached her house.

"No way!" I could tell that she was smiling through her mock horror.

"Then I'm coming over." I rang her doorbell. "Expecting someone?"

"No. Hold on a sec."

Door opening, her jaw dropped and I howled with laughter as I took in her hot pink jammies that looked a decade past due for the trash. Her tank top read *I am woman, hear me roar*. Figuring the damage was already done, she turned around, presenting me with the full picture and I found a *Sweet Cheeks* fading away on her bottom.

"Prickly but sweet, it's completely you."

She groaned, but backed and allowed me entrance. "Shut up!"

"What? It's kind of cute," I said while shutting her door. "I have to agree with you though; you're definitely overdue for new jammies."

"If you don't like them then feel free to take them off." She crossed her arms at her chest and smirked.

I grinned. "Do you really want me to do that?"

"No?" Disappointment reigned only momentarily as she started past me, heading toward the stairs. "I guess I'll just have to do it myself then." She pulled her pants off at the bottom of the stairs.

Standing there in lacy black underwear and her top, she

said, "Catch!" She threw the garment at my face. "Hold on to those while I get rid of this shirt will you?" I watched as she paused halfway up and reached for the hem and yanked her top over her head. All I could do was stand at the bottom of the stairwell, staring up at her. "Maybe we can burn these when I get back. It's been a while since I've had a fire in the hearth." She threw me her shirt and that's when it clicked that she wasn't wearing a bra. The woman may have worn ridiculous looking jammies, but what was underneath was far from ridiculous at all.

"Sure," I said, but my feet were already moving in her direction.

I hung a right at the top of the staircase like I saw her do and it wasn't hard to locate her. She was rummaging through her drawer and humming to some tune I couldn't make out.

I leaned up against her bedroom's door-frame and smirked at the sight.

"You play dirty, you know that?" I said, making her jump.

She turned, covering her tits with her arms. "And you've grown soft since Austin."

"Are you trying to get me riled up?"

"If it works." She approached me and stopped when we were toe-to-toe. I kept my hands to myself. "Which it seems to be." She looked at my crotch. "So what's it going to take to make you give in, big guy?"

I laughed. "If you want to play, all you have to do is ask."

"What if I don't want to ask?" She ran her finger along my jaw and down my neck, making me shiver. She stood on the tips of her toes. "What if I want you to take what you want?" she whispered over my lips.

I growled and she shut me right up by kissing me hard, her arms winding themselves around my neck as she pushed her tits into my chest. I could feel her hardened nipples through the thin material of my shirt.

My hands went straight for her ass and palmed it as she began to walk backward toward her bed.

"Let's do this right." She pulled away, biting her lower lip. Her hands went for my belt and after tucking the condom I had with me between my lips, mine went for my shirt.

Standing in my underwear, my dick aching to feel that silken heat of hers again, I pulled her into me.

"If we're doing this right, then allow me." I grabbed her by the waist and with a girly yelp and giggle, I lifted her off of her feet and threw her down onto her back atop her mattress. "Fuck you're gorgeous." I slid my underwear off. Her eyes widened and she blushed at my nakedness—or was it the fact that I had stroked myself a few times after donning the condom that made her so bashful?

I crawled up between her legs, taking in the sight of her body. She was tiny, but flawless. My head bent to take one of her nipples in my mouth, tantalizing it with my tongue and teeth while I massaged her other. Perfect handfuls they were. She moaned, her hands feathering through my hair as I switched to her other breast and gave it the same attention.

My mouth followed my hand as it caressed the indentation that followed the middle of her abs all the way down to her navel. Goosebumps broke out all over her torso.

Blowing a puff of hot air on her mound granted me with an arch of her pelvis. The musky scent of her arousal permeated my senses, making my mouth water for a pure unadulterated taste of her.

Slow and torturous, I slid her underwear down her legs, making sure to pay them some attention too. Her musk was more potent now that she was bare to me and I took my time admiring the small tuft of hair she had left on her mostly bare pussy.

I looked up at her and our eyes connected.

"Y-you don't have to do that."

Here she was apprehensive when I felt like a kid in a candy store at Christmas. "I want to."

"But…"

"Nic, is this new to you?"

She blushed. "No?" She bit her bottom lip. "Well, only once."

"Seriously?" She nodded. "Why?" I allowed a finger to skim her folds, delighting in the heat, the wetness that had begun to manifest.

"It never really did anything for me."

Damn. What she meant was that no other partner had taken the time to show her how good it could be. The selfishness of those past partners made me mad. "Really?" She nodded again. "Well that's about to change." I lowered my head and licked up her slit.

"Oh God, Mike! This…this is…oh, God, yeah!" Everything else afterward came out in an assortment of moans, groans, and mewls once my mouth fused to her core.

Never did anything for her, my ass!

Her thighs twitched with each stroke of my tongue, her breath caught when my fingers found her sweet spot. With a flick of my tongue onto her clit, her body went rigid.

"I'm coming!"

She tried to pull away from me, but I wrapped my arms around her thighs, pulled to keep her against my face and latched onto that swollen bud of hers, shaking my head from side to side which made her cry out in ecstasy.

Her passion-filled cry rang out in my ears as her body shook with her orgasm.

Pulling away, I kissed her inner thighs as I stroked her heat with my fingers, bringing her down from her high before ascending her body to bring her back to the brink once more.

Before I could pay my respects to her tits again, she pulled me up and attacked my mouth and moaned. Having her taste herself from me like that, and her not pulling away in disgust, was erotic as all hell.

"Does it do anything for you now?" I smirked, giving her another light kiss.

Nicole's face broke into a grin and she nodded. "Very much." Her feet rubbed the back length of my legs and my dick, hard as granite, begged for release, poking at her slickened slit.

Arching her hips for me, I slid in slow, watching her eyes glaze over.

Our momentum was fast-paced and frantic, our search for release, imperative. The sweat of our bodies mingled and we glided together with perfect synchronization and ease.

"Fuck!" I said, when her inner walls began to contract around me. My balls tightened up against her ass and I let myself go, body shaking with the force of our combined releases.

I flipped us over so that I wouldn't crush Nicole with my body and she lay over me, her head on my chest. I began to play with her hair, eliciting a sigh of contentment from her.

"I may have enjoyed our stunt in your office, but I have to say that this beats all," she said.

"Is that so?"

She lifted her head and winked at me. "That was fun."

I agreed, but wondered why she felt inclined to put it in those exact words. Soon enough, I discovered why she had.

Nicole tried to exit the bed. I pulled her back to me, settling her with her bare back to my chest and I nipped her earlobe. "You're not getting away from me as you have with your others," I whispered. "I happen to enjoy my cuddles and, like I said before, I'm not playing."

"I just thought." She sighed. "Never mind what I thought."

I kissed her temple, tightened my hold around her and buried my nose in her hair. Her body relaxed and her fingers interlaced with mine. I knew that I shouldn't, but I closed my eyes for a moment. I didn't expect to fall asleep with her in my arms, but I did for the second time today. It had felt so natural to do just that.

It was midnight when I woke to an empty bed and music coming from downstairs. Reaching for my boxers, I tiptoed to investigate. I stood in the entrance to Nicole's den and leaned on the wall as I watched her.

She sat, wearing nothing but my dress shirt and I presumed her underwear, her guitar in hand. When her voice faded at the end of her song, she turned enough to see me. She smiled and, as opposed to being tense like last night, she was relaxed.

"I'm sorry, did I wake you?"

I shook my head and walked up to sit on the couch beside her. "Couldn't sleep?" I tucked a stray strand of hair behind her ear and kissed her cheek.

"Not exactly." She smiled. "Inspiration struck. It's most likely the curse of me picking up my guitar again after being away from it for so long."

"So last night…"

"…was the first time I picked up a guitar and played in almost two years."

"Why the sudden impulse?"

"I think it's because of you." She looked down, appearing nervous and tweaked a few chords.

I tilted her chin up and gave her lips a chaste kiss. "Play something for me?"

"I don't…"

"How about that song you played last night when I walked in?"

She scrunched up her nose. "That song sucks."

"I loved it." I wasn't going to let her know that I had heard it before then. Not yet.

Her lips tilted up to one side in that nervous quirk of hers. "Okay."

She hiked up her feet onto the coffee table, giving me a nice view of her legs and began to strum.

I smiled, nodded my encouragement to her and off she took me on a whirlwind serenade with one of my favorite tunes.

CHAPTER 23

On my way home the next morning, I felt guilty for imposing the same end to my time spent with Nicole as she had bestowed upon me yesterday afternoon.

I walked through my front door and rushed to get changed, not bothering with a shower since I had been lucky enough for another round in Nicole's bathroom before we had called it a night.

Exhausted, but nowhere near as tired as I was upon waking yesterday morning, I shaved and dressed.

Ready to go and face my sister's wrath, I texted Nicole.

> *Beautiful,*
> *I'm sorry I couldn't be there when you woke up. Had to go to Dani's.*
> *Forgive me? I'll call you later.*
> *Hope you have a great day,*
> *Mike*

Upon entering the Landen household, I was met by the boisterous cries of twin babes. Peering into the living room, Jordan was trying to mute things out with a head-splitting volume on the television.

Jake popped into my field of vision, running from one end of the kitchen to the other with a baby and bottle in hand.

"Someone's in trouble!" Jordan said in an amused tone and turned the TV off.

"What makes you say that?"

"Mom said so." He smirked. "What'd you do now?"

"I'll let you in on it when I know myself. It looks like they could use a hand in there." I walked into the kitchen and made my presence known.

"Mike." Danica's eyes were piercing me.

Here we go! "Here." I extended my arms and made to grab Gabby, my niece. She went from panic to calm and lay in my arms, her dark baby blues taking me in. "That's right, Uncle Mike's here." I smiled down at her tiny form.

"A baby looks good on you, bro." Jake handed me a bottle and then popped one in baby Marco's mouth.

"Thank God!" Danica massaged her temples. "I couldn't think. One was tough, but two? Having them at the same time is one thing, but did they have to be on the same schedule for everything else too?"

"Sit down and relax, sis. Jake and I have it under control."

"Let's talk since you're stuck here for the next half hour, at least," she said.

"I'd rather not, but I don't think I have a choice do I?"

"Nope."

"Before you start asking questions, here's the deal," I said.

"You mean I won't have to force it out of you?"

"Let me talk, woman." I sighed. "I like her, Dani, I mean, really like her." Christ! Could I have sounded any more like a nervous teenager?

I told Danica about what had been going on since the night she had gone into labor up until the night before last.

"When you called yesterday, I thought I was alone."

"What happened?"

"I know that she's been hurt bad in the past, she's told me what happened with Dean, but I got mad. Anyway, when she hesitated and became distant, I gave her the brush-off and went home alone. I was so exhausted that I passed out on the couch. When I woke to take your call, she was curled up against me.

"I know I should have kicked her out after I was done talking to you, but she wouldn't wake up and then I realized that I didn't want her to leave, so I let her sleep and I slept some more.

"When I woke up, she was gone, but she left me a text, apologizing for leaving without waking me. She'd come by because she knew I was upset, Dani." No one but my family and Ben had ever done that.

"There's just one problem." I sighed. "I know she's not one for playing people, but I can't shake the fact that this is more for fun than anything serious with her. I like her too much to hurt her, and I'm scared shitless of getting hurt again. I don't need another Tracey, though I know Nicole wouldn't do that to me. She knows how it feels to be on the other side."

"So you mean to say that you're falling for the short, scrawny, brunette that sported pigtails, funky jammies, fuzzy slippers, and braces; the same girl that you terrorized while we were growing up?" Danica asked. I gave that some thought, but didn't answer. "Well, are you?"

"Yeah, I guess I am," I said. "I hate arguing with her, but I love it at the same time. She challenges me in everything; even over that stupid pitch of Winthrow's."

She looked puzzled. "You like arguing with her?"

A short laugh escaped me. "I know it sounds ridiculous, but yeah." I smiled. "The air gets filled with so much tension that when it breaks, we're left with…"

"Heat," Jake supplied.

I nodded. "Lots and lots of heat."

"Men!" Danica shook her head. "I love you both, but I'll never understand either of you. Well, at least not completely." That garnered a chuckle from her husband and I. "So what do you plan on doing if she's only in it for fun? You can't keep going like this and falling for a girl who won't worship the ground you walk on, even if she is my best friend."

"I don't know." I looked down at Gabby who'd fallen

asleep on her bottle. I rubbed her cheek and she started suck-ling for her food again. That was the crux of the matter, wasn't it?

Danica broke the silence. "I have an idea."

CHAPTER 24

Filled with optimism for where things could head between Nicole and me, I got in my car to head home.

What amazed me was that Danica hadn't had a clue about those tracks her best friend had recorded years ago, but she did know that Nicole had harbored a strong love for music and had managed her own music store.

When I made my sister listen to the songs, she understood why I had kept the CD for myself. She would have done the same.

Sitting in the driver's seat, I checked my messages before taking off and saw a text from Nicole.

I'll forgive you if you give me a repeat performance of yesterday. –N

My lips tugged upward into a smile and my finger hit the dial button.

"Is breakfast tomorrow morning included?" I asked the moment she answered.

"Perhaps." Her voice held a semblance of relaxation. "I could possibly be persuaded to include lunch and dinner for today as well."

"You'll be too busy for that," I said, self-assured.

On a harrumph, she said, "Really?"

My voice went husky. "Yes, really."

"Now you've got me curious."

"I bet. Listen, I have a few things to tend to, but I can be there in about an hour, unless you rather I come by later?"

Even to me I sounded like a damn whipped fool.

"No, that's perfect." My relief was immediate.

With my phone dropped in the middle console, I put the car in drive, all the while smiling as if nothing could get me down.

It was time to get to business.

I was in the kitchen, cutting up some vegetables for a salad to go with dinner when Nicole's doorbell rang. Moments later, she came waltzing into the kitchen with a large vase of flowers and an even larger smile.

Whistling at the impressive display, I said, "Someone's well-liked."

"Except that I can't think of a reason I'm getting these." She stuck her nose into the roses and closed her eyes as she took in the scent. "They're gorgeous."

"What's in the envelope?"

"I don't know. Flowers never come with envelopes this size." She dug into it with a puzzled expression. "It's a CD."

"Nothing else?" She shook her head. "Pop it in."

I followed her to the den where she put the disc in her stereo and pressed play. The soft sound of the guitar kicked off and I saw her face drain of blood. She turned to me in shock when her voice came from the speakers.

"I haven't heard you sing this one. I thought you didn't have any other songs?"

"I don't." She sat on the armrest of her couch, nibbling at her thumbnail. "Well, nothing new. I wrote this in high school."

"Why is it recorded?"

"Dad had a dream for me. He brought me in to record a demo after school one day and then he died a few days later. I lost the CD about a week after he passed." She looked down as if reliving it all and I noticed fleeting emotions of sadness and pride cross her features. "I have no clue where I'd left it."

"It must be nice to get a piece of history back."

"It is, but it'd be better if I got the whole damn thing. The problem is that I have no clue who knew it was mine to begin with. The CD wasn't labeled or anything."

She went silent and listened, eyes closed. When the song ended, she powered down the stereo. With a smile and a glint in her eyes, I followed her back toward the kitchen.

I prepped, she cooked, and at some point, she began to hum to the tune that had played in her den some fifteen minutes before.

My duties tended to, I found a seat at the kitchen island and watched her. The woman appeared content, which had me smiling.

It's working.

In bed that night, I cradled Nicole's head on my shoulder, our bodies fitting to perfection. Absorbing the heat of our skin-to-skin contact, an epiphany hit me. I wasn't falling for this woman…I had already crashed.

When did this happen?

An image flittered in my mind of the previous night, when everything had changed. Her armor had been stripped down enough for me to catch a real glimpse of the complex woman that now lay next to me.

With that image in my mind, I kissed her hair and fell asleep.

CHAPTER 25

According to Nicole, the following morning, I needed to be on the "up and up" because she had plans for us. If I only knew what she'd meant by that.

I was lathering my hair with shampoo when a pair of breasts with hardened nipples pressed against my back, arms hugged me from behind.

Without a word, Nicole grabbed the bar of soap and proceeded to wash my body, paying detailed attention to my cock which began to throb with need.

"Nic?"

"Shh."

I was on the verge of exploding when she turned me to face her and sunk to her knees to take me in her mouth. Despite the hot water streaming between my shoulder blades and back, I felt a sheet of goosebumps blanket my entire body and shivered.

My eyes rolled to the back of my head and I hissed when her tongue circled the tip of my shaft. "Fuck, that feels good."

Her hands massaged my balls and the tip of my dick hit the back of her throat. She moaned around me and my hips jerked at the feel of that sinful mouth of hers. Gentle teeth grazed my length and my hands grasped her hair, finding purchase in an effort to keep me grounded. Nicole was about to send me flying over the edge without a parachute.

When I hit the back of her throat a second time, she tried to swallow me. The action milked my cock and that was my undoing. I tried to pull out, but she grabbed my ass and pulled me back in, taking all I had to offer. She hummed her satisfaction, causing my body to shake with one last tremor.

When Nicole pulled away, she looked up with a self-satisfied smirk. It was hard for me to maintain my footing. The woman could have brought me to my knees with the simple sucking of my cock, and I wouldn't have complained one iota.

"Up and up!" She pointed down at my dick and giggled.

My grin was slow and lazy. "You're evil." I pulled her up to her feet and wrapped my arms around her.

Kissing her hard, she moaned into my mouth as my tongue met hers.

After indulging in her body for a few more minutes, we called our shower interlude a done deal.

Finding ourselves at the breakfast bar, Nicole set out a bowl of fresh fruit, yogurt, toast, and an assortment of jams and jellies. I grabbed the coffee for us and filled two mugs.

The doorbell rang.

When she came back, she held a yellow manila envelope in her hands and another one of her confused expressions. "It came by messenger service."

"On a Sunday?" I asked.

She shrugged her shoulders. "Weird, I know." She opened the envelope and pulled out another CD. "What the hell is going on?" Forgetting about breakfast, she headed to the den and popped the disc into the stereo, knowing what it would contain. She wasn't disproved as the first strums of guitar strings filled the air. "It's another one of them," she said when she noticed that I'd followed her. I smiled. Instead of the same look of shock she had worn last night, she sported a goofy grin.

"There's a note with this one." She handed it to me. I read it, although I knew what it said, seeing as I had written it.

An angel called and her songs kind of stuck...

"What's it mean?" she asked.

I shrugged my shoulders. "Your guess is as good as mine. Are they some of your lyrics?" I asked. She shook her head indicating the negative, lip singing to the words that poured out of the sound system. Was this one a favorite of hers? "Maybe it's a poem?"

"A one-liner?"

"No, I'd say it continues by the ellipsis." I showed her my observation.

"There's more?"

"Well how many songs were on that CD?"

"I don't know." She paused to think. "Five or six? It's been so long."

"My guess is that you're bound to find out."

"I think you're right."

CHAPTER 26

Sunday was spent with Nicole; laughing, talking, relaxing, not to mention the sex we indulged in had been explosive.

At the end of the day, however, she had been adamant that no one, mainly the office folks, know that we were intimate. Reluctantly, I agreed.

By lunchtime on Monday, my excitement had turned into impatience as I waited on what was to come. Irritated that Nicole had left with a few of the office ladies for an early lunch, I ended up being the one to sign for her latest delivery.

Within minutes of the courier guy leaving, Nicole walked in. I was already at my desk, watching her as she bent to stick her nose into the pink colored roses. She picked out a bloom, grabbed the card from the bouquet and the yellow manila envelope that I had set against the vase before trotting into my office.

"If the rest of the deliveries have bouquets like the last three and they wind up here, I'll have to explain myself to the girls." She giggled. "Then again, these are beautiful and I've never been spoiled like this before." Her eyes sparkled.

"Did you check the card?"

She shook her head and handed me both the tiny white envelope as well as the larger yellow one. "Here, you open it. I'm too wired!"

I unveiled the CD from the yellow manila envelope first

and popped it into my computer as she closed my office door. I took the small note, made as if to read it and smiled before passing it for her to read.

"For years she remained a mystery—an enigma…" She read aloud. "These cards are confusing." She waved the piece of paper at me.

I laughed. "Just wait it out. In the end, these things always make sense."

Her eyes narrowed. "Why aren't you jealous?"

"Am I supposed to be?"

"Well, I mean, you've been around for all three deliveries and we've been…you know. I'm getting gorgeous, not to mention, expensive roses from a pure stranger which tells me it has to be a man. These words aren't indicative of a love poem but…"

"Hmm," was all I managed.

"I have no clue who this person is, but my gut tells me it's someone I know."

"For all you know, he could be sitting right under your nose." I smiled at the irony of my words seeing as she was standing, leaning against my desk as I sat in my office chair. Under her nose was quite literal at the moment.

As the week went on, things grew busier, but Nicole and I made time to steal away a few moments during our lunches. She hadn't mentioned any more deliveries, but then again, that's because I hadn't scheduled any.

We hadn't been intimate since Sunday and despite my physical hunger for her, I was content just being near the woman and getting to know her better.

Thursday arrived and Danica was scheduled to come in, eager to find out what Winthrow's new proposition had been about. I knew how to pick my battles when it came to my sister, so I'd given in to her request.

Nicole had been avoiding me all day, disappearing at lunchtime which meant we didn't get our usual quiet time. I was annoyed, but when she came waltzing in with Danica at her side, I understood why she'd gone without notice. After all, my sister was her best friend, and I knew they hadn't seen each other in nearly a week.

"So about that Fleishman account and Winthrow's pitch," Danica leaned against my PA's desk, "I think we should go for it."

What?

Heads peeked over cubicle walls and that's when I realized I had spoken aloud. Too loud.

I growled. "Can I see you in here for a moment?" Nicole rushed to her desk and attempted to sit down, but I latched on to her elbow and kept her on her feet. "You too." My eyes pierced hers.

When both women were seated in front of my desk, I slammed my office door, making them jump.

"Would you please explain to me why you know it's about Fleishman, when we haven't discussed it yet?" I leered at Nicole who shrunk into her seat at my tone.

"Calm down. I told you he'd have a fit." Danica had the audacity to giggle as she looked at Nicole, but my PA didn't seem as entertained as my sister was. She didn't react to her friend's words, or speak for that matter.

"I'm glad that you've learned to keep that mouth of yours shut for once," I said to Nicole.

"Just you wait a damn minute!" Danica got up to her feet. "Nicole saw something in that proposal that warranted my attention and I happen to agree with her. I know that George has had some cockamamie ideas in the past and Dad entertained most of them, but this," she threw the document down on my desk in front of me, "for once, is good."

"I agree with you that to do it all in one shot would be risky, as we're still trying to get our feet under us again. If we implemented a portion of what George proposes in here," she pointed toward the document, "then we might be able to grow stronger. We can tackle the rest later. Just because you know Nicole doesn't give you the right to undermine her opinion. She's more valuable to us than you think and she's got a degree–"

"Don't you start with me on her qualifications, Danica! I'm well aware of her degree. What I'm not happy about is how you two decided to go behind my back and make a decision without my knowledge, when I had already agreed to meet with you this afternoon to discuss this."

"What decision?" she asked. "She presented me with the package and that was it. We discussed a tentative plan of action based on her conservative approach and nothing more."

"Exactly! Don't you think that I should have been present?"

"We already knew your stance," Nicole said in a calm manner.

"It's another reason why I should have been involved!" I glared down at her.

"Don't you try and intimidate her," Danica said. "I'm drafting up a plan and I'll have it to you by the end of the day tomorrow and we're sticking to it."

"Not happening," I said with finality.

"You don't get to make all of the decisions, Michael," Danica said. "Didn't you say that the majority of the board was in accord with this idea, Nicole?" I looked at her and saw her hesitant nod. "So there! If we take her approach, we will be fine, big brother. Our financials aren't as bad as you think, and that's in large part thanks to you for turning things around, but I had a hand in that too. The Fleishman account is one of our largest, and if this works, and I know it will, it'll be one lucrative win for us. Enough to ensure that the other offices remain open." She was right, but the woman kept talking. "I think Nikki should run point on this with Winthrow as the second."

"And now you're taking away my PA?" My tone had grown incredulous.

"Wait a minute!" Nicole got up and when I turned to look at Danica, my sister had her arms crossed over her chest with a smile of victory on her lips. "I never said anything about being interested in managing this project. It wasn't even my idea!"

"So you're all for it, but you're not going to guide it into fruition?" I asked Nicole.

"I'm a PA, what do I know?" She shrugged her shoulders.

"You're more than that," Danica said, trying to boost her friend's confidence and pointed at me, "and he knows it!"

CHAPTER 27

By the time all was said and done our monster blowout had captured the attention of the entire office.

When Danica stormed out—satisfied, I might add—everyone went back to work as if they hadn't witnessed our latest squabble.

"Nicole, we need to talk." I closed the door before she could leave.

With my PA standing in the middle of my office, I leaned against my office door, running my hands over my face. This was bound to go one of two ways: great or horrible. I was hoping for the former.

"I'm sorry," she said when none of us said anything, and her voice came out squeaky.

"You're sorry?" I hissed. "Nic, you went above your boss' head and introduced a proposition from one of our satellite offices without my expressed consent! People have been fired for a lot less!"

"I know." She looked at me, but I still couldn't meet her eyes because I felt the rage still simmering in the pit of my stomach. "When Dani called and asked me to lunch, I agreed. Then she showed up while you were on your con-call and pushed me to bring Winthrow's presentation with us so she could revise it before your meeting with her. I didn't think she'd take it as far as she did."

"And that's where you fucked up! I know you mean well, and I know you're trying to help, but–"

"That's exactly what I was doing!" Her voice had gone sharp. My eyes flew to hers. "I can't believe that you dismissed something without looking at it first. I mean, these people work for you, don't they? If you can't trust them, then how the hell do you expect to even make WI last?"

"Are you saying I'm incompetent?"

"It's not what I'm saying at all, Michael, and you know it!" She sighed. "I believe you're the one who told me to open my eyes and look around. Well, from where I'm standing, you're the one blinded this time.

"Just because your father took the wrong risks with Winthrow before doesn't mean that his ideas are all bound to fail. Dani thinks it's good and so do I. Most of the board members are in agreement. The fact of the matter is, this company of yours will fail if you don't do anything substantial enough to set you apart from the competition. Maybe not today or tomorrow, but further down the line, it'll happen.

"Your tactics are sound, but they're also safe. Too safe. You tell me to take risks and push for others to do so, but you haven't, have you?" She turned and plopped herself down on a chair in front of my desk and buried her head in her hands. "Now I'm running point on this whole thing, when it should be George. It's not what I asked for. It's not what I want."

"And that's my fault?" My gaze narrowed on her.

She looked up and met my eyes. "Yeah, it is. You've said that Dani and I wanted this and put me smack in the middle of it." Her knuckles turned white on the chair's arms. "Well, I have news for you. I'm not doing it!"

"So you're backing out and refusing a directive from your boss?"

"I sure as hell am!" She got up. "I don't care about what you and Dani have to say about it. I was thrust in the middle of World War Three with you two just now."

"You did that on your own, honey." I stepped toward her.

"And I'm ending it, right here and now." She stepped up to me and eyed me head on. "This was George's idea and he should be the one running point."

Anger faded into arousal, all thanks to the mixture of emotions and our heated discussion.

"Maybe I should just quit." Her eyes conceded defeat.

"I won't allow it." I sighed and wrapped an arm around her waist.

"I'm screwing it all up for you."

"You know you're not," I said, my voice softer, our faces growing closer.

Her hands landed on my chest. "I can't do this, Mike." I knew she meant the project.

"Why not?" I kissed the soft spot under her ear.

She whimpered, her fingers fisting my shirt in an attempt to stay grounded. "All we do is fight. At first, it was fine, for the most part. Now that things are better on a personal level, it's the business side that's suffering."

"I can't help it if you infuriate me." I nipped at her jaw.

"See?" She pushed me back, but stayed in my arms, our eyes meeting.

"I need you, Nic…here, especially."

"But you don't trust me." She looked away.

"What makes you say that?"

"The way you blew your top in front of Danica and me said more than enough."

"Dani and I argue all the time and I still trust her with my life and our company. As for you, I trust you," *with my heart* went unheard, "and George has too much on his plate, so you will run point on this project and maintain your PA duties. The man can advise. I doubt George will have a problem with that." I kissed her senseless.

She melted into my arms.

"Don't you think it's kind of odd that instead of being fired, that I'm running a project that some of your other employees with more seniority should be given the opportunity?" she asked, breathless as my lips nibbled her jaw.

"Hmm…" I continued my assault and heard her breath catch when one of my hands groped her ass.

"I mean…"

I pulled away and looked at her with a smile. "Shut up, Nic, and let me fuck you."

Her eyes widened. "Uh…okay?" Her surprised expression dissolved only to be replaced by a cocky grin.

"You're in so much trouble already and yet you look like you're about to sass me. You're unbelievable!"

She began nibbling my jaw, upward to my ear. "You know you like it." Her teeth snagged my lobe, pulled, and upon release, she leaned back and gave me a wink.

"You're right. Now off with your underwear, woman."

"What underwear?"

Holy fuck!

"Trouble," I growled, "it should be your middle name." She giggled into my neck as I picked her up, setting her on my desk and reclining her until she lay back. "I should think about getting a couch in here."

"Why?" She wrapped her legs around my waist and when I searched with my fingers for her underwear, she hadn't lied, she wasn't wearing any. I groaned into her cleavage.

"Because if I ever find out about your lack of underwear again, I'll have to give you lessons on propriety in the workplace, and I'll be in need of something much more comfortable than my desk, since I'm pretty confident that there'll be numerous infractions." I grinned at the blush that spread onto her face and neck. "Plus, all of these lessons would give you more work with keeping my desk organized. I wouldn't dream of adding on to your already-busy schedule."

"Mike?" I gave her an inquisitive glance. "Get to it already."

Within seconds, my pants were undone and I thrust into her soaked heat.

"You're sure about this?"

We'd discussed going without condoms on Sunday, when she divulged that she was on the pill and that none of us had gone bareback before.

"Yeah!"

"You undo me, Nic." An odd expression flittered

across her face and she pulled my face down for a sweet kiss.

It wasn't going to take very long. This whole buildup with raging emotions had done us both in, but it seemed like the right way to end things.

I didn't pound into her because we needed to be quiet, especially after drawing so much attention earlier. Instead, I went deep, controlled, and was thorough.

I held off for as long as I could. When I felt her tremors, her nails digging into my shoulders through my shirt, I fused our mouths together, hoping it would muffle enough of our sounds.

Pulling out, I continued to kiss Nicole, smiling over her lips when she whimpered at the loss of me. She pecked my mouth and accepted my help to sit up along with the box of tissues. I retreated far enough so she could hop off my desk and straighten herself out while I got myself back together.

"I may have to continue with my impropriety if your methods of discipline are like that." She gave me a soft kiss as she straightened my tie. Her hands brushed over my shoulders, ridding my shirt of wrinkles like a dutiful partner. "There, handsome and ready to kill it!" She gave me a dazzling smile and my heart flipped at her simple gesture of coupledom. It's too bad it wasn't official, but I didn't want to dwell on that. Not yet.

I smiled back at her. "There's only one thing missing."

"What's that?"

"A good luck kiss."

She laughed a hearty laugh. "You just got lucky."

"I did, didn't I?" My smile turned into a grin. "I guess that'll have to do." I turned and was about to reach for the handle on my office door when an abrupt hand turned me around and Nicole's lips fused themselves to mine.

"How's that?" she asked when she pulled away.

"You're lucky that I have five minutes to skedaddle, or else I'd have you up against this door and to hell with who hears us. I'll see you later, you minx."

Flicking the tip of her nose, I was out of there before the notion to stay and take her as mine again overtook me.

CHAPTER 28

The next day, I woke up feeling chipper, and walked with an added bounce to my step. That was until I attempted to play a trick on Nicole by jumping up from behind and surprising her.

"No…It's just…It's fun…I'm having lots of fun, Dani, but…No, it's not that at all." I heard her talking to my sister. "It feels weird talking to you about this. I know I always talk to you about everything. It's just…" Her face was in her hand and she sighed. "Yes, of course I like him! I'd be crazy not to." She continued. "Yeah, I'm scared as hell…What? Fine. I said fine!" She groaned. "No, no…I can't. Dean? I can't, Dani. There's too much…it's too much. It would never work. You can't be serious. You know what…never mind. I've got to go. Your brother is about to get here and– well, no. I don't know what I'll say to…"

Without her noticing me, I made my way to my office and shut my door. I couldn't listen to any more. Everything was blowing up in my face, or so it seemed. I hadn't even finished executing my plan with Danica's help, and now I wondered if it was even worth it, based on what I had heard.

I had a delivery planned for later today, but now I wondered if cancelling everything would be better. I could just take her CD and dump it on her desk and let her know that I was the one who'd held on to it all these years and be done with it all.

Maybe that's what I should have done all along.

A soft knock on my door sounded and Nicole poked

her head in. She smiled in greeting. "You're later than usual."

"Slept in." I got up and stuffed my travel laptop into its bag. "I've got to go. I just came in to grab a few things. Can you cancel my meetings for today?"

"Everything okay?"

"Yeah, I'm just not feeling well."

Nicole nodded.

I made to leave.

She grabbed my arm to stop me, but I shook her off. "Don't. I'm fine." I kept my gaze averted. "Call me if something urgent comes up, otherwise, have a good weekend."

I left the office like I had a fire up my ass and headed straight home.

When I got there, I was shocked to find Danica's car in my driveway.

"What are you doing here?"

"Oh wow! Nikki didn't lie when she said you weren't yourself."

"She called you?"

"Why wouldn't she? She's worried about you."

"I need you to go. I'm in no mood to entertain."

"Then you're lucky that I'm in a mood to talk."

When is she not? I snorted my annoyance.

I left her in the driveway and stuck my key in the front door to let us in when Danica's words stopped me in my tracks.

"She's falling for you, you know." I didn't answer. "You've got her against the ropes. She's fighting it and she's covering it up good, too. If I didn't know her well, I would have believed everything she told me this morning."

"Yeah, well, I didn't catch the entire conversation, but I understood plenty." I gestured for her to come in.

"She's playing it off like it's all fun and games and that you two are just friends. I know both sides of the story, and from what I can see, it's not a game to either of you," she said. "So my question is, what are you going to do about it, because I don't think Nikki can do anything. She's too scared and her past with Dean is too fresh."

I ran my hands through my hair. "What can I do?"

"Fight! Tell her how you feel."

"You know how she is. It took her months after my move here before she believed me about the whole player thing. She'll never believe me with this either."

"That's where you're wrong."

"We had a plan…I had a plan at the end of this whole thing. I just don't know if it's worth it."

"Do you like her?"

I shook my head. "I love her, Dani." I groaned and hung my head, my elbows leaning onto my knees. "I'm doing this all wrong! She should be the first to know that, not you!"

"You're right about that one."

"Which?"

She sat down beside me and grinned. "That you're doing it all wrong."

W hen all was said and done, my deliveries were never cancelled. Instead, I switched things up. Thanks to Danica and her cupid playing abilities, I had renewed ambition.

I picked up my phone and texted Nicole.

> *I need you to pick some documents up for me at Dani's. Jake's holding on to them. Can you bring them over?*

Within seconds, I had my reply.

> *Okay. I'll handle it on my lunch break. How're you feeling?*

I smiled.

I'll be better when I see my package.

Let me explain what I did…

I'd instructed Danica to head to the office and sit down with Nicole in order to discuss the proper financial allocations for the Fleishman project. A messenger was tasked to get to Nicole before she left the office on her errand, delivering a single red rose, accompanied by the remaining verses of my poem, and two CDs containing two more of her songs.

She's on her way to pick up the package. Danica texted.

Everything was coming to a head with perfection.

CHAPTER 29

My doorbell rang and my pulse kicked up, knowing who stood on the other side of that door.

"Come in." I tried to relax into the couch with the stereo on low, but still audible.

"I've got what you asked me to get." Nicole rushed into the living room, waving the sealed envelope, but stopped dead in her tracks with a gasp as she heard the music.

"Mike?" Her voice had gone breathless, her eyes glossy. I crossed the floor to her, taking her into a tender hug. "It's you, isn't it?" she said into my chest. "Please tell me that it's you, because I've been racking my brain about this; about how we've been together quite a bit lately, how our fights aren't as frequent, how you haven't been jealous one bit, and even happy when I tell you about all of these deliveries. It's not normal." She pulled away to look at me. "Whenever I think about the last time I saw that CD, I'd been spending a lot of time at your place. Dani was helping me deal with things, and Mom was broken and…the CD was always in my bag until one day, it wasn't."

I took a deep breath and sucked it up. It was time. "You caught me." I shrugged my shoulders.

"You stole it?"

"No." I kissed the top of her head. "I found it under Dani's bed while I was looking for some of my CDs. She used to steal my music, remember? I thought it was one of my mixes, so I took it and kept it. I love these songs, honey. I had no clue who the artist was, but I've listened to your music a lot over the years."

"But it wasn't yours to keep," she said, her tone sharp.

"Nic, I didn't know whose it was. It didn't seem like anyone missed it, because no one asked me about it."

"Where is it?" she demanded. "Why didn't you just give it back when you knew it was mine?"

"It was a way of keeping you with me," I said with simplicity. *Yeah, and if you wanted to keep things simple, you would have burned yourself a copy of the CD and handed her the original.* "Just like you didn't believe me about the player thing, I doubted that you'd believe me if I told you I felt something more than lust or friendship for you. So I decided to do something special to prove it."

"Don't you think that should have been up to me to decide?" she asked. "Instead, you made me think…God, I don't know what to think!"

"You seemed to have enjoyed it as it happened!" I bit back.

"Yeah, when I thought about it being someone else."

"So you're disappointed." I harrumphed. "I should never–"

She shook her head. "I should go."

"Nic…" I began, but she pulled out of my arms, and all I wanted to do was pull her back in until she saw the truth, until she gave into how I felt for her, until she felt the same. She hadn't given it time to sink in. She didn't give me time to let me explain myself and how hard I had fallen for her over such a short amount of time, either. There was so much left to say.

"I have to go." She turned to let herself out.

Please don't! But my mouth couldn't speak what should have been said.

Her car door slammed and its engine revved and before long, silence engulfed my house and I knew she was gone.

Standing with nothing but Nicole's words surrounding me, my brain began to process.

I had to do something.

There'd be no more waiting.

There'd be no more watching life as it passed me by, while everyone else seemed to get their happily ever after.

I knew what I wanted, and whether she knew it or not, Nicole was it for me. She'd just have to deal with that fact, and if I had to, I'd spend whatever time she gave us convincing her that we were made for each other.

It was time for me to fight.

CHAPTER 30

I drove the ten minutes to Nicole's house, breathing a sigh of relief when I found her car in the driveway. I hadn't worked out what I was going to say, but I knew I had to speak with her and not let everything go unresolved. God help me, but I was going to wing it.

I knocked on her door. I rang her doorbell.

"Who is it?"

"It's me."

"Mike, I can't talk to you right now."

"I know!" I said, looking at my feet. I guess I wasn't going to get through her door. An idea crept into my head. "I just need you to listen." I ran back to my car, sat in it and started its engine. Grabbing my cell, I dialed her number.

"Listen to what?" she asked through the receiver, and I could hear the emotional exhaustion in her voice. I'd be lying if I said I didn't feel the same.

The first track of her songs began to play through my car speakers.

"You hear that?" I asked her and didn't expect a response, but I got a sigh. "That song is what drew me in to you." I skipped to the next track. "This one…it helped me through a tough time in my life. When Mom died, this song meant the world to me and kept me together." Next. "This one lulls me to sleep, but not because it stinks. On nights when my brain was too busy worrying about exams, the next big football game, or work, it soothed me enough to relax and fall asleep. It still works. Hell, I've been using it since Austin, because all I do is think about you, Nic, and I've been having a hell of a time trying to sleep unless you're next to me." Next. "This one is my favorite. Actually, I have two favorites now, but this one was the first. I managed to convince Tracey to use this song for our wedding dance. I wish I hadn't." I could have sworn I heard a groan on the other end of the line, making me regret my words, but I needed honesty. "She accepted because it meant so much to me. I just never realized that the words matched what I wanted and not what I had." Next. "This one makes me happy, because I realized it was you I'd been listening to when I heard you singing that first night I dropped by. I can't help but smile when I hear this song, because all I see when I listen to it is you, and how you have so many dreams you have yet to see realized…dreams I want to help you achieve. And that leaves me with this one!" I hit the next button one last time. "This song is my official favorite of favorites by you, Nic. When I hear this song, it brings me back to the night I realized I loved you for the first time." I heard her gasp in the phone. "You were wearing my shirt, looking natural, content and comfortable…completely in your element. You were perfect to me in that moment, Nicole. That was the song that sealed the deal. It's when I knew that I needed you in my life." I swallowed hard. "I don't want you to say anything just yet. I just wanted to say my piece and let it simmer. At the risk of losing you altogether, I'm leaving your CD on the doorstep. Even if it means losing the one and only piece of you that I could ever have." I exited my car and propped the item against the bottom of her door, keeping my phone to my ear. "I'll be at home if you need me. Trust me when I say I never meant to upset you with what I did. I love fighting with you, but not about things like this. I love you, Nicole."

I hung up and jumped into my car, shifted it into reverse, and peeled away before I lost the nerve.

I felt so empty, so confused. Lost. I needed to do something to get my mind off of things. A swim seemed like a good idea. I hadn't done laps in my pool in weeks.

Not bothering to lock the door as I walked through the threshold, I stripped off my clothes, shedding one layer at a time until I was standing naked as the day I was born by my pool's edge.

Numb.

I dove in, feeling the cool water wrap around me, making my outsides feel just as chilled as my insides.

I don't know how long I was swimming for, and I don't care. There was no one to be around, no appointments, no places to go. The only person I cared to see was in her home, locked away, battling emotions I had no clue what they entailed.

"You must be one pissed off son of a bitch!" I heard when I surfaced at the end of a lap, my muscles aching with exhaustion. Ben sat on a poolside footstool, leaning onto his knees with an assessing gaze.

"Or a sorry one." I tried to catch my breath. "What are you doing here?"

"Danica called me. She's been trying to get a hold of you, but you haven't picked up."

"So you know?"

"Your sister filled me in on enough. It explains why I haven't seen you in a while." He smirked. "I take it that it didn't go so well."

"Yeah, well, I should have known it wouldn't work." I snorted. "I thought this time was going to be different. It's bad that it took me a long time to figure out that Tracey wasn't the one for me, but this…" Fuck, did it hurt on a new level.

Ben nodded in understanding. "Listen, I've got to go and get a few orders sorted out before the dinner rush, but drop by later, we can talk."

"Maybe."

"If you're not there by ten, I'm hunting you down."

"Right." My chuckle was humorless.

"Seriously, man." He turned at the entrance from the patio and looked at me. "It'll be fine. Something tells me that if she's as smart as she is, she'll figure it out, and she'll be back."

"I won't hold my breath. I don't think it's what she wants, she's too fucking scared."

"Scared is a good reason, but not good enough."

"Practice what you preach, Carpenter. Wasn't it you who's been telling me that you're not interested in dating women because you're scared?"

"Not scared, try petrified." He gave me a dry chuckle. "I found my love and lost her, man. I'm not in a rush to do it all over again."

"Later."

"Remember, no phone call or no showing your ass means I'm popping by to be your drinking buddy at quitting time."

"Yeah, yeah."

"By the way, put some clothes on." My first real laugh of the day escaped and my best friend took his leave.

CHAPTER 31

After Ben's departure, I got out of the pool and grabbed one of the few towels I kept out in an outdoor cabinet for such times.

I headed inside and up to my room, wanting to soak up the heat from my shower, washing off the residual grime of chlorine and emotion down the drain.

With the water turned off, I wrapped a towel around myself. It was then that I swore I could hear something coming from my bedroom.

Everything looked normal, with the exception of my bed.

At its foot lay a red rose, a CD case, and an MP3 player on a docking station which was playing soft music. Nicole's voice filled the room through the tiny speakers and I found myself smiling. She'd been here. I picked up the case and looked it over. The titles to the songs were inscribed on the back, and there was a note written on its cover.

> *Michael,*
> *This is for all the times you need a smile, the times you need to sleep, the times your soul needs soothing, and the times you need love. If all else fails, you have me.*
> *Love,*
> *Nic*

I smiled, but despite the sudden boost in happiness from her declaration, I was disappointed that the woman whose voice I could hear, accompanied by her guitar, wasn't here in the flesh.

Why did she go?

I checked my phone.

Ben had been right.

Danica had left me several messages. Along with those, I had two from him, and five missed calls from Nicole.

I got dressed in an old t-shirt and a pair of cargo shorts, ran my brush through my hair and fixed it so I didn't look like I had just gotten out of bed.

Heading downstairs, trying to figure out what to make for dinner, I decided that takeout would be the best option.

When my feet hit the landing, en route for the kitchen where I stored the menus, I froze. Nicole stood by the picture window, looking out onto the world, her back mostly to me.

"I wasn't sure if you'd call back, so I came." Her voice was strained softly with emotion. She had her arms wrapped around herself, her hands rubbing up and down as if chasing a chill away.

"Thanks for the CD."

Thanks for the CD? I chastised myself for the comment. Couldn't you come up with something better?

My feet took me toward her and from the moment my arms wrapped around her waist, I felt the tension in her body dissipate. She leaned her back into my chest with a sigh of relief.

"Were you worried that I wouldn't want you?" I whispered in her ear, buffing my cheek against hers. Her small nod broke my heart. "You're mine, Nic, I'll always want you." I gave her a squeeze.

"How do you know?" She turned in my arms and faced me. Tears trickled down her cheeks. "I mean…I loved Dean too. What makes us so different? What makes you think that I deserve it? That we'll be happy? That we won't hurt each other?"

"Let me ask you something." I kissed her forehead. She closed her eyes, soaking in the small amount of comfort she could get from me. "Do you want to be happy? Are you looking to hurt me? Do you not feel deserving?"

"Yes. God no! And no." She tried to look away, but my hands cupped her face, trapping it so I could see the pain reflected in her eyes.

"Dean really did a number on you, didn't he?" I didn't so much ask as I pointed out. "I'm happy you answered the first two with the right answers, but what bothers me is your last one.

"Honey, you deserve more than you think. I see it, Danica sees it, and I know that everyone else in your life can too. You deserve the world, Nic, and as much as I know that, chances are, I will disappoint you at some point because I'm just a man, I'll spend the time you give us making you feel deserving, and giving you everything I know you need."

I brushed her damp cheeks with the pad of my thumbs.

"I'm sorry about how I reacted earlier."

"It wasn't the reaction I was going for, but I got what I wanted in the end." I smiled down at her.

"And what's that?"

"You."

With one hand sliding around her waist, the other cradling the back of her head, I pulled her closer. Savoring the moment, I leaned in and she gave herself over.

When her lips met mine, that familiar electrical sensation hit me tenfold. It was like all the missing links in my life were assuming in their rightful place.

Her hands rubbed up my chest and found their way on either side of my neck, her thumbs tracing my jaw. It was a sweet kiss, one filled with passion, but no aggression. We took our time, tasting and delighting in the closeness, the warmth.

The smile that graced her face when we pulled apart made me want to kiss her again and again until I knew it was going to be etched there permanently.

"I love you," I whispered and pecked her mouth.

"I-I love you too, Michael."

I held her gaze. "Don't say it if you don't mean it." I was serious.

"Oh, I mean it," she said with confidence. "It's the hardest thing I've ever had to say."

"I know the feeling," I smirked down at her, "but I'm glad it's out."

"So what do we do now?" She hugged me.

"I don't know about you, but after not having lunch, I feel like ordering myself and my girlfriend a pizza, settling in with a movie, maybe a fire, and some serious you-and-me time." I wiggled my brows when she tilted her head up to look at me.

"I have a feeling that I'm not going to want to leave here tonight. Maybe I should go home and pick up a few things."

"You won't need them." I gave her my best mischievous grin. "I plan on having you naked most of the time anyway. I have a lot of proving to do when it comes to convincing you what you deserve, and I don't care if Danica tears me a new one come Sunday, when I'm a no-show for our family dinner."

"Is that so?"

"Mmm." I pressed my lips to hers and stayed there. "It is."

CHAPTER 32

Nicole was right where I wanted her: naked and vulnerable on the plush rug by the fireplace. Tonight, she would be shown thoroughly, and convinced undeniably, of my love for her.

Something niggled at me though, and I couldn't quite figure what it was. I was forgetting something.

Pushing the feeling out of my mind, I proceeded to dote on my woman like no man ever could.

With a series of kisses down her neck, I moved to suck on her succulent breasts, her nipples growing taut for me. Her hands were in my hair, urging me to satisfy her, and I loved that she tried to fight for control, even in the most tender of moments.

I wasn't going to rush.

Not this time.

My fingers trailed after my lips, causing her moans to grow husky as she lost herself in my ministrations.

Skipping her wet folds, I trailed kisses to her inner thighs, nipping them, marking her as mine. The smell of her arousal drove me to hurry things up, but I resisted the urge.

Dipping a finger in her depths, I slid the digit over her g-spot. She came undone.

I took in the face of pure bliss displayed before me. "Beautiful."

It was time for a taste.

A second finger joined the first and began massaging, Nicole greeting me with the most pleasant of unfiltered sounds.

My lips surrounded her clit and began to suck and titillate, as I felt her internal tremors continue, until she spilled over again, this time, in my mouth.

I lapped her juices up, moaning my pleasure and dying to feel her wrapped around my cock. Damn, it hurt to be so fucking hard!

"Oh, Michael," she whimpered as lucidity came back to her. My fingers continued to pump inside her slick channel, my lips trailed back up from her heated pussy to her chest. "Baby, I love you! I love you, Mike! I…" Her words ceased, as a surprise to both of us, she climaxed again with a loud cry and her pelvis arched hard into my hand.

"I love you too," I whispered on her lips and kissed her hard. In a swift motion, I thrust my cock deep inside her, feeling the tremors of her third orgasm all around my shaft. "Fuck!" I said against her mouth. I wasn't going to last long if this kept up.

Her internal walls contracted and released around my girth as I kissed her lips, my fingers running through her hair.

She arched her hips into mine. "Please!"

I smiled down at her before shaking my head. "This is my time, honey." I pulled out, leaving the tip inside and held her gaze as I pushed back into her with smooth velocity.

"Oh, God!" Her eyes grew wide. "Again?" A strong twitch fluttered around my cock announcing the commencement of another whirlwind orgasm building.

Slowly, I delighted in the feel of her tightness wrapped around my member, her tremors squeezed me in a rhythm that almost matched the thrum of my heart.

Her hands came from the back of my head and cupped my face.

When her next climax became imminent, I was a goner. Her lips parted and her moans were like a song meant for me.

"Open your eyes, let me see you."

She did just that.

My hips jerked and as she flew over the precipitous edge, she took me with her.

Nicole's whimper of loss as I pulled out had me smiling. I reached for the couch throw and covered us as I remained settled between her legs, leaning on one arm, kissing away the stray tear that had come out during our climax. I couldn't stop touching her. Her skin was softer than the best of silks and satins I'd ever run my hands on.

"That was…" I nuzzled her cheek.

"…amazing," she finished for me.

"Beautiful." I looked at her and smiled. "Simply beautiful." She lifted her head and brushed my lips with hers.

For a while, we indulged in some innocent and sweet kisses, remaining by the fire, the idea of a movie long forgotten. Not much was said, we were content being close to one another, soaking up the unbelievable outcome of the day.

My lips were delighting in hers when I heard the front door open and shut.

Fuck!

"Hey, buddy, I'm– Holy shit!"

And that's when I remembered what that niggling feeling had been about.

Ben.

CHAPTER 33

The look of embarrassment and horror on Ben's face had been priceless. The man had been rendered to a blubbering mass of profuse apologies. He seemed more bothered by it all than Nicole was.

When Ben managed to put one foot in front of the other, he strode out the door, but not without mumbling a "lock the door next time" which brought on a fit of giggles to a humored Nicole. I couldn't help but laugh along with her.

The Ben incident had prompted me to carry her to my bed where I laid her down and made sweet love to her again, followed by gathering her in my arms and falling asleep.

Dilemmas.

They weren't all bad.

A naughty woman hovered above me. Words to an old 2-Live Crew song played about in my head, filling me with all sorts of dirty ideas. The sight was undoubtedly amazing, yet I couldn't get my hands on it.

Restrained.

Spread eagle in a starfish position, Nicole had me bound by ties. How she managed it, I don't know, but there was no doubting that I'd been out like a light when we finally settled in to sleep last night.

"I never imagined seeing this first thing in the morning!" I smirked at that upturned ass of hers that was displayed mere inches from my face. "Honey…" My words failed when her mouth covered my already erect cock and plunged down until it had hit the back of her throat. "Holy fuck!" My back bowed.

Lifting my head, she moaned as I got a lick of her glistening pussy lips. The vibration all around me made my hips buck, following her on the upstroke.

Nicole backed her ass up, as if knowing I had to strain to get to her. I was beside myself with elation at this shocking wake-up call and I knew that I'd have a little more fun of my own later today when she least expected it.

I ate her out like a man starved, gaining a certain fondness for the sixty-nine. If I had the use of my hands though, I would have pulled her back a little more so she really sat on my face, but I made do with what I had and, according to her squirming and moans, it was enough.

When she climaxed at the mercy of my mouth alone, I knew that I'd shoot my load right there in her mouth and our fun would be over.

The moment came, blindsiding me and I exploded. The sexy vixen swallowed me whole, or so it felt like it. She worked my length so that I stayed hard before turning to face me with a sly smile on that devil mouth of hers.

Nicole straddled my hips, impaling herself on my shaft. The sight of her naked gorgeousness made my arms flex against my restraints. I wanted to touch the goddess before me, so desperate to tweak those nipples, ravage her mouth, anything and everything I could get to.

"You seem to be in a pickle," she said with that sexy laugh of hers. "Good morning." She leaned forward and nibbled on my lower lip before kissing me. I felt her squeeze her internal muscles around me and my eyes widened as she straightened herself up, sitting atop my cock.

"Please loosen the ties," I begged. She shook her head with a teasing glint in her eyes and began to ride me.

The way her abs undulated reminded me of a belly-dancer. Damn, she was one hot mess first thing in the morning, and I was about to go out in a blazing inferno just watching her.

"I-I need to touch you."

"I think you need to let me do the touching, handsome." She winked and ground herself down on me. I groaned with my eyes rolling into the back of my head. "Furthermore, I don't think you're suffering that much, are you?"

"Fuck!" My voice croaked when I saw her hands reach up and tweak her nipples. "Fuck me!"

Her hips switched momentum and movement. "Mike…I…Oh!" I felt the first unbridled clench of hers around me. "I want you to watch me get off on you, baby. Watch me please myself, as I please you." Her voice had gotten higher as if she was putting effort in postponing her climax.

I gave Nicole a quick upward thrust of my hips as she lowered herself, her eyes widening. She came with a loud crying moan, coating my shaft with her juices, making her ride that much slicker.

Her rhythm continued to speed up and she let go of her tits with one hand, leaving one to please her top as she trailed a path down the middle of her stomach, all the way to her…

She isn't! Oh fuck, she is!

She began to massage her clit as her movements grew demanding. Her hips alternated between rotating and grinding, a pattern that was quickly driving me to lose my sanity.

"You feel amazing." I wanted to grab and fuck her until neither of us could see straight.

She moaned and met my eyes. "I'm burning right now, Mike."

"Nic," I said with desperation, "you're so fucking hot. Please!"

I wasn't quite sure what I was asking for anymore. To be freed? For her to never stop?

In the seconds I was trying to figure things out, a hand moved behind her and began massaging my sac.

She plunged herself over and over on my cock with so much velocity I could feel her bottoming out.

"Oh, God! Oh, baby! Oh fuck!"

It felt as if lava was about to erupt. The heat, the sweat, the sound of slapping skin, her moans, the way she wielded her body over mine as she took anything and everything she needed without my protest. She had me roaring my release to the heavens once more.

Nicole must have felt that same heat, because by the time my loudest cry faded, she had already begun praising the higher powers above, albeit with a few profanities, but it made the culmination of our morning sex that much better. The unfiltered sight of her coming undone was the cherry on top.

Nicole scooted up my body to undo my wrists, letting me slip out of her. I couldn't help but indulge in her tits which dangled in my face. She jumped when I nipped her the first time, and looked down at me with a surprised but amused glint in her eyes. I gave her a grin and just as quickly, latched on to her other nipple, which caused her to moan and she ground herself on my stomach before proceeding to my other wrist while my free hand roamed down her side to cup one ass cheek.

"I don't know if we'll be seeing much of the outside world today." I laughed into her bosom while rolling her onto her back. "That was…" I shook the haze from my head. "Woman, you've fucked the words right out of me." Color bloomed over her chest, up her neck and into her face. "And you're so much hotter to me right now with that blush. I'd let you fuck me mute if we both still had enough energy."

Her deep belly laugh exploded. I'd pay a fortune to hear that laugh again. It was the kind of laugh that was genuine, the kind that set a heart aflutter and warmed you to your core.

"I'm glad you enjoyed the show."

"Like you wouldn't believe." I pressed my lips to hers.

"Is there any chance for an encore performance, say, around lunchtime?"

"I'm sure I can be persuaded." She wrapped her arms around my shoulders and kissed my forehead before I settled my head onto her chest, hugging her torso, as I tried to regain my wits after a rather stimulating awakening.

CHAPTER 34

We spent the day secluded from the outside world, lounging. Thanks to that one night at Nicole's place, aside from naked, I knew there wasn't anything sexier than seeing her parading around with my shirt, so that's all I allowed her to wear.

It worked wonders when I saw her bare ass peek from the bottom of it, as she'd reached up in the kitchen cabinets for a bowl. I took her on the kitchen island that time.

Her glorious cheeks made another appearance when bending over to grab her phone out of her purse to check her messages. I made sure she knew I appreciated the view then too.

All day long, I began to find excuses to make her reach up or bend over. By the time she'd caught on to my antics, she was just as riled up as I was and forgot why she had been vexed to begin with.

The pool got some mileage too. I watched as she swam about and couldn't keep away from her naked form, so I grabbed her and fucked her up against the tiled edge, thankful that my neighbors weren't that close.

It had been an amazing day. But like all good things, they come to an end, right?

The doorbell rang and Nicole was chasing me around the house with a spoonful of chocolate sauce. We were in the middle of dessert, which had turned into a food fight of sorts.

"You're not getting away from me that easily, mister!" She came up behind me with a cloth to wipe at the spatter I had gotten on her cheek and plowed into my back when I opened the door to see who it was.

"Baby!" Tracey cried before she attempted to jump into my arms.

I caught her by the shoulders and kept her at arm's length.

"Tracey?" Nicole came to stand beside me.

"What the fuck are you doing here?" I asked my visitor, dropping her like a hot potato.

"I came for you." She tried to make another advance and that's when Nicole stepped in front of me. "Move, bitch."

How the fuck did she find out where I lived? "You need to apologize to my girlfriend, turn around, and leave me the hell alone."

"You know I can't do that," she said.

"Why the hell not?" I asked, annoyed, and slid my arms around Nicole.

"Because I still love you. I realized it when I saw you in Austin. We're meant to be together, Michael." Her eyes were intent on Nicole.

Call me crazy, but I couldn't hold back the laughter that bubbled up. When I looked over at Nicole, the woman had turned a shade of maroon.

"Get the fuck out!" Nicole yelled.

"Or what, your tiny ass will get rid of me?" Tracey asked, looking down on her.

Amazonian versus Sprite. The vision was comical, but the reality, not so much.

Nicole pounced, but the arm I wrapped around her waist acted as a metal band, preventing her from getting to her target.

"One more word, Trace, and I'll let her loose," I said. "She might be small, but she packs a punch. It's over. It's been over for nearly two years now, so go on and get out of here."

After a lengthy stare down, the woman conceded. "Fine, I'll go. But you will be mine again, Michael. She can't keep you happy. You know I can."

"You didn't keep me happy, Tracey. It's why I left, remember?"

We watched as my ex overdid it with the swinging hips on her way to her car, got in and drove off.

Things lightened up, but weren't that much better after Tracey's visit. It was as if a dark cloud hung over Nicole.

She had been hurt before and despite knowing my story, it didn't cure her of all insecurities. And I didn't expect them to dissipate right away either. Hell, I still had some of my own.

By the time we hit the sheets for the night, I couldn't keep my thoughts to myself anymore.

"You know," I combed my fingers through Nicole's hair, "I've never felt like this with anyone else, not even Tracey. The fire, the passion, the raw tension," I shook my head, "it was never there. Not like this." I grabbed one of her hands and intertwined our fingers.

"What were you thinking?" She gave a rather unladylike snort that had me chuckling.

"I don't know." I sighed into a soft kiss to her temple. "It makes me wonder how great things can be for you and me."

"I'm not going anywhere." She snuggled further into my side. "You'll have to cart me off to the loony-bin in a straightjacket to get rid of me, and that's if you manage to dissolve the superglue that's laid on thick against our bare skin, fusing us together."

I laughed at the visual. "Now, now…no need for invasive maneuvers. You'll be lucky if you can keep me off of you in the office." I hugged her tighter to me. "I can't see myself ever letting you go.

"I remember wondering one night, before things went south with…" Nicole propped herself on my chest with crossed arms and listened. "I wondered if what we were was it, if there wasn't anything more. It wasn't the bliss some people talked about. I pretty much thought–"

"That bliss was a myth?" she supplied.

I nodded. She understood. "It's like waking up or going to bed and turning to see your partner and deciding that being with them was better than being alone. You convince yourself that it's all there'll ever be, and that you're okay with it."

It was her turn to nod in agreement. "I used to tell myself that it could be worse. With Dean, I was taken care of from a financial standpoint, but I didn't care, because with the shop, I had it on my own too. The more I think about it now, the more superficial everything was between us. I'm not mad at him anymore, but I'm mad at myself for staying with him for so long, for giving into my weakness toward him."

I reached up and cupped her cheek. "He was stupid for not seeing you as anything more than a toy. Frigid, my ass!" I winked at her and she buried her face in my chest. Her lips pressed a lingering kiss against my chest.

"And how is the temperature then, doc?" she asked.

"You're the best I've ever had," I kissed her, "the hottest," another kiss, "the most beautiful, caring, loving person–"

She kissed me in an effort to shut me up. "Great answer." She smiled against my lips.

I grinned. "Great question."

CHAPTER 35

I woke up with a start. The quiet of the night had been broken by a large crash. Nicole heard it too and in my sleepy haze, I held her against the mattress, inspecting her from top to bottom to make sure she was fine.

"I think it came from downstairs." She swallowed hard. "Outside."

"Stay here," I told her, "I'll be right back."

I made to get out of the bed, but she grabbed onto my arm. "Maybe we should call the police."

I tried to sound reassuring. "No point if it's nothing. It'll be fine."

She let her hand fall to the sheets. "Hurry back."

"With you in my bed, how could I not?" I grinned, covering my manliness with my underwear, hoping that she wouldn't pick up on my apprehension.

I walked downstairs and my instincts were to look at all my front-facing windows. They were intact. I hurried to the front door and sighed when I confirmed that it was indeed locked, my alarm active. I looked out of the window beside the front door and saw it. Nicole's car windows were smashed.

"Nic," I called out. "Honey, I think you better come down here."

The sun was beginning to creep up higher in the early morning sky by the time the cops had left with Tracey's name as our suspected culprit after our brief explanation as to what had transpired yesterday. Nicole's car was taken away by a tow truck.

Nicole and I had spent the better part of the day unwinding from last night's events when she brought up the family dinner at Danica and Jake's.

I played with her hair. "I want to stay here with you."

"But you haven't even checked in with her, and I know that she called you on Friday. Christ, she called me before I came over."

I flipped her under me, on the couch. "I'll go if you come with me."

"Oh no, you don't!"

"I can convince you." My fingers found her sides and tickled her until she cried mercy. "So what'll it be?"

"Fine, I'll go, but you have to take me home so I can change."

"No more shirt?" I asked with a pout that befitted a small child.

"No, no shirt!" She giggled. "At least until later." She kissed my cheek. "I promise I won't disappoint."

"You haven't yet, honey," I smiled down at her.

Nicole was right.

That light green sundress of hers looked fantastic, but it's what she'd surprised me with when I got her to sit down with me before heading out that got me going. Thanks to my roaming hands, I discovered that the woman had barely covered herself with some skimpy piece of lacy floss.

Needless to say, I indulged in her a little before hurrying us out the door for some family time, which was bound to include an interrogation I no longer dreaded because I had my girlfriend with me.

Jordan ratted out my presence as per usual.

My sister appeared in the kitchen's entrance fuming until she saw Nicole, and then a smile broke out.

"Finally!" Jake said as he peered over her shoulder, an all-knowing grin on his face. "I told you, baby." He kissed Danica while handling Gabby.

I heard a cry from upstairs and knew that Marco must have just woken from his nap.

"I've got it," Nicole said and rushed off.

"Traitor!" I called up at her and she stopped to look down at me.

"She's your sister," she grinned, "you deal with her while I deal with your nephew."

When she disappeared, I realized everything had gone silent and everyone's attention was on me. "What?" I shrugged my shoulders.

"You could have at least returned my calls," Danica said.

I rubbed my hand at the back of my neck. "I was busy."

"Oh, I bet!" She smirked. "So I take it that you're together now?"

"Yeah." I grinned.

"It's about damn time!" She rolled her eyes at me before giving me a hug. "Take care of her. She's been through a lot…and so have you."

"I know, baby sis, I know."

Nicole made an appearance with baby Marco in her arms, and I was taken with the sight. She looked perfect, at ease with the newborn in tow. The pang of want to my gut was overwhelming.

I wrapped my arms around her as she cradled the little guy and kissed her temple. "A baby looks good on you," I whispered so only she could hear.

"I plan on getting a lot of practice time when it comes to making one of these." She bounced Marco in her arms and looked over her shoulder at me, smiling.

"You want kids?"

She nodded. "But I never felt the need before." I understood why.

I loved kids and wanted my own, but the proverbial 'baby fever' as they call it had never materialized when Tracey and I were together.

Nicole holding my nephew, so tender as she was, cooing and kissing him, made that urge to have a namesake of my own that much stronger. I could picture a little boy with dark brown hair like mine, her bright green eyes instead of my boring blue ones, a day where Nicole sat on the piano bench, teaching him to play…

"So Tracey's back in town." Danica pointed out, knocking me back to the present and shifting the conversation into uncomfortable territory.

"How'd you know?"

Jake snorted. "She stopped by yesterday. Real piece of work, that one."

"I know. Sorry."

"I sent her packing," Danica said. "I think she's got a few screws loose though, so watch out."

I grumbled. "That's an understatement."

"We think she might have wrecked my car," Nicole threw in.

"What happened to your car?" Jake asked.

We filled my sister and Jake in on the events of early this morning. "Are you sure it's her?" Danica asked.

"Who else would it be?" I asked.

Somehow, another name popped into my head, and I couldn't believe that I hadn't thought of it before. Nicole and I must have been on the same wavelength because we turned to one another with wide eyes.

"You don't think…" I started.

She shook her head, but didn't appear too convinced. "He doesn't even know where you live."

"Tracey found out somehow, so could he. And he'd recognize your car."

"There are loads of silver Honda Accords out there, Mike."

"And only one with your license plate." My gaze was stern. "Why are you so quick to dismiss him?"

"I just don't think he would do something like that."

"What about when you told me–" Dani started but shut her mouth.

I found my girlfriend giving my sister a shut-up-if-you-know-what's-good-for-you look. Nicole met my eyes, but she never elaborated.

"Fine! Let's just wait and see what the cops have to say," I conceded.

Why was Nicole so quick to brush her ex off? Her dismissal of the overall situation pissed me off more though. She made it seem like there was no threat against her, when in reality, there could very well be.

The whole situation worried me. What if it wasn't her car, but her head next time?

I shuddered at the thought.

"Hey, you okay?" she asked. We were sitting so close on the sofa that there was no way she hadn't felt the tremor.

"Fine!" I said, my sullied mood apparent.

Okay, so I might be worrying more than I should, but at least one of us was.

"It'll be fine." She pecked my lips. "You'll see."

I hope so.

CHAPTER 36

Monday rolled by with far too many meetings keeping me out of the office all day. I found myself missing Nicole, rushing to get back to her.

Instead of a beaming smile to greet me when I got to the office, I sure as hell didn't expect the sight of a pair of wide shoulders leaning over my woman.

Dean.

The man had his hands holding onto her arms, forcing her into him.

Too busy snickering at the inappropriate display before them, the men and women that were viewing the spectacle hadn't even paid enough attention to notice Nicole's panicked demeanor. The fact that no one had budged to stop the bastard, when it was so evident that Nicole wasn't interested, set me off.

My feet moved, as if a puppet manned by some unseen force, taking me in their direction. I ripped the man away from Nicole by his shirt collar, the fabric tearing as seams were forced.

"Just what the hell do you think you're doing?" I growled.

A large fist came at me in a flash. One minute I was a seething ball of anger and the next, I was a complete puddle of dazed mush on the floor and the side of my face was throbbing.

Nicole took the opportunity to move toward me and crouched down. I accepted her help to get back to my feet.

"Leave now or I'll have security throw you out. And don't ever let me catch you with your hands on Nicole again," I said, filled with venom.

"She wanted it."

"Dean!" Nicole started.

"Did you?" I looked at her, already knowing the answer.

"What? No!" She looked at me as if I'd lost my mind. "He forced himself on me!"

"That's what I thought I saw." My eyes never left Dean. "Nic, call security and have this man escorted out. He'll be lucky if I don't press charges."

"You threw the first punch. Remember that." The man was referring to our scene at the bistro as he proceeded toward the elevators. "I'll be seeing you, Nikki."

Nicole didn't deign him with an answer to that last statement as he left without another word.

As soon as he was no longer within sight, she turned toward me and tried to grab my face, but I pulled back and her hands froze mid-air. She looked torn, and I was past mad.

"What the fuck was he doing here?"

"I don't know. I was on the phone with a client and when I turned around to drop a file on your desk, he was right there."

"Are you okay?" I asked and this time, when her hands came up to frame my face, I let her touch me.

She nodded with a sad smile on her face. "I'm fine."

"Hey, boss?" I heard from someone on the floor and I grabbed her hands to lower them.

"Yeah!" I called out to Randy, one of our finance executives and turned to him.

"I've got something for you to take a look at before I send it out," he said.

Squeezing Nicole's hands in mine briefly, I said, "I'll be right back, and then we're going home."

"Don't you mean you're driving me home?"

"No!" My tone brokered no argument. I turned to the man that had asked for my attention. "Randy, in my office."

He acted fast and I turned to Nicole again. "I don't care where I sleep, but I'm not letting that asshole get near you again."

She sighed. "We'll talk about this later."

"Wait for me."

"I can't do much except pay a small fortune to get home by cab, so yeah, I'll be right here," she said with ample sarcasm and muttered something about a rental.

From the time Randy left my office to when we walked into her house, Nicole hadn't said much but answer my questions with a quiet yes or no. She was in the kitchen, fetching us a drink and slamming every cabinet door she opened in the process.

Something wasn't right.

"Nic?" She jumped, but kept her back to me as she poured our drinks and handed me my glass before walking past me. "Nic?" I followed her to the den.

She took a generous sip from her glass before setting it down and picked up her guitar.

"Nicole!" This ignoring bit of hers was getting on my last nerve. "Will you at least look at me? What the fuck is going on?"

"Mike, just go home."

"Go home?"

"That's what I said!" she said over her shoulder, strumming the guitar strings. "I don't need a babysitter."

"Is that what you think I'm doing?"

"It's exactly what you're doing, Michael." She turned to pierce me with her emerald eyes. "What else would you call it? I'm a grown-ass woman! I can take care of myself."

"I'm well aware of that," I said and set my drink down, crossing my arms at my chest.

"Just because my car was bashed in, and my ex shows up at the office, doesn't mean that I'm in any imminent danger.

I have a security alarm. I have pepper spray. I know not to let strangers in."

I burst out laughing.

She looked vexed at my reaction.

I moved to a crouch in front of her.

"I don't find any of this funny, Michael."

"Neither do I." I cupped her face in my hands. "I know you're fine and fit to be on your own, honey. It still doesn't make me worry about you any less." She looked down, to her feet. "Look, if you want me to go, I will."

She never answered, but I took it as a yes.

I rose to my feet, massaging the bridge of my nose with my index and thumb. My headache from that asshole's punch had intensified due to my frustration.

Her hand covered mine when it landed on the front door's knob. "Don't go like this."

"It's okay, I get it. I'll go home, take a few painkillers and take it easy. I'll call you later."

"No."

"What do you mean, no?"

"You're not leaving." She closed the distance between us and pushed me against the door.

"Nic," I sighed, "I'm not in the mood to hash this out. You want to be home and I plan on letting you enjoy what you want, which is peace."

"Who said I wanted that?" She smirked up at me. Was this woman sending me mixed signals, or had Dean's punch affected me more than I'd originally thought? My brows furrowed. "I might have not wanted a babysitter, but I never said anything about not wanting my man with me. After all, I have to take care of him, since my ex was the one to give him that nasty bruise on his cheek."

"Are you sure?"

Her hand came up to lightly finger the swelling on my face and I flinched. "Mike, let me take care of you. I haven't seen you much today. I could use a bit of alone-time with you. Plus," she winked at me, "I need to forget about what that bastard tried to do."

Without another word, she guided me to the couch and made me sit. Leaving me there for a moment, she came back with a glass of water and a couple of ibuprofen.

"So, about forgetting that bastard?" I asked, pulling her down to me after setting the glass of water on the side table. She straddled my lap as I gazed up at her face while my head rested on the back of the couch. "There are a few things you need to do first."

"And those are?"

"I haven't had a kiss from you all day. I–"

Her lips crushed mine.

Well, something has to be said about asking and receiving…

CHAPTER 37

I wish I could say that the rest of the week had gone well, but it seemed that at every turn, something new popped up, and shit was hitting the proverbial fan on the work front. Spending my evenings with Nicole at my side seemed to be the one thing keeping me sane.

I missed having Danica around the office. With her being home, I was assuming a lot of her duties, and combined with my very own, it left me very thin energy-wise.

"Are you sure about this?" Nicole asked. "I can always tell Dani that we'll go some other time."

"Go." I pressed my mouth to hers. "I've got a lot to look after tonight. I'd like to be out of here by nine."

"It would go quicker if I stayed."

"No, it wouldn't." My lips pressed against the side of her neck. "You're a distraction here when no one else is around. Besides, if you skip out on Dani, she'll be in here before you know it, dragging you off, kicking and screaming."

She laughed. "True, but I bet we could get her to go away screaming herself with some of the things that you've been coming up with these last few days." She pressed her front into my chest suggestively.

I groaned. "Honey, you have to go."

"I should, shouldn't I?" She pulled away with a pout. "Will you be coming over tonight?"

"You know I will." I smiled. "Now move that sweet ass of yours so I can get on with it, and get back to you at a respectable time, if you can call nine-ish that."

"Okay." She backed away from me. "I know

when I'm not needed." She turned and walked to my office door.

It didn't take me long to reach her and press her against the wall next to it. "Forget something?"

"Not to my recollection." The light dancing in her eyes told me that she was in a mood to tease.

"I need my kiss, Nic!" I wrapped a hand behind her neck and crashed my lips to hers. Before long, our bodies were pressed against each other's. Much to my disappointment, I pulled back. "In case you didn't know this, I always need you, honey. More than you'll ever know."

"I think I've figured that out." She rubbed her pelvis against mine, my dick quickly running out of room.

"Devil woman!" I grumbled. "I didn't mean it in that way."

"I know, handsome. Hurry home." She kissed me one last time.

"I will. Have fun."

"Only because you asked me to."

Nicole winked and left my office.

I was on my way to my car when my cell rang. I looked at the caller ID and slid my thumb across the screen to answer. "Dani, what's up?"

"Get your ass over here now!"

She hung up before I had the chance to ask her why. The woman sounded none too pleased for whatever reason, and it seemed like I was going to be cursed with the brunt of her temper.

I redialed her number. "You better tell me what the fuck is going on. I have a woman to get back to, and after the night I've had, I'm not feeling your tone."

She snorted. "Yeah, well, I'm sure Tracey can wait."

"What?"

"Come out with it. The bitch told us everything!"

"What the hell are you talking about?"

"I'm just glad that Nikki held herself together long enough to leave without anything physical happening."

"Dani, what happened? I haven't seen or spoken to Tracey since the weekend when she showed up on my doorstep."

"Sure!"

She didn't believe me? "Are you fucking kidding me?"

"Do you take us for fools, Michael? Get your ass here now. I can't believe I helped you land my best friend. How could you!"

"I didn't do anything!" I yelled into my phone. "I'll be home soon. Where's Nicole?"

"It doesn't matter."

"That's where you're wrong. Where is she, Dani?"

"Forget about Nicole right now, Mike. I'm not going to tell you a damn thing until you explain yourself."

She hung up.

CHAPTER 38

Danica launched herself off my front steps and toward my car as I pulled into my driveway.

"You have a lot of nerve!" she said when I stepped out of my ride. Why were my house lights on?

"Hold on a minute." I held my hand up to halt her words. "Don't you go and attack me when I have no fucking clue as to what the hell's going on!"

"You let her move in!"

"Who?"

"Who else? That fucking ex of yours, you lying, two-timing bastard!" She pushed me in the chest and slammed me into the side of my car.

"Excuse me?"

A car door slammed behind me.

"Danica!" Jake came running out toward us, grabbed his wife and held her away from me. "Calm down."

"Don't you dare tell me to calm down!" Her eyes shot daggers at her husband. "My brother is behaving like a jack-ass and I'm calling him on it!" She turned her glacier gaze back to me. "I told you not to hurt her, and what do you do? You let your ex move in!"

"I'm only going to say this once, so listen carefully," I said. "Tracey has not moved in, nor will she ever. What the fuck gave you that idea?"

"Have you not been home?" she asked.

"Not until now. I've been staying over at Nicole's for the past few days," I told her. "Planned on staying there again tonight. Nicole can tell you that. Where is she?"

"I don't believe you."

"I don't need you to believe me. Now tell me where Nicole is." I was losing what thin thread I had left on my patience.

"Baby, I think he's telling the truth," Jake said.

"I am." No one said anything. "Fuck this! I'll find her myself." I wanted to jump in my car and go, but I remembered the lights I had seen illuminating my home and headed toward the house. I paused to turn and look at my sister with my hand on the doorknob. "When I broke it off with Tracey, it was the end. I love knowing that my own family thinks so little of me. Tell me this, Danica. Why the fuck did you even help me win your best friend over if you thought I'd fuck around? Why worry about me getting hurt if I'm such a bad guy? I don't need this bullshit. I need my fucking girlfriend, dammit!"

I shoved my keys in the tumbler only to find the door unlocked.

What the fuck?

"Baby!" I heard as I slammed my front door, leaving my sister and brother-in-law out in the proverbial cold.

This must be the twilight zone.

"Oh, hell no!" I stopped her in her tracks. "What the fuck is going on?"

"I told you that we'd be together." She tried to throw herself at me again.

I held her back. "And I told you, there wasn't a chance in hell. You broke into my house!"

"I found the hide-a-key." She shrugged her shoulders, as if she hadn't committed an offense. "You keep it under the flower pot on the front step, just like you did in Austin."

If that wasn't a sign to avoid a hide-a-key, I don't know what was.

"I'm not your baby!" I said. "Get the fuck out of my house before I call the cops." I moved to open the door, but it opened before I'd reached it and in came a livid Nicole.

The woman ignored me completely and stomped to

Tracey, grabbing my ex's arm, and pulled her toward the front of the house.

"Let go of me you bitch!" Tracey screamed.

"Not on your life, slut!" Nicole retorted.

I slid my hand down my face, stopping to pinch the bridge of my nose. *Christ, this is like some bad episode of Maury Povich.*

"You have two choices. Either you leave on your own, or I make you."

"I'd like to see you try!" the woman said.

"Gladly!" Nicole proceeded toward the woman. "If I ever see you near me or Michael again, I'll slap you with a restraining order so damn fast, it'll make your head spin."

Tracey was the first one to lash out, slapping Nicole across the face. The contents of my stomach began to churn, but before I could move to separate the two, Nicole's claws came out.

She reared and slammed her fist into the woman's cheek, flooring her literally onto her ass.

"You have no clue how much you'll regret that!" Tracey said as she attempted to get to her feet, unsteady in her movements.

"Try and bring me up on charges for assault and I'll guarantee you that you'll lose. Mike saw you and look around, lady, there's no guessing whose side he's on. I'll claim self-defense."

"She's right." I crossed my arms, taking a stand beside Nicole. "Go back to Austin, Tracey. The next time I see you, I'm filing an injunction."

"You can't be serious!"

"As a heart attack," I said.

"But what about my stuff?"

"Grab what you left in the entrance and the rest is in the mail." Damn, if kicking her out like this didn't feel better than when I first left her ass.

The woman huffed before letting out a loud growling

shriek. "You two deserve each other! You can both go to hell!"

"On the first point, you're right. On the last, I've been there already, with you, and I don't care to revisit."

Nicole snorted a laugh at my statement.

Tracey started for the door and I hoped that it would be the last we ever saw of her.

"Hell might have been an understatement; Lucifer's lair would be better matched to her." The front door slammed shut.

Nicole's words made me snicker. She had no clue how right she was.

I turned to the fierce woman beside me and cupped her chin to take a look at her face. "By the way, that's quite the right hook you have, honey."

Nicole pulled her chin out of my grasp and backed away. There was a discernible hand print on her cheek, but what worried me more was the cold distance she was putting between us.

Her brows were pulled together. "I'm going to need some time, Mike."

"What?"

She kept backing up until she'd reached the door. "I know that you had nothing to do with what happened tonight, but this is too much. I need time to process."

"But, Nic–"

"I have to go," she said and made her escape.

The shock of her behavior had me frozen in place long enough to register a car revving as it left the front drive.

One thing was for sure, it felt like the beginning of the end for us, and I had no clue how to rectify the situation.

The one thing I did know, though, was that I needed to find Nicole and fast. And when I got a hold of her, she wasn't running from me.

Sitting in my car, I dialed Nicole's number. No answer, as

anticipated. I figured I'd start with the most obvious of places and headed toward her house. When I arrived, her home was plunged in darkness and her rental car wasn't in the drive.

Where are you, Nic?

I drove around for hours, checking out a few of her favorite haunts, including the commercial space she used to rent.

Nothing.

Knowing that she'd have to come back home at some point or another, I settled on heading back there to wait.

But first, parked at the curb outside the location that used to be her old music shop, I sent her a text, thinking that at least she'd be forced to read it.

> *Nic,*
> *I don't know why you think you need space.*
> *We need to talk, honey. Call me as soon as you*
> *get this. I'm worried.*
> *I love you.*
> *M*

I never got a response.

CHAPTER 39

Nicole's lack of contact was a direct hit to the solar plexus.

One thing was for sure, I needed help, and I needed it bad.

But first, I had to talk to my sister.

Before I could connect the call, my phone rang in my hand.

I answered before looking at the call display, "Nic…" and put the car in drive.

"No, it's your sister."

"Dani, I didn't let her in, I swear." My voice cracked.

"I think I know that now." She sighed. "Are you sure there's–"

"Don't even finish that sentence." I growled. "She's gone now, thanks to Nicole."

"What?"

I chuckled at the memory of the spitfire nymph scene. "Yeah, Nicole came roaring in like a lioness and made Tracey leave."

"She didn't!" Danica guffawed. "I knew she was on a mission with the way she stormed in without giving Jake and I a second glance."

"She did." I sighed. "Sis, I need your help. I don't know what went on when you two were with Tracey, and Nicole left before I could ask her what happened. She said she needed space and ran out like her hair was on fire. She could barely look at me, let alone stand my touch."

I heard Danica release a loud breath. "You called her?"

"Yeah, and she won't pick up. She hasn't even answered my text. What the hell happened earlier? I'm losing my mind here and I have nothing to go on!"

"We went over to your place. Nicole had it in her mind to surprise you with a quick text telling you that there was a change of plans and that you guys would be staying at your place tonight. So much for romance, because when we got there, Tracey was making herself at home."

"What did Tracey tell Nicole for her to leave me? I know Nicole didn't believe I let her move in. So what else was there?"

"I'm sorry, but I fell for her whole moving-in scheme," Danica started. "There wasn't anything else but…"

"What?" I pushed.

"She said something about how things shouldn't be that hard before she left." Danica sighed. "I called you right after that."

"Dani, do you know where Nicole is? I checked her house, the place where her shop used to be…I don't know where else to look."

"I got a text from her about fifteen minutes ago." Danica's voice shook.

"Where is she?"

"Mike…"

"Please tell me she didn't…"

"She's at Dean's," she affirmed. "Well, at least that's where she was when I got her text, and then I called her to bitch about her brainless move."

"Where does the bastard live? I swear, if he's touched her, I'll rip his arms from his body and feed them to him for breakfast."

"I don't know. Listen, when I spoke to her, I tried to convince her to talk to you. She refused. So I tried to convince her that she needed to go home, that she was about to do something stupid and ruin something great she had finally found with you if she stayed there."

"What did she say?"

"She said that it was already ruined." My breath caught at my sister's words. "There's one more thing though. I got the sense that she wasn't over at Dean's for the same old thing."

"What makes you say that?"

"She sounded different. Pissed. Almost like a woman on a mission."

Yeah, that seemed to be the theme to her personality tonight.

"Where are you?" Danica asked. "Are you okay?"

I rubbed a hand down my face, pinching the bridge of my nose and took a deep breath, released it. "No, I'm not okay. I'm just about to turn up her street. Hold on." I pulled the phone away from my ear as I rounded the corner, using both hands on the steering wheel to park by the curb.

Nicole's rental was in her driveway and I caught sight of her walking up the walkway to her front door. That's when I noticed smoke coming from her roof, towards the back of the house. "Holy fuck, Dani! Call 9-1-1! Get in your car, bring Jake. Get to Nicole's as fast as you can! I've got to go."

"Wait!"

I ended the call before Danica could say anything more. I threw my phone on the passenger seat, jumped out of the car and ran toward Nicole.

"Nicole, no!"

The woman turned to face me, but it was too late. One second I felt the ground beneath my feet shake and the next, the shattering of glass could be heard before the big bang made my ears ring. A massive wave of heat knocked me onto my ass and Nicole went flying dozens of feet onto her front lawn.

"No!"

Nicole lay in a heap, unmoving as I rushed to her, collapsing to my knees.

A blonde woman stood across the street, watching the whole thing and I repeated the same order I had given Danica.

"Call 9-1-1!"

I knelt at Nicole's side and paused. I didn't know if I should move her, but surely, leaving her on her stomach couldn't be good for her breathing if she was having issues from the shock of the blast.

Careful not to jostle her too much, I flipped her onto her back. Her color was ashen, her nose was bleeding, and she had a gash on her forehead. I felt for a pulse, finding one that was weak and thready, but it was there, and that was enough to quelch my ever-growing fear.

In the distance, I could hear the sirens getting closer. When I turned to see if the blonde woman was still there, she had disappeared.

Helpless and alone, I began to pray, holding Nicole's hand in mine as we waited for help.

Please, honey, please be okay.

CHAPTER 40

With a distraught Danica and Jake standing behind me, the paramedics worked on bringing Nicole around. They tried for a while before finally giving in, securing her to a stretcher and proceeded to load her up in the back of the ambulance.

Firefighters were busy running around, trying to control the blaze, but I paid them no heed, too consumed with worry for the woman I loved.

"Sir, we're leaving now, if you'd like to jump on in," the female attendant said.

I didn't hesitate.

Throwing my car keys to Jake, I jumped in to sit beside Nicole who remained unconscious.

I spent the rest of the night at the hospital, my ass perched in an uncomfortable chair, listening to the beeps and hums of monitoring devices.

Every so often, a mechanical voice interrupted the rhythmic pattern over the PA system.

The police had been and gone, taking my statement. I'd given them as much as I could remember, what with my mind wanting to shut down from the exhaustion and stress of the day.

Nicole had come to a few times, but only to fade back into slumber.

Danica and Jake headed home, with much reluctance on

my sister's part, after Nicole had been examined and admitted. I had to promise to call them if there were any important changes in her condition.

Nurses woke Nicole at regular intervals throughout the night due to a moderate concussion, but she was so out of it that she never noticed my presence at her bedside. The doctor assured me that it was nothing to worry about, and his additional medical jargon did nothing to assuage my overwhelming worry. I knew that nothing short of Nicole waking and seeing the look of recognition on her face when her eyes met mine would make me feel better.

Sitting vigil, I struggled to keep my eyes open, despite the discomfort in my ass, back and neck. It seemed that the medical professionals had a keen sense for sleep disruption and it didn't apply strictly to patients. Without fail, I would begin to nod off and a nurse or doctor would walk in, interrupting the few moments of rest I managed to find.

Morning came and I hadn't slept more than a wink.

I was standing by the room's window, watching as the outside world came to life for yet another day, when I heard Nicole stir with a moan.

I rushed to her bedside and grabbed a hold of her hand. "Good morning, beautiful." Tears burned my eyes, and I forced them back.

"Hi." Her voice croaked. "What happened?"

"You don't remember?" She tried to shake her head but winced. "Don't move, you have a concussion. What's the last thing you remember?"

"I left your place confused and wandered around for a while. I remember getting a call from your sister...I came home." She swallowed hard and her brows furrowed. "You were there."

I nodded and managed a sad smile. "That's right."

"You yelled at me."

"I came over because we needed to talk," I started. "I saw

smoke coming out from your house and I came after you. There was an explosion."

"My house!" Her eyes teared up.

I shook my head, hating myself for being the bearer of bad news. "I'm so sorry, honey, it's gone."

Her body began to shake with silent sobs and I couldn't take it. I buried my head in her pillow, the sides of our faces touching as I whispered consoling words in her ear and ran my fingers through her hair.

Nicole's arms came around my shoulders and she buried her face in my neck, and that was my undoing.

"I was terrified," I told her, my body beginning to shake. "I thought I'd lost you for good."

"I'm here." She pulled me closer. "I'm fine." Her hands came up to cup my face and pulled me back. Her eyes bore into mine. "And I'm yours, if you'll still have me. I know I don't deserve it with the way I ran off instead of sticking around and talking things out like you asked. I know I'm a wreck. I'm scared of anything that has to do with settling down and–"

"On one condition," I said with determination. "If you ever have doubts about us, you come to me first. No more running. I don't know how long we'll be together, but I do know how great things can be, and after last night, I know that I can't live without you, Nic." I took a deep breath and continued. "I have no clue if forever is in the cards, but it's what I want when I think of us. Last night, not being able to know how you felt, what you were thinking...I hated that."

"Me too, and it's my fault."

I cupped her chin in my hand. "It's both our faults. You could have stayed just like I should have stopped you from walking out my door."

"I love you, Michael, but you're killing me right now." I arched my brow in question. "Kiss me?"

I didn't hesitate.

The moment our lips met, she pulled me down on top of her. I pulled away and combed my fingers through her hair.

"I love you too. Now let's get the doctor in here so he can send you home."

"Shouldn't you be getting ready for work?"

"I'm not leaving you, honey, but I do have a question for you." Her brows arched. "Have you thought about where you'll be staying when you leave here?"

She grinned. "Is this where you convince me to live with you?" She feathered her fingers through the hair at the back of my head.

"Perhaps." I nuzzled her nose. "Do I really need to ask?"

"Hmm." She gave me a chaste kiss. "Not really."

I chuckled. "It's settled then. You're moving in with me."

"I like the sound of that."

Me too, maybe too much.

CHAPTER 41

It took the better part of the morning before the doctor came to release Nicole. By then, all the woman had was a bad headache, aching muscles, and her stomach rumbled with hunger because the hospital's food selections proved to be less than stellar.

Armed with the physician's advice on what to watch for that would indicate worsening of Nicole's condition, he signed her release and handed her a prescription for pain killers.

Sporting hospital scrubs, my girlfriend looked down at herself with a scowl when she exited the bathroom in her new duds. "I look frumpy."

"You look beautiful." *Alive.*

"Are you blind?"

I grinned. "Only to everyone else out there."

Her annoyed expression melted and she stopped in front of me, smiling. "I love that silver tongue of yours."

"It's the truth." I wrapped my arms around her. "Let's get out of here."

"I need to do something about clothes and my ID. My God! The insurance–"

"Whoa, whoa, whoa!" I kissed her temple. "We'll get to that soon enough, honey. Right now, let's just get you home and settled. I wouldn't mind a nap."

Her fingers played with the hair at my temple before cradling my cheek.

"You didn't sleep last night did you?" I shook my head. "Can I ask you for a small favor?"

"As long as it's within reason." I kissed the inside of her wrist.

"Can you drive by the house on your way home?"

I contemplated her request. "Are you sure?"

She nodded. "I need to see it."

"Okay."

Turning the corner where last night's horror had greeted me, this time, it was Nicole's nightmare that awaited us.

The premises was surrounded with yellow caution tape, twirled onto pegs surrounding the perimeter of her property. The only thing left was the charred framework of her house, nothing else.

With the car parked, Nicole let herself out.

"I can't believe this," she said after a long moment of silence. "How am I supposed to move on from this?"

I came to a stop behind her and wrapped my arms around her waist. "We'll figure it out." I kissed the back of her head. "I'll help." She leaned her head back onto my shoulder. "We'll make some calls, see what your options are."

She turned to face me and I caught her solemn expression. "I don't think this was an accident, Mike."

"Honey, let's see what the authorities have to say about it first, okay?" I closed my eyes and breathed to stave off the rage that was building up inside. I didn't have the guts to say it out loud, but I doubted an investigation was needed to let us know that she was right.

"Who would do this?"

"I don't know." I sighed, *but I have my suspicions.* Some of those ponderings made sense, others, not so much. "Let's get going."

CHAPTER 42

Nicole was at home with Danica who dropped by with the babies while Jake was out on business. With nothing to wear but the clothes on her back, which had been borrowed from my sister, I told the ladies to keep the windows and doors locked, along with the security alarm activated, and left them for some overdue girl time.

I had a plan.

After a busy afternoon wandering about downtown, the back of my car was filled with an added something that was sure to brighten Nicole's day, along with my other treasures.

I got home to find a police cruiser in the driveway and rushed in with as many, but not all, of my parcels.

Had something gone wrong?

Storming through the entrance I called out to Nicole.

The woman in question came out from the living room to greet me with baby Marco in her arms and her jaw dropped. "What's this?"

My body went slack with relief and I gave her a sheepish look. Shrugging my shoulders, I said, "I just thought I'd pick you up a few things while I was out. What's going on? Did something happen while I was out?"

She shook her head. "It's arson, Mike."

"We have reason to believe that the arsonist may be trying to get to you through Nicole," Detective Mercer supplied. "Can you think of anyone you might have done business with, maybe someone disgruntled enough to go to extremes? It could be a previously dismissed employee, a client…"

The cops were trying to cover every possible angle, that was for sure. For a second time in as many days, I was questioned within an inch of my sanity.

"This isn't the first time that Nicole's been a target," I said after Mercer was done with his questions. "If you talk to Detective Shane Peters, he's the one who's heading the investigation for her car."

The man nodded. "All right. Miss Baxter, you've mentioned your exes have been back in the picture recently." Nicole nodded. "We'll start looking at the few names you've both managed to provide. In the meantime, I need to wait on the arson unit to finish up with their investigation. I'll keep you posted if any other leads turn up from canvassing your neighborhood. No one's come forth yet, but it doesn't mean that there isn't someone out there who's noticed something suspicious."

"Thank you, Detective," I said, squeezing Nicole's shoulder as she still held my nephew, tucked against her chest.

The cop sighed. "If something else comes to mind, you have questions, or if anything happens that you think is related to this case, call me immediately." Mercer extended his hand which I shook.

The man turned toward Nicole and offered her a sympathetic smile. "We'll find this guy, Miss Baxter."

Nicole nodded. "Thank you."

After the man left, I turned from shutting the door, and Nicole pointed over her shoulder with her thumb. "So about those."

"Go check them out." I took a fussing Marco from her and sat myself on the couch beside my sister, who was bouncing Gabby on her knee.

"What did you do?" Danica asked me.

We watched as Nicole rushed to the bags I had left beside the couch. My sister's breath came out in a whoosh when Nicole pulled out a few items of clothing. "Oh no! You didn't!" Nicole looked at me. "I have money to do that, you know."

"I know. I was only going to buy a few things at first, but then…" I gestured to the bags. Yeah, I'd gone a little overboard.

Danica giggled. "Since when does a few things translate to a whole new wardrobe?"

"What?" I laughed. "I think I'm going to enjoy watching her wear what I got her."

"You're going to make my ears bleed with that kind of talk." My sister turned to her best friend, squealed her excitement and plopped Gabby on my lap beside her twin. "Let me see!"

Nicole reached for the Victoria's Secret bags and started pulling out pieces of lace, satin and silk. She turned to me with an arched brow. "Is there anything you didn't get?"

"I'm not sure. Oh! Hold that thought, I left something in the car."

The women looked at each other and after helping me put each baby down in their respective car seat, I rushed toward the front door. They were giggling over the sound of rustling tissue paper and crinkling of shopping bags when I exited the house. I never realized, until then, how much I'd missed hearing the sounds of joy and excitement in my home.

I got to the trunk of my car, popped it open and pulled out the large parcel.

With one foot in the door, I said, "Close your eyes." I entered the house, shutting the front door behind me. "Dani, make sure she listens, and I don't want to hear anything from your mouth either."

Danica giggled. "Scouts honor. This should be good."

I walked into the room and Danica began to bounce on

the couch when she saw my parcel. Nicole squirmed in her seat as I sat on the coffee table in front of her.

"Open your eyes, honey."

The look on her face when she saw what I held was priceless. "You didn't!" Her voice was breathless. I nodded. "But why?"

"Because I know you're happiest when you're playing." She reached to open the case and pulled out the guitar, her fingers skimming its surface reverently. "I can't have you living here and not have your music. You'd be miserable, and I'd miss hearing you."

"I could have paid for all of this," she repeated her earlier words and strummed the chords on the acoustic, her nose scrunching up, most likely because the instrument wasn't tuned, "but I love you so much more for doing it."

CHAPTER 43

I helped Danica get the babies into her car and waited until I saw my sister's taillights round the corner before heading inside, finding Nicole strumming away on her new baby.

Leaning on the wall, I watched her for a short while before moving toward her. She smiled at me and set the guitar down on the coffee table when I crouched to sit beside her.

"I don't deserve this." She shook her head, but her grin remained.

"You deserve so much more." She shifted to her knees and straddled my lap as I leaned back to look at her. "That smile of yours," I ran my fingers through her hair, "it makes you look even more beautiful."

"You need to stop that. You're already getting lucky."

I laughed. "That wasn't my intention, but it is one hell of a payoff."

Her fingers grazed the stubble on my jaw, which I had yet to shave off. "Let's get you to bed. You look beyond exhausted."

"The doctor did tell you to take it easy. I'll go lay down if you come with me."

"I think I can swing that." Her lips brushed against mine and she pulled away before I could deepen the kiss. "It's not like I plan on going anywhere. I have no house and my boss won't let me work until next Monday. That's more than a week off, you know."

"I like the fact that you're staying here." I nuzzled her nose. "And I'm not reneging on you going back to work sooner. They were doctor's orders more than mine, but you won't hear any complaints from me."

"But you're going to fall behind." She got up and pulled me to my feet.

"Honey, I love that you worry about me, but you have enough to worry about with the fire, the insurance, and the investigation right now." She sighed deep and I turned her around to face me at the bottom of the staircase. "How's this?" I squeezed her hands in mine. "I'll let you take care of my schedule and emails, but that's it, and it'll be done from here." She gifted me with a beaming smile. "Happy now?"

"Very." And she led me up the stairs.

The door to my en suite opened and I was blessed with a vision of Nicole wearing a satin number that I had purchased for her.

"I think someone has an aversion to traditional jammies." She giggled.

My gaze was slow in its appraisal. "Wow!" I swiveled my ass so I sat on the edge of the mattress, motioning for her to come closer.

Nicole sauntered over with a lascivious smile. "You like?"

"Very much." I pulled her down so she straddled me and gave her a deep kiss. "How are you feeling?"

"Good." She pecked my chin. "Great, actually."

I ran my hands over the back of her thighs, over her ass until they met the satin covering her back. Her lips met mine and trailed a path of liquid fire down to my neck.

"Honey…"

"Shh." She nipped my lower lip. "Let me."

"I don't think so." I flipped her so she lay under me, holding on to the back of her head so not to jostle her too much, seeing as quick movements still made her dizzy and intensified the pounding in her head.

Crashing my lips to hers, her hands found their way up

the back of my shirt. I retreated enough to let her pull the garment over my head. With one arm supporting me over her, I used my other hand to skim the flesh of her leg and halted when it reached her ass.

I heard the buzzing of my phone on the bedside table and Nicole hesitated. "You should get that, it could be work."

I groaned. "It can wait." Whatever it was, Danica would be able to handle it for today. She'd said as much before leaving earlier.

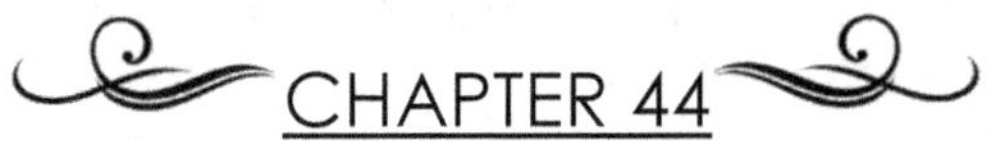

CHAPTER 44

The next morning, I smiled at the sight before me.

"Good morning, handsome." Nicole's lips quirked upward, her eyes clouded with the remnants of sleep.

"Hi, beautiful, been up long?"

A wicked grin was present on that delectable mouth of hers. "Long enough for a few ideas to come to mind."

"Is that so?" I rolled her onto her back and hovered above her.

She nodded.

Her lips met mine in a feverish kiss.

I trailed my hand down her side and rested it on her hip. My lips glided down her neck, over her collarbone and onto her shoulder.

A groan escaped when her hand met my engorged cock.

"I need you, Mike."

I snorted. "Try and keep me away. I plan on spending the next hour making sure you know I need you just as much."

Kneeling back, I pushed my underwear down from my hips. My desire for her was so extreme that I didn't give a shit about her panties, pushing the material to the side and plunging into her depths.

Her legs came up to wrap around my hips and her arms surrounded my neck, holding me close.

Arching her hips into mine, we found a rhythm that took us to heights unknown. Our bodies hummed in the delight we were able to provide one another.

Following our escapades, Nicole and I ate an early lunch and headed in to the office. I wanted a status report on a few ongoing projects prior to our grocery store run.

Upon our return, we managed to get the perishables stowed away, as our conversation steered toward the previous day, and Nicole's and Tracey's altercation in the very room we were in.

She grinned. "You liked that, huh?"

"Hell, yeah!" I kissed her cheek as I put away a can of soup in the pantry. "Watching you put that woman in her place had me wanting to do all kinds of things to you."

With a wry grin, Nicole retreated toward the kitchen table and leaned back on it. "Like what?"

"How about I show you?" I pounced.

My lips crushed hers as I held her face between my palms.

When her arms came around my neck, I lowered my hands to undo my pants. They dropped to the floor as I pushed up the skirt of her dress.

She reclined enough until she was lying down on the tabletop, wrapping her legs around me.

"Hold on," I guided myself to her heat, "this is going to be a hard one."

I grabbed the edge of the table with both hands, up by her head, and began to ram her like a man starved.

"Oh, God, Mike!" I could feel her throbbing around my cock almost immediately, as I thrust up to hit that sweet spot of hers.

Her moans grew to cries, and when she clenched down on me with her climax, I felt her teeth biting into my shoulder.

Edging on the side of pain, the sensation spurred me on, rather than making me pull away.

I sent her reeling into her second orgasm within seconds.

"God, don't stop!" Nicole's eyes opened and her head

lifted to catch my lower lip between her teeth and she sucked it into her mouth.

She was so intoxicating that it was impossible not to give her what she wanted.

And so I lost myself in her. Completely.

When the tremors ebbed, I collapsed over her. She cradled my head in her cleavage.

"Oh hell, Mike!" Her chest heaved. "I don't know if I'll be able to walk after that."

Her laugh grew hearty and I joined her.

"That right?"

"Hmm."

We shared a soft kiss and I pulled back to look at her. "It won't pain me one bit to have to carry you around."

"You might have to."

My house phone rang, jarring us from the moment.

Who the hell can that be?

"I'll get it."

Pulling away and yanking my pants up, I grabbed the cordless phone that sat on the kitchen island.

I read *Ben* on the display.

CHAPTER 45

"Go," Nicole said. "Take Jake with you. I think he could use a night out with the guys. I'll hang out with Danica while you're out."

Despite not being one to turn down a night out, I found it hard to leave her.

"Are you sure?"

"You need some time with them. You haven't seen Ben all that much lately. He needs his best friend, and so do you."

She was right.

I picked up Jake on the way to meet up with Ben at Fairfax.

When my brother-in-law and I arrived, I was shocked to see that my best friend had corralled an entire group of men, most of them I'd grown accustomed to hanging out with since my move back to Jacksonville.

"Hey, man." Ben greeted me with a slap on the back and thrust a beer into my hand. "I figured it was about time we all got together."

"Hey, Ben? Incoming!" Paxton nodded toward the rear of the establishment. There was a table of women, one of them closing in on my best friend.

"You should go for it," I told Ben when he'd turned the woman down and she'd gone to rejoin her clan.

Being hit on was a constant for him, yet he refused every single woman that ever approached.

"I don't need that. She's in here every weekend, leaving with a different guy. I'm a family man, you know that."

"Yeah, but what's wrong with getting the kinks out with a good lay?" I asked and Jake nodded in agreement.

"I don't need a quick fuck." He took a drink from his beer. "And my shit works fine."

"Doesn't mean you don't need a woman. I mean, it's not like you don't have your pick of the litter around here. Hell, from what I've heard, women love a man who can sling drinks like Tom Cruise, and if that doesn't do it for them, there's always the firefighter gig. Chicks dig uniforms." Jake gave a subtle laugh and Paxton nodded. "A hand will never be enough in the end, buddy."

"But you're forgetting something," Brent added to the conversation. "Meeting women in a bar doesn't exactly shout out marriage material."

Brent had a point.

Having grown up together, I knew Ben better than any of the other guys. The man was like my brother.

What happened to him had been tragic, what with the freak accident that had cost him not only the love of his life, but his baby girl too. It took a while to get the man back on his feet and build himself into the guy he was now, but damn, how I wished he was moving on faster to rediscovering the guy he was before he lost everything.

"Seriously though," I gave him a sobering look, "you need to open yourself up a little more. Maybe not here per se, but I think a good woman would be all you need to make things right for you again."

"What the hell happened to you?" Ben asked. "You're like the old Mike again."

"What do you mean?"

"Nikki's really sunk her teeth into you, huh?" Ben stated more than asked.

"What?" Brent started laughing. "You and Nicole?" I nodded. "Well shit! How the fuck did that happen? I thought she hated you."

I grinned. "There's a fine line."

I gave them all the four-one-one on what's been going on, including the psychotic happenings that led to her house being torched and her moving in with me.

"You should have seen the two of them a week ago," Ben added between bouts of laughter. "Sorry about that, by the way."

"I think you were more embarrassed than she was." I chuckled. "We had a good laugh about it after you left."

"Wait a minute!" Jake said, his gaze on Ben. "You walked in on the two of them?"

Ben nodded and took a sip of his beer and Jake said, "Damn!"

Ben cleared his throat. "It was the day Dani sent me to check up on him since he wasn't returning her calls. I walked in, thinking the poor guy would be moping, and there they were, in the buff, in the middle of the fucking living room floor, snuggling of all things! Like I said, bro, you need to lock the door."

"And you need to learn to knock," I retorted.

"Would have been a better show if I'd seen a bit more action." He snickered.

I took a sip of my beer and pointed its tip toward my best friend. "You should have been there ten minutes earlier then," I quipped, making him laugh while the rest of the boys hooted and hollered.

Most of the men had headed home, leaving it to Jake, Ben and I.

Jake had gone to the men's.

"So what's going on with you?" I asked Ben.

The man shrugged his shoulders. "I don't know. It's been busy lately." I nodded. "How's it going with Nicole, really?"

I grinned. "She's perfect. If it weren't for all those side issues with our exes, I think we'd be well on our way to marriage and babies."

The man sputtered and wiped his mouth with the back of his hand. "Did I hear you right?" A laugh was my response. "Fuck, Mike, you never talked about kids with Tracey."

"It just proves that she wasn't right."

"That's an understatement!" he mumbled. "So what's going on with Nicole's place? I heard the Chief say it was arson, that the old propane tank in the back is what blew the roof off the place."

And nearly blew my woman to bits with it. "Yeah."

"You know that things will take forever to get settled because it's a criminal case, right?"

"It doesn't matter. I want to ask her to stay."

"Seriously?"

"Yeah, why, you got something against that?"

"It's not that." He seemed to deliberate something for a moment. "Never mind..." The man went from sporting a ponderous look to grinning like a loon. "I'm just shocked at this complete turnaround. I'm happy for you, I really am. It's been a long time coming."

I couldn't help but notice the loneliness that emanated from the man.

Here I was happier than a pig in shit, when my best friend was still licking his wounds instead of living out a happy life.

Still, the fact that his happiness for Nicole and me was genuine and unforced had me feeling less guilt. Along with his humor, it demonstrated that the remnants of my formerly-lively best friend were making a more frequent appearance. Maybe there was hope for him yet.

I took a sip of my Bud. "You know, if it's someone outside the bar you want, I might just have the person for you."

"Not happening, Mike."

Jake plopped himself down on a chair to rejoin us. "What's not happening? By the way, Gabby's got a fever, so we've got to run, but I want to hear this first."

"Mike thinks he can play match-maker," Ben explained.

"She's right up your alley."

"Who is she?" Jake asked.

"A colleague." I swallowed the remainder of my beer. "She's pretty quiet, but a complete sweetheart."

"Good," Ben said, "why don't you date her?"

"Because I'm happy with my trouble-making kinky spitfire." I grinned, making Jake laugh. "Just think about it, all right?"

"Fine!" I knew he wouldn't, though. A man like Ben wouldn't take handouts. He could find his own woman. "Now get lost. Say hi to Nikki for me and make sure to pay those legs of hers some undivided attention while you're at it."

Jake shook his head. "I'm glad to see your smart-ass mouth is back, but you're begging for it, Ben."

The man guffawed. "He knows I'm kidding."

I laughed. "You're lucky you're on my good side, or you'd be on the floor nursing your jaw instead of that beer."

Yes, Ben was definitely on his way back.

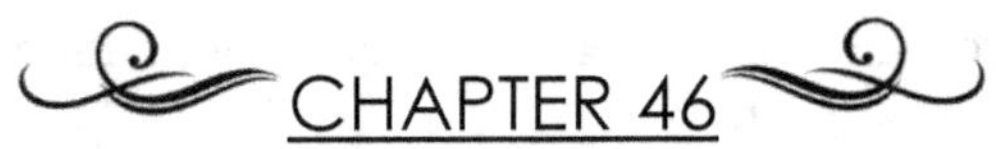

CHAPTER 46

After a grueling day at the office, I found Nicole on the couch, head bent, laptop on her lap and her cell in her hand at her side, as her other massaged the bridge of her nose.

"What's going on?"

Her head snapped up. It was clear she hadn't seen or heard me come in and the look on her face showed pure exhaustion.

"I just got off the phone with the insurance company."

"And?"

The flat line of her lips said it all. "They said the investigation needed to be closed before I can get the funds and do anything with it."

I sat beside her, closed the top on her computer, and set it down on the coffee table along with her phone. Pulling her into my arms, I kissed her hair. "You know there's no rush for you to get out of here, right?" I kissed her hair.

"I know." She pulled away and looked up. "It's just–"

"If you think that I'll grow tired of you, then you're mistaken."

"You might change your mind a month or two from now, when–"

"Just stop!" Her mouth snapped shut at my sharp tone. When I continued, my voice had softened. "I've been thinking about something." Nicole's brow arched, but she remained silent. "Why not sell the land and keep the cash?"

"But then I'm still living with you."

I smiled. "Exactly."

"But…"

I sighed. Did I have to spell it out for her? "You're not getting what I mean, honey. I want you to stay…permanently."

"Are you kidding?" Her voice squeaked, but her lopsided grin made its appearance.

"Not even a little. Nicole, move in with me. Live with me. Be mine. I know this is quick, but I want to wake up to you every morning. I want to go to bed with you beside me every night. It's no different than what we've been doing since before all hell broke loose."

"Mike…" She cupped my face in her hands.

"What do you say?"

"I've always wanted a pool." She giggled. "So, your house, huh?"

I shook my head and corrected her. "Our house. Now, kiss me."

She leaned in and paused before closing the rest of the distance. "You're sure?"

To prove how sure I was, I grabbed her face and leaned in to kiss her hard. On a moan, I took advantage of her opened mouth to get a better taste of her.

Tastes like home to me.

CHAPTER 47

Nicole had the right idea. Working from home sure held its benefits, what with the lack of disturbances.

I was going through a client's latest changes to a campaign we were asked to undertake when I heard the doorbell.

Nicole got up from the sofa. "I'll get it."

I waited for Nicole to come back or call me, but all I heard was muffled conversation.

Around the corner, Nicole's shoulders were slumped, her arms hugging her torso as Detective Mercer held his silence, his gaze ever watchful.

"Detective?" I offered my hand which he shook. "I take it you have news?" I wasn't pleased with Nicole's coloring, or the defeated look in her eyes that had combined with an onslaught of tears.

"We have a name." I waited for Mercer to continue. "A man named Guy Turner was apprehended. I need Nicole to come down to the station to see if she recognizes him."

An hour later, that's where we ended up.

"That's him?" Nicole asked when we saw Guy Turner through the one-way mirror of the interrogation room as Detective Peters joined the suspect.

I snorted at the frumpy-looking giant. If I had to guess his occupation, I'd say he did something in construction, what with the torn-up knees of his jeans and the dust speckling his shirt.

"That's him," Mercer confirmed. "Does he look familiar?"

She shook her head, indicating the negative.

"Try and think, honey." I pulled her into my side.

"I've never seen him before, I swear."

"I'm guessing he was a hired hand," Detective Mercer said. "We've got a warrant for his email and phone records. We're hoping that'll tip us off as to who might have paid him. We're waiting on the judge to give the nod to access his bank records too."

"How'd you find him?" I asked.

"Someone from Miss Baxter's neighborhood called it in. The man drives a company truck," Mercer explained. "It's his company, and he's the only one working for himself. We found empty gas cans in the back of his truck. We've got forensics running comparative tests to see if the accelerant matches."

Moments later, a clerk came in and handed Mercer a piece of paper. I didn't like the grim line that formed on the detective's face, or the way he marched to the interrogation room. He whispered something in the other detective's ear. Peters nodded, then Mercer walked out of the room, and left Nicole and me alone.

"Who's Lisa?" we heard Peters ask through the intercom.

The man refused him the answer he wanted with a cocky smirk. "I think it's time I lawyered up."

"This is your chance to talk, Turner. Maybe we can work out a deal." Peters tried again. "Now, who is Lisa Granger to you?"

"She must be pretty important since she's been blowing up your cell since you've been here." Mercer's words made Turner tense.

"I'm not telling you two a damn thing. I want my lawyer and phone call."

"Oh, my God!" Nicole's ass hit the seat she stood by and she bent forward, elbows on her knees, covering her face, her breathing having gone erratic. "I can't believe this!"

What the hell? "Nic?" I crouched down in front of her, my hands on the sides of her thighs. "What is it? Are you okay?"

She shook her head. "I can't believe this! It can't be!"

"Talk to me, honey."

"Lisa Granger…Fuck, it's Lisa!" she repeated. "I have to speak to Peters and Mercer now!"

Peters came to the door after I pounded on it for nearly a minute. "Can you please tell me why it is that you're pulling me away from my interrogation?" he asked as Mercer came back to join us.

"I think you're both going to want to hear this." I turned from the two men to Nicole. "Honey?"

"Can I see a picture of Lisa Granger?"

Peters' eyebrows pulled up and Mercer asked, "Why?"

"Because I think I might know her."

CHAPTER 48

Mercer was having Lisa brought in as soon as they could locate her.

With time to burn, Nicole grew antsy, so I took her out for a coffee to distract her.

An hour sitting on a park bench in silence was disturbed when the precinct called my cell, prompting our return to the station.

We entered the same room we were in earlier, only for Nicole to stop dead in her tracks with a gasp when the interrogation room came into view. Turner was gone, but someone else sat in his spot, somewhat familiar to me, but I couldn't quite figure out where from.

"It's her."

"So this is your ex's fiancée?" Peters asked. Nicole nodded. The man sported a look of confusion. "What's she doing with Turner?"

Nicole shrugged her shoulders. "I wouldn't know."

"Why would she have a beef with you?" Peters asked.

"She's got a man," Mercer said, "well, two, apparently, if her texts were any indication."

"I don't know why, Detective, but..." Nicole stopped to think.

Peters prompted her. "But what?"

She shook her head. "Forget it. I'm so tired that I think I'm reaching at things. She's just the woman my ex cheated on me with, and that's that."

"I think you need to share." Mercer nodded in agreement

with his partner. "What may not seem relevant now may just be an answer for us, Nicole."

Nicole turned to face me. "You remember the night of the fire?"

"I don't think I'll ever be able to forget it." I nodded. "What of it?"

"I could have sworn someone was following me when I left Dean's."

"Why haven't you told us this before?" Detective Peters asked.

"With the shock of what happened that night, it never occurred to me to think more into people connected with those we gave you names of," Nicole said. "I knew Lisa could get a little crazy, but I never thought that she'd be capable of anything like burning my house down."

Mercer nodded. "Well, we've looked into both of your exes and they've checked out, alibis and all."

Peters headed toward the interrogation room and paused to face us with his hand on the doorknob. "I'll see what I can get out of her and I'll be in touch. You should know that Miss Granger's here of her own cognizance. If she chooses not to talk, we have nothing to hold her here until we have substantial proof that she's behind this. As for Turner, the only way he'll be turned loose is if someone posts his bail."

"What about the evidence?" I asked.

"The lab's backed up because of another case, but we're looking into other things to try and speed things along," Mercer said.

"But you found text messages?" Nicole asked.

"Nothing conclusive." Mercer's lips were in a tight line. "We can tell that they were plotting something, but they don't actually spell it out. Even if they did, a lawyer could very well argue those messages inadmissible because there can't be proof that they were indeed the ones physically texting."

My arm squeezed Nicole's shoulders in reassurance when I felt her body tremble against mine.

Siding with Mercer's recommendation, I opted to take Nicole home. Our answers would be the same, whether they came from a phone call or in person.

Ten minutes passed as we rode in the car and the silence was deafening, if at all possible.

I grabbed Nicole's hand and said, "It'll all be okay, honey." She gave me a feeble nod. "I've got an idea."

"Does it include locking everyone from our past away?" she asked without much humor.

I chuckled. "You might be on to something with that, but no. There's something I want to show you before we go home."

CHAPTER 49

I drove us to a place I often visited in my youth. Not having been back since I was in high school, I'm not sure what possessed me to bring her here, or where the notion had come from, but it seemed like a good idea.

I parked the car and made to get out.

"Where are we?" She exited the vehicle.

Grabbing the blanket from my trunk, I held out my hand. "We're not there yet, we're walking the rest of the way."

She assessed the scenery as she took my hand.

"I don't have to worry, do I?" Her lips quirked up a bit at the sides. "You're not going to rape, kill, and leave me out here, right?"

I laughed out loud. "Hardly." I brought her hand to my mouth so my lips brushed her knuckles. "I used to come here in high school. There's a trail I hiked to burn off some steam. It leads to a small creek. I thought that you'd appreciate it."

"You thought right." She smiled and kissed my cheek. "Let's go."

It wasn't a long hike, just enough to get the blood pumping and release some of the pent up stress from the last few days.

We got to the creek and Nicole stopped walking, transfixed with the scene. "This is beautiful." I wrapped my arms around her, pulling her back to my front. "How'd you find this place?"

"I went out of the way to disappear as a kid. This is where I ended up. I kind of got stuck on it from there on out.

When Dad and I argued, or things became too much, I biked it all the way out here and hiked the rest of the way."

"Seriously?"

I kissed her head through her hair. "Yeah."

"Have you ever brought anyone else here?"

"Never."

She turned in my arms. "Not even Tracey…or Ben?"

I shook my head. "It never occurred to me to share this place with anyone else until now."

"How long do we have until darkness?"

"Long enough."

I set the blanket and pulled her down to sit between my legs so I could hold her.

She let out a long sigh, the tension ebbing from her body. "Thank you." She lifted her head and kissed my chin.

"For what?"

"For this, taking me away from things."

I gave her a squeeze. "I thought you could use the distraction."

"I'm so sorry for everything." She shivered.

"You have nothing to apologize for."

She pulled away to look at me. "But–"

My lips stopped her words.

She shifted to straddle my lap without ever breaking our kiss.

Withdrawing slightly, my forehead pressed to hers. "Let's just enjoy this place."

She kissed me before getting up to her feet. "How deep is this creek?"

"I don't know, why?"

She kicked her shoes to the side and shimmied out of her jeans. "Because I feel like a swim." Pulling her t-shirt over her head, she turned to me with a grin, and threw the item at me.

"We've got a pool at home, honey."

"But this place is special." She gave me her back and

reached for the clasp of her bra before peering at me over her shoulder. "Are you coming?"

I grinned. "I might just watch. The view's fantastic from right here."

Nicole graced me with her first real laugh of the day. "Your loss then."

She walked toward the creek, shedding her loosened bra and then, just when I thought she'd head into the water, she peeled her underwear down her legs and walked in—gloriously naked.

I didn't wait, hitting my feet and racing through my stripping.

The woman broke the water's surface and smirked as she caught sight of me wading into the freezing water. "It takes a naked woman to get you in here, huh?"

"No." I walked up to her. "Only you can convince me to get in here. Now get over here and keep me warm." I reached out and grabbed her arm to pull her to me.

"I have a little something in mind to keep you warm, but it doesn't involve us being in here."

"Good." I smiled. "I think I know exactly how I want you to warm me up."

I felt her cold hand grip my cock and squeeze. "Does it entail me doing this?" Her hand began to stroke.

I groaned. "More or less."

She nuzzled my jaw before nipping my chin. Her free arm wrapped itself around my neck as she continued to jerk me off.

"Baby?" she whispered.

"Hmm?"

"I love you."

"I love you too, honey." I gave her a peck on the mouth. "But I'll love you even more if you let us get out of here before my junk turns into an ice pop."

Nicole's eyes darkened with lust and her smile grew lascivious.

"Sounds delicious, but you're right. I can do more on dry land."

Her body lay prone on the blanket as I covered it with mine. Taking my time, I slid into her, capturing her moan with my mouth. The evening sun shone over us, helping us dry, and warming us from the chill of the water.

"Look at me," I said over her lips.

She did as I requested.

I pulled back, then thrusted in, savoring the feel of her wrapped around me. Her hands were threaded in my hair while our eyes remained connected.

She arched her hips into mine as we immersed ourselves into a rhythm that outdid all others.

I loved the sight of her. The setting sun made the red streaks in Nicole's chestnut hair look as if it were on fire. Her cheeks were flushed and her lips puffy from my kisses. She was breathtaking.

"Why are you looking at me like that?"

"Because I don't think I've ever been with anyone as beautiful as you."

"There's that silver tongue of yours again." She ran her fingers over the day's regrowth on my cheeks and I gave her a quick peck on the mouth.

My pace slowed to savor the feel of her digits as she proceeded to trace the contours of my jaw, my nose. She didn't leave much of my face untouched. I grabbed her wrist and kissed the inside of her palm.

"Michael."

"Nicole." I was trying to make sense of the slew of emotions that flashed through her features. I ran my fingers over her cheeks, smoothing them over her lips.

"How did I get this lucky?" she asked.

"I ask myself the same thing every day."

She pulled my head down toward her face and nuzzled my nose with hers.

I sped up the pace a bit, consumed by the fire in my gut. I knew that Nicole felt it too, with how tight she clung to me.

Wrapping our blanket around us, I cradled her into my body.

"You've ruined me for anyone else, you know that?" she mumbled into my neck.

"Good." I buffed my cheek into the side of her head. "I plan on keeping you for myself until well after we're old and grey."

She pulled away and looked down at me. Her eyes searched mine for any hint of hesitation or humor. "You're not joking."

I smiled. "No, I'm not."

She settled into me again. "I can't say that I mind that idea."

We were cooking dinner together when the doorbell rang.

"I'll get that." I kissed Nicole's cheek in passing.

Upon opening, I was shocked to see who was standing on my front step.

"What the fuck are you doing here?"

"Where is she?"

"Get the hell out of here or I'm calling the cops." My blood pressure rose along with my rage. How the hell did he know Nicole was here?

The man pushed through and entered despite my warning.

"Dean!" Nicole said from behind me.

"Who the hell do you think you are?" He stormed past me. I hurried to get between the two of them, but held silent. "It's not enough that you sent the cops to question me, but now you have to drag Lisa into this?"

"Get out!" Nicole's shaking index finger pointed toward the door.

I reached for my cell. "I'm calling Mercer."

"Don't bother," Dean said. "You won't get away with this, Nikki."

"Is that a threat?" I growled with my thumb pausing on the call button.

"It's a fucking promise you can take to the bank, asshole." He snarled and turned to walk away.

"Note to the wise, jackass," I began. "I suggest you ask your woman about why she's being questioned. I bet you'd be shocked at her answer. Better yet, you might want to talk to the cops instead, since she seems to have an entire agenda you don't know about."

Dean turned when he reached his car. "Whoever it was sure missed their mark when they hit your house."

Nicole launched herself toward her ex as the bastard got in his car. I held on to her until he'd peeled off, surprised at the fact that I hadn't gone after him myself.

Nicole's body went limp in my arms when Dean's car disappeared from sight. "Will this ever end?"

"It'll all be over soon." I turned her so she faced me and took in the tortured look in her eyes. "That man creeps me out."

"I'm thinking that restraining order might not be a bad idea after all."

"We'll see about doing that, then. Just promise me that if he comes around again, that you won't open the door. If I'm not around, call the cops."

She nodded. "How'd he know where I was? I'm so tired of this." Her forehead made contact with my chest and her hands fisted my shirt.

"I don't know, but I'll be damned if we don't get to the bottom of this soon."

As Nicole finished up with cooking dinner, I called Mercer and Peters to check in and see what they'd managed to get on Turner and Granger.

"Mercer's got a hunch about something," Peters said. "I'll keep you and Miss Baxter posted in the morning on anything new. Aside from the labs, we're waiting on a court order to search Lisa Granger's premises. She might have come in on her own, but she sure as hell wasn't cooperative when we started asking questions about your girlfriend and

her relationship with Granger's fiancé. She couldn't deny her relationship with Turner, though."

"Don't you need something substantial to get a search warrant?" I asked.

"Yeah, we do," Mercer said. "Turner decided to be a bit more talkative when he saw the fiancé pop in to pick up his woman. He let a few things slip with his frustration. By the time Turner shut up, we had enough to go to the judge."

"At least that's some good news," I said.

"Is there something else I need to be worried about?" Danson asked.

"I don't like the way Nicole's ex keeps popping up," I said. "Any way we can get a restraining order on the guy? I have a hunch that something else is brewing."

"We can do that," Danson said. "Peters and I have been talking. We have an idea I want to run by you."

After listening to the man, I thanked him, then hung up.

Walking into the kitchen, dinner was served, and Nicole was waiting for me at the table.

"So?" she asked.

"No results on the labs yet." Her face fell and her features darkened. "Turner did manage to incriminate himself further by pointing the finger in Lisa's direction, though. Mercer's only going on a hunch, but Peters said they've put in for a search warrant of her property. They're going to go ahead and get a restraining order done up for Dean, though. We'll need to go in to sign the necessary papers."

"So what you're saying is that they don't have any answers."

"Not really. I'm—"

She got up and left the table without another word, or allowing me to finish speaking. Moments later, I heard a door latch shut.

CHAPTER 51

Letting myself into our bedroom, I heard the water running in the bathroom. There was low music in the background and I smiled when I heard Nicole's sultry voice singing along to the tune.

I knocked on the bathroom door.

The water stopped. "Come in."

When I opened the door, Nicole was in the bath, a vast amount of bubbles surrounding her.

I offered her a solemn smile. "Is this what you do when something's bothering you?"

"Sort of." She looked away from me.

Taking a seat on the edge of the tub, I said, "Honey, I know there's little progress right–"

"Look, I really don't want to think about it right now."

"Okay." I grabbed her scrub sponge and poured body wash onto it. "Turn around, I'll wash your back."

I ended up taking my sweet time with that sudsy sponge.

When I was done, I leaned over to give her a chaste kiss on her forehead and pulled away enough to study her face. The stress lines had slightly dissipated from her face, but were still distinguishable.

"I'll wait out there for you." I nodded my head toward the bathroom door.

"Hmm." She smiled and wrapped a hand around my wrist.

"What are you–?"

With her other hand gripping my shirt and a swift pull, I didn't stand a chance. I ended up in the tub with her, clothes and all.

A hearty laugh burst from her. "Why don't you stay?"

"Why you little…" I kicked off my shoes before I got to my knees to try and get out of the tub.

Her hands grabbed on and tugged my pants. "Let's get rid of those wet clothes and you can join me."

"Seems you got laundry started." I made haste of my shirt and proceeded to help her out by shimmying the material of my slacks from my waist while she pulled on my pant legs.

Once freed of my clothes, I leaned in to shift so I could sit behind her, but her leg came up, resting a foot on my chest and pushing me back. Her eyes glittered with mischief.

Two can play at that game!

I rubbed up her calf, grabbed it and pulled her toward me.

"How about I wash the rest of you now that I'm in here?" I asked.

She slid her body over my lap and wrapped her arms around my neck. "I thought I'd have to work harder to convince you."

"You know I can't say no to you." I pecked the corners of her mouth and ran my hand from her cheek, cupping the back of her neck, my other running from her collarbone, down the front of her body. Her eyes closed and she tilted her head back.

"Where should I start?" I asked.

She moaned when I squeezed her nipples. "There!" She hissed as I pinched them again, a little harder this time. "Yes!"

"I see." I nipped the side of her neck.

Her hands gripped my shoulders for balance as I tantalized her breasts.

My hands grasped her torso, the muscles of her stomach rippling, her skin twitching as I moved my touch further south.

Her nails dug into my shoulders as I applied a bit of pressure with my thumb and circled her clit.

"Baby, I need you."

"You have me," I whispered into her ear. "I'm yours, always."

Her hips began to ride my palm and I felt a hand of hers gliding down my front to capture my cock. Nicole squeezed before her hand began to slide over my length. Her thumb traced the slit at my tip and I shivered. She lifted her hips and next thing I knew, I was inside her, her legs squeezing me closer, increasing my depth.

"I love the way you fill me." She nipped my jaw. I thrust into her and watched her eyes darken. "I love the way you hold me, like I'm the most precious thing to you. The way I respond to you is like nothing I've ever felt. I love the way you react to whatever it is I do to you." I moaned when she ground her hips into mine and tightened her pussy around me. "Yeah. Like that."

"Nic…" My voice sounded strangled from desire. "You're killing me here."

"Definitely like that. I love it when you take charge, but damn, do I love it when you give in." She rotated her hips. "You know what I love the most?" I grunted. "I love the way you love me." She pulled away to look at my face, her movements halting altogether. "So many times you could have just given up on me, on us, but you didn't. You're an amazing man, Michael. No one's ever been able to make me feel this way. You infuriate me to no end. You make me laugh when I need it. You always know what I need before I even figure it out. You love me for me."

"Where are you going with this, honey?"

"I'm just stating how I feel, handsome." She pulled my face to hers and pecked the corner of my mouth. "Now kiss me and let me take care of you instead of it being the other way around. I need this."

The moment our lips met, her hips gyrated over mine. My arms tightened around her, with my hands fisting her hair, keeping her close. Her arms surrounded my shoulders and I reveled in the feathering of her fingers over my spine, the feel of her surrounding me as we soaked each other in.

"Don't stop," I begged, letting her do as she wanted.

She kissed my nose, my eyes, and my cheeks. I felt her muscles tightening around me and she pulled away enough for our eyes to meet.

She came undone, taking me along for the ride. Her mouth connected with mine in a sensual crash to bring us down from our high.

"Feel better?" I asked over her swollen lips.

"Much." She nuzzled my nose. "What do you say we get out of here?"

"I can't think of a better thing right now than you, me, a bed, and some sleep."

I had a feeling that the next week was going to be our toughest one yet.

CHAPTER 52

As predicted, things progressed from bad to worse as a new week dawned.

On Monday, I woke up to a slaughtered cat on my front step.

On Tuesday, my car's tires were slashed and someone had taken a dislike to the front garden—every bloom having been beheaded, torn apart, and scattered to litter the front lawn.

On Wednesday, the precinct called us with the worst news yet.

After obtaining a subpoena and going through Lisa's and Turner's financials, they were able to find irrefutable proof that Lisa was the mastermind behind the arson and Turner was her puppet. The forensic results were in, linking them further to the case. By then, however, Turner's bail had been posted, and the man was walking free.

Lisa may have been on premises during their search on Wednesday, but at some point, the woman had given them the slip, further proving her guilt.

It was just Nicole's luck, that when the authorities finally had answers, they weren't able to locate Lisa or Guy. Even odder was when they delivered Dean's restraining order as well as to question him about his fiancée's whereabouts, the man couldn't be tracked down either. Stationing officers at each of their residences and places of work had turned up nothing. All three had fallen off the grid.

With everything going on with Nicole, instead of working from home, my sister had returned to her CFO role as of

Monday. It allowed me to come and go with more ease from the office. Danica seemed happy to be around, but I knew that she preferred to be at home with her husband and their new babies.

As for Nicole, the woman proved her stubbornness in negotiations. She managed to convince me that she should come back to work on Friday. I have to say that I was relieved, because work was piling up, and it would be easier to keep an eye on my girlfriend instead of having her be at home alone.

Later than her usual arrival time on Friday morning, Nicole called me from home, in hysterics. I cursed myself for not pushing to drive the both of us in, but I had understood her need to reclaim her independence.

Rushing home and barging through the front door, I found my house in shambles. The smaller furniture was overturned and an assortment of glass, crystal, and frames lay shattered on the floor.

I swallowed the panic that stirred my gut and pushed down the bile that was quickly rising in my throat. "Nicole!"

"Upstairs!" Her voice was muffled, strained with sobs.

Taking the stairs two at a time, I found our bedroom door shut and locked. "Honey, it's me, open the door."

I heard the shuffling of furniture before the latch popped and she opened the door to throw herself into my arms.

"What the hell happened?" I asked.

"Someone was in the house."

"I see that, but how the hell did that happen when I asked you to lock the door and set the alarm when I left?" I sighed. "Did you not do that?"

She shook her head. "I didn't think. God! You weren't gone for very long and my phone rang. I came up here to get it, and next thing I knew, someone was in the house, trashing the place. They tried to get to me, but I shut myself in here," she gestured toward the bedroom, "and locked the door."

I noticed that my dresser was askew. "You moved that thing in front of the door?" The thing could barely be moved by me alone, it was so large. She nodded into my chest. "Did you call the cops?" She shook her head. "Nicole." I grumbled. "Fine, I'll put the call in right now." I reached into my back pocket for my phone.

"I know it's them."

"Did you see them?"

She looked up at me. "No, but I know there was more than one person. I heard them talking. They knew who I was. They said my name." She broke down again.

I pulled her into my chest and kissed the top of her head. "Okay." I ran my hand over her hair. "It's okay, I'm here." And enough was enough.

CHAPTER 53

Mercer and Peters had been and gone with our statements, along with the CSI team. I had sent Nicole to our bedroom to lie down an hour ago while I tended to the crew of investigators.

After tackling a few work-related issues, and despite my unsettled stomach, I fixed us a light snack rather than a lunch.

Nicole's arms came around me as I was setting everything on a serving tray.

"What are you doing out of bed?"

"I can't stay up there."

I turned and wrapped my arms around her. "In that case, what do you say that we get out of town? Peters said it was fine as long as we stayed somewhat local, and I have just the place in mind."

She shook her head. "We can't. We've got work and what about–"

"I hate to ruin that picture perfect work ethic of yours…"

"…but you're the boss." She rolled her eyes.

I kissed the crease in her forehead and said, "I see that you're learning."

A few hours later, the car was packed and we were ready to go after I put in a call with Mercer and Peters, letting them know we were taking them up on their recommendation to get out of Dodge. With them in the know as to our whereabouts, a plan was put in motion.

"So, where to?" she asked, buckling herself in.

"It's a surprise." I smiled. "I think you might just love this."

I hadn't allowed her to help me out with packing the car. We drove for a few hours before I pulled down an old dirt road.

"This isn't one of your hiking expeditions, is it?"

I laughed. "Wait and see. We're almost there." I was surprised she didn't recognize the area, but then again, a lot had changed over the years.

I watched from the corner of my eye as Nicole squirmed in her seat beside me, the mixture of excitement and anxiety exuding from her.

Fifteen minutes off the main road, there it was in all its glory.

"Oh, my God!" Her hand squeezed my thigh. "I've forgotten about this place."

"Welcome to the Withers family cottage."

"But I thought your dad sold it?"

I snorted. "He did, but Danica and I bought it from the owners a few years ago. We kept it under wraps because we didn't want Dad to know about it. He hated this place, but Dani and I loved it. So did Mom."

"We used to have so much fun here," she said. "I have so many memories of this place."

"Me too." I chuckled at the mental picture rolling about in my mind. "I remember a certain girl who was too busy admiring my chest to hand me a bottle of water."

Nicole groaned and got out of the car. "You were mean." I followed her retreat and waited for her to say something else. "It was a good thing you had your looks back then."

"That was the last summer before we moved away," I pointed out.

"Yeah." She sighed and looked up to take in the whole of the place and smiled. "It's still as beautiful as I remember."

"Come on!" I pulled her to the cottage's door and opened it.

After taking care of the dinner dishes, I found Nicole standing out by the beach with a blanket wrapped around her. The sun was setting and she looked at peace for the first time all day. Trying not to freak out that she was out by herself when the Detectives had told me to keep her in my sights, I slowed my rushing pace to a walk, wrapping my arms around her when I got to her.

"What are you doing out here by yourself?"

She pressed her body into mine. "Just taking it all in."

"Are you okay?"

"Yeah."

"You sure?"

She hesitated. "I think so."

Not convincing. I turned her so she faced me. "What is it?"

"I'm sure it's nothing but paranoia what with everything that's been going on."

"Meaning?"

She sighed. "I feel like I'm being watched. Kind of like that night with the fire."

My body stiffened. I hugged her tighter to me. "Let's go inside."

She nodded and started for the cottage.

I took a long scan at the surrounding woods and debated.

I really should tell her.

"Hey," I felt her hand on my arm, "are you coming?"

"Yeah." I wrapped an arm around her shoulders and started us toward the deck.

"Is everything okay?"

"It will be."

She stopped in her tracks, gave me an assessing gaze and her lips thinned. "What's going on Michael?"

She was on to me.

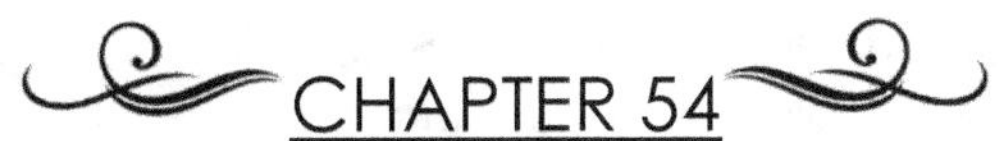

CHAPTER 54

"I know something's up," she said as we entered the cottage.

I locked the sliding glass door behind us and stared at the lake, taking a deep breath in preparation for what I was about to tell her. "Nic…"

"Michael, what's going on?"

"I thought it was a good idea." I groaned and ran a hand through my hair. "Maybe I was wrong."

"Wrong about what?"

"I should have told you from the beginning." I looked down, guilt ever consuming.

"Michael, you're freaking me out here, what the fuck is going on?"

"Peters thought it was a good idea that I take you away for a couple of days. He said that it might help him with finding–"

"Are you trying to tell me that I'm bait?"

"To put it mildly," my gaze met hers, "yeah."

"So me feeling like I'm being watched…"

I nodded. "It's most likely one of Mercer's guys but it could be–"

Her face turned a bright crimson. "How could you?"

"Mercer and Peters thought it better that you didn't know," I said. "I wanted to say something, honey, believe me, I did."

"Then you should have!" Her laugh came out lacking any humor. "Mike, I've been losing it since my house burned down. I'm trying so damn hard to keep my head above water and I thought I'd be fine, but I'm not."

"I know, Nic." I reached out to her.

She backed away. "Don't!" She shook her head. "You can't make this better by holding me, or with your sweet words and kisses, Michael. You know how I feel about being played."

"It wasn't my intention. I want this to be over as much as you do. I know it hasn't been easy. I've seen how it's affected you, and it hasn't been easy on me either. I've been worried sick about you…about us."

"I need some air." She walked toward the front door. "I can't stay here right now. I need to think."

I grabbed on to her arm. "You're not running from this."

"I'm not running, Michael, I need space."

"I can't let you go out there, Nic. I'll go to another room and let you be, just don't go outside."

With a defeated look, she conceded. "Fine."

"He's right, you know."

We turned to face the voice.

I found myself face to barrel with a rather pissed off looking Lisa standing behind it, and that's when the feeling of familiarity from the police station came back. Everything clicked.

"You were there." I moved to stand in front of Nicole.

Nicole's hand reached for mine and within seconds an idea struck me as I squeezed it.

I moved her hand to my back pocket. Nicole tried to snap it back, but I forced her to cup my ass cheek and guided her fingers over the edges of my phone until she stopped pulling away.

"You might want to move," Lisa said. "You don't want to know what happened to the last guy that stood in my way." Her laugh bordered psychotic.

"Lisa, what did you do?" Nicole asked.

"Sweetheart," Lisa called out, "can you bring in the rope?

Turner made his appearance with what Lisa had requested, and my head began to spin.

"Where's Dean?" Nicole asked the question that had just come to my mind.

"Why do you care?" Lisa said. "Oh, right! It's because you two are still fucking, right? I followed him, you know. He's been following you like a lost puppy. Should have known he was still up to his old tricks, that you'd want back what was mine. Tell me, does your man here know what you've been up to? Look at me when I'm talking to you, bitch!"

Nicole gasped, sliding my phone back in my pocket. "You know that's not true."

"Don't lie to me!" The woman gestured toward me with her head. "Tie him up first."

I didn't wait, pouncing on Turner and praying to God that Lisa was a lousy shot if she decided to pull the trigger.

Turner crumpled onto the old kitchen table and the thing collapsed to the floor in pieces with me on top of him. Chaos ensued, and next thing I knew, people were barging into the cottage from different entry points.

In the midst of the commotion, I looked around to make sure Nicole was all right and felt Turner's punch to the side of my head.

It sent stars and spots across my vision, but I still had a fight to finish.

I laid into the man, swinging like a lunatic and didn't stop until someone pulled me off of his unconscious heap. Seeing red, I reared and tried to swing at my detainer, but a familiar face halted my fist before it could make contact. Detective Peters.

"Drop the gun, Lisa," an officer said.

When I turned, I nearly crumpled to my knees, but the adrenaline kept me from doing so.

Lisa was standing with a fist in Nicole's hair, the gun wedged into my girlfriend's side. She was using Nicole as a shield.

"Lisa…" I began.

"What do you see in this slut anyway?" The woman snorted her disgust.

"Lisa," Nicole's eyes were swollen with tears, "please don't–"

"Shut up!" she screamed. "Dean and I were happy. Why the hell did you have to come along and ruin things? We were happy, dammit!"

"Where is he, Lisa?" Nicole asked.

"He's dead!" Peters answered for the woman. My heart skipped a few beats and then hammered in my chest. "Lisa, drop the gun. You don't want to do this."

She shook her head. "You know I can't do that."

"Yes, you can." Peters moved toward her as I felt someone else's grip take hold of me. He pulled out his gun and pointed it at her. Nicole winced, but what I saw in her eyes was more than just fear.

Anger. No, fury.

And determination.

I could tell that Nicole was thinking something, and whatever it was, I knew that there was a possibility that things wouldn't go well. Good shot or not, Lisa's aim was flawless at point blank range.

"Don't!" I begged Nicole. I held her gaze, pleading with her in silence so she didn't do anything rash, to let the cops handle the situation.

Nicole teetered on her feet causing Lisa to dig the gun into my woman's side harder. My life, my love, whimpered, but took a deep breath with her eyes shut, maintaining whatever calmness she had left.

"Make another move and I will shoot you, Nicole," Lisa said. "You should have burned in that fire."

"Lisa, drop the gun now or I'll be forced to shoot. You don't want to do this, I know you don't. I know you loved Dean. Wouldn't you want a real chance with Guy here?" He nodded toward the still unconscious form of Turner who was now cuffed and lying on his stomach.

To show her degree of insanity, Lisa turned her armed hand and shot Turner in the back.

In a quick flash, Nicole made a move and multiple shots were fired.

The moment may have felt as if it had dragged on forever, but in mere seconds, it was over.

Both women lay on the floor of my cottage kitchen, blood pooling everywhere. There was no movement from either of them and I kicked at the officer that held me back. He turned me loose and I rushed to Nicole's side as Peters hurried to Lisa's, kicking her gun out of reach. The detective felt for a pulse, looked up at Mercer who was standing by the back door, and shook his head.

My eyes widened at the possibility that Nicole might have suffered the same fate.

"Nicole!" I grabbed her face, tapping her cheeks, squeezing her shoulder. She wasn't waking up. "Where the fuck is all this blood coming from?" I palpated her body in search of a wound that seemed invisible. "Honey, wake up. I need you. I'm sorry. Why did you do that? Fuck, Nic, wake up, dammit!"

Peters came to me and pulled me away from her. "You've got to let them work, Withers," he said as I fought him to remain at Nicole's side. I turned to find three medics standing there, waiting to do their job, and that's when my knees gave way.

Mercer came up beside me and put his hand on my shoulder. "They'll take care of her." All I could do was nod and watch the three as they worked on Nicole. Each second without a response from her was killing me.

The medics checked her vitals. They inspected her front and then rolled her over. That's when I saw the wound in her side.

"Flesh wound," the female paramedic called out. "I'll clean and cover it and then let's get her loaded up and out of here. She's lost quite a bit of blood."

As she finished securing the last of the medical tape, the woman treating Nicole turned to her colleagues. "Let's roll!"

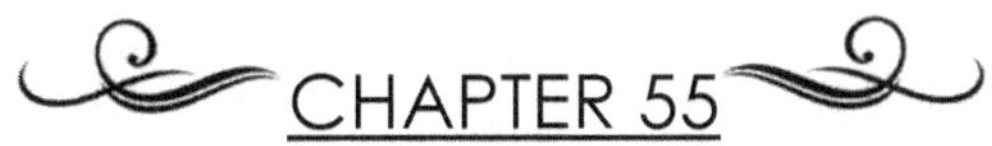# CHAPTER 55

I followed the ambulance in my car as the medics refused to let me ride with them because they were full up.

On arrival at the hospital, Nicole was pulled into surgery.

I called Danica and Jake to let them know what had happened.

The doctor made his appearance and asked for Nicole's next of kin while I was busy pacing the room. Panic overwhelmed me in that instant.

"She's fine," the man was quick to reassure me and proceeded to confirm what the paramedics had said was right. "It was a flesh wound and she's lost some blood. We didn't see anything else, which is great, and she's awake."

"Can I see her?"

The man nodded. "She's been asking for you."

He escorted me to a room. I wasn't sure what to expect, and was shocked at what I saw.

Nicole was sitting up in bed and, if it weren't for her pale coloring, I would have pegged her as a healthy person. It was a drastic difference from the sight I remembered in my cottage's kitchen, or the ambulance where she'd been looking like she was knocking on death's door.

"Thank God!" I rushed to her side and grabbed onto her shoulders. "Honey," I kissed her hair, "I'm so sorry."

"Did they get her?" Her voice was slurred and hoarse. "No one's telling me anything."

"She's dead, Nic. What the hell were you thinking? Why didn't you let Peters handle it? Why'd…"

The surge of emotion was too potent and I broke, my ass

meeting the edge of her bed as my knees gave way. My body shook with sobs.

Nicole's arms wrapped around me and tightened. She didn't say anything, only held me as I let it all out, my face buried in her neck.

"I thought you were gone." I sniffed and wiped at my eyes with the back of a hand. "When I heard those shots and saw you lying on the floor, I thought I'd lost you for good this time. You scared me, worse than the fucking fire."

I pulled away and stared into her eyes. Her hands came up to my face and tried to dry my tears. She was crying too.

"I can't seem to keep you safe." I tried to avert my gaze.

"Don't you dare blame yourself for this, Michael Withers!" There was that stubborn lilt to her chin, and that stern tone of hers. "I'll never blame you for anything more than taking me away for a weekend with a hidden agenda. One, I might add, that worked."

"Yeah, well…"

"I love you, Michael," she said, "more than you'll ever know. I was mad and yeah, I felt betrayed, but Peters' plan worked. It's over."

"Nicole," I cupped her face in my hand, "I have something to ask you."

"You do?"

I nodded and got to my feet. "This isn't the way I planned it," I took a deep breath, "but I can't wait anymore, not after today."

"Michael," she pulled me back toward her and shook her head, "if you're about to ask me what I think you are…please, not here, not like this."

I nodded and sat back down. "Let's go away. I don't care where. Let's just disappear for a while, for real this time." I leaned my forehead against hers. "I need you, Nicole."

"You have me." She pressed her lips to mine. "You'll always have me."

CHAPTER 56

Two weeks went by and between working from home, and dealing with the authorities who were working on closing Nicole's case, it's safe to say that things were chaotic.

With the trauma Nicole suffered from the cottage incident, she'd been having nightmares. Can you blame her? Hell, I had my own.

Visions of alternate outcomes of that day and losing Nicole plagued me when the darkness fell and slumber prevailed.

I hadn't been to the office or run any errands, refusing to leave Nicole's side for more than what was needed, so that meant that Danica and Jake, even Jordan, had been helping a lot.

Today was the first day where Nicole forced me out of my own house.

Ben came over at her request and dragged me off to Fairfax. She told him that if he didn't come and fetch me, she was going to strangle me and do away with the evidence.

Yeah, we'd been fighting. A lot. Cooped up around the clock for a few weeks was bound to cause friction between any two people.

"You need to give her time to breathe." Ben handed me a beer, knocking me back to the present from the thoughts of our latest dispute. "She's fine, but she needs you to be."

I snorted at his statement. "She's not fine, she's got night terrors."

"It makes sense, with everything she's been through," he said. "What about you?"

"What about me?"

"You look like you haven't slept in weeks. What are you doing to deal with everything that's happened? I know it hasn't been easy on you either, so don't feed me any bullshit."

What was I doing? I'll tell you what I was doing. I was busy looking after the woman I love. Knowing that she was safe and within reach put me at ease. I knew it wasn't healthy for me to be so obsessive. If she were home alone right now, I would have been in the middle of a panic attack, but Danica showed up before I left.

"What's going on in that head of yours?" my best friend asked.

"I'm terrified."

"Of what?" I saw the look of recognition cross his face after a moment. "You're scared of losing her."

I nodded. "I don't know what to do. I know that it's over now, but I'm scared that I'll lose her without the chance of living my life with her." I took a healthy sip of beer. "I saw what happened after you lost Candace."

"Buddy, just because it happened to me doesn't mean that you'll go through the same thing."

"I know." I looked down. "I just know how it was with you. I don't think I'd survive if I lost Nicole."

He seemed to ponder that and looked me straight in the eye, speaking with conviction. "You'd survive." He paused to take a drawn out breath. I wish that I could be as convinced as he sounded. "It's not easy, but you'd find a way. With great friends and family, it's hard not to keep going, but let me tell you something…You're not going to lose her; not in the way that you're imagining. But you will if you keep this up. You're choking her, Mike. She needs time to deal with things on her own, find her feet just like you do. She'll let you know when she needs you. Women tend to do that."

I nodded and decided to change the subject. "I need your help."

"With what?" He took a pull from his drink, his brow arching.

And so I spilled my thoughts over a couple more beers.

Ben dropped me off. Leave it up to the man to put things back into perspective when his life wasn't even close to being whole.

It took me everything I had to walk, instead of rush, through the front door when I realized that Danica's car was no longer in the driveway, which meant Nicole was alone. The panic churned my gut, but I managed to keep it at bay.

Ben was right. I couldn't keep doing what I'd been doing. I was ruining what Nicole and I had.

"Hey!" Smiling with her greeting, Nicole got up and gave me a large hug and then kissed me nice and slow. I hadn't had a kiss like that since the hospital. Damn had I missed them. "Did you have fun?"

"I wouldn't call it that, but it was good. Listen…" I pushed her back and held her hands. "I know I've been a real jerk this week and I'm sorry. I didn't mean to–"

"I understand. I'm fine. I know it might not seem like it with the nightmares right now, but I'm okay. I'm worried about you, though. You haven't been sleeping, Mike. You've barely been eating. Now that the cops have closed the case, I think we need that trip you were talking about."

"Aren't you sick of spending every waking moment with me?"

"Only when you're in this depressed funk you've been in. I can't stand seeing the panic in your eyes whenever I mention one of us leaving the house. You can barely stand being in a different room without looking like I'm about to vanish. I need my Michael back."

I pulled her tight against me, filled with relief that things were looking up once again. "He never really left." I kissed her hard, then pulled away and pressed my forehead to hers. "I've missed this."

"Me too." She smiled. "So what do you say that we get back to it?"

"I think there's no better idea."

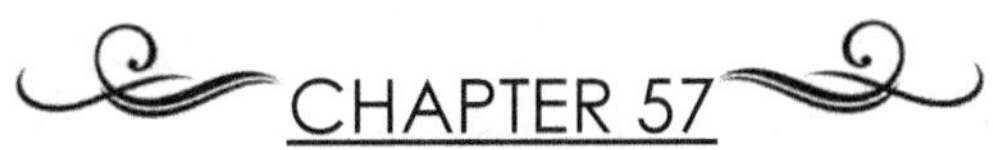

CHAPTER 57

Nicole wouldn't agree to take off and fly somewhere, so I figured out an alternative.

Early Saturday morning, the car was once again packed, and Nicole was waiting in it for me as I locked up.

"All good?" she asked when I started up the car.

"Yeah." I grinned. "Are you ready?"

"Let's get to camping, nature boy!"

"Make fun all you want, but you chose this above a weekend spa getaway."

"That's because this whole thing was about you and me being alone." She poked my side. "And face it, handsome, your reign of celibacy will be over before bedtime tonight."

I laughed. "Sick of the make-out sessions are you?"

She crossed her arms at her chest and pouted. "As hot as they are, I think we've outgrown them."

Two hours later, our tent was set up and Nicole was getting our lunch ready.

Dumping the firewood I had gone to get, I watched as she stood at our makeshift kitchen counter: the small collapsible table I'd brought with us. She seemed content with us being out here in the bowels of nature, camped out in pure solitude by a lake and its intermittent patches of sand no one would qualify as a beach.

I walked up to her and snuck my hands around her waist, nuzzling her hair, enjoying that little thing she did with her ass. Pressed up against her, my hands went to her hips and I made sure she felt my reaction to her subtle teasing.

"If I didn't know better, I'd say someone's hungry for more than just these sandwiches." Nicole's laugh was husky.

"You have no idea." I pulled her hair to the side, kissed her neck, and reveled in her reaction when she tilted her head sideways to open herself to my ministrations. "It's too bad we have to eat."

She turned and faced me. "What do you mean?" She wrapped her arms around my neck. "You've never been one to care about which order sustenance fell in." Her lips devoured mine and I gave just a little.

"Honey, let's eat." I said between kisses, slowing things down. "I'm starved."

As if on cue, my stomach growled and I thanked it for the small reprieve.

Her smile didn't reach her eyes, and her arms fell away to her sides. "All right."

Throughout the day, Nicole made advances which I kept shutting down. I could tell that she was resenting me for doing so, when my desire was as clear as the cock trying to burrow a hole through the crotch of my pants, but I held strong.

I had a purpose.

I bet you're wondering why it is that two people, who normally can't keep their hands off each other, haven't been intimate in over a week when I had all the reasons to jump her now.

I'm being honest when I say that we avoided it at first because of Nicole's injury. Now, however, I knew that if she asked, I was out of excuses unless I wanted to volunteer the truth, and I wasn't ready to tell her just yet.

"What's going on, Mike?" she finally asked as we cuddled in front of the fire well after the sun had set.

"What do you mean?" I mumbled into her hair before kissing it.

She turned toward me. "You know what I mean." Her eyes rolled with annoyance. "What's the problem? I know it's not my injury. You were there when the doctor gave me the all clear. Why are you pushing me away?"

I tried to pull her close again, but she pulled back. I sighed. "Nic…"

"Don't you 'Nic' me! Tell me! I know it's not that you don't love me, so what is it?"

"Honey, I…" The words wouldn't come, so I made another reach for her.

"Don't!" Nicole backed further away and pushed herself to her feet. "What do you want, Mike? Do you want to dictate how things go? Do you want to be the boss at home like you are at work? You know it's not going to work."

I shook my head. "It's not that."

"Are you telling me that I don't do it for you anymore?" She peeled her t-shirt over her head and chucked it to the side.

Fuck me!

She couldn't have been further from the truth, and she knew it. I'd been wandering around the campsite with what felt like a fucking permanent case of blue balls throughout the entire day.

"Nicole," I began with a shake of my head, "don't do this."

"Don't do what?" She popped the zipper and button to her shorts and dropped them. "This?"

I cleared my throat, the bulge in my shorts aching to no end. "Don't." My voice croaked with lust. I got up onto my knees. She backed up a step to stay out of my reach.

Nicole stood before me, her clothes tossed to the side on pine needles and leaves. Bared physically, with the exception of her undergarments, and without a doubt, stripped emotionally. She was beautiful, even with the hurt spread across her features.

"Mike, I need you." Her fingers skimmed over her stomach, toward her panties. "I need your lips on my body, your hands touching me. I want you to–"

As much as she turned me on, she was infuriating me by moving me further away from what I had planned. "Dammit, Nicole! Enough!" She jumped at my words. I got up to my feet and marched to her. "Just stop this before we both walk away feeling like idiots, all right? Don't ruin this weekend before it starts."

"Ruin it?" She snorted, her arms going rigid at her sides. It was as if she'd forgotten she was practically naked. "You've already managed that, Michael. I'm not the one at fault here."

"Nic."

"Stop calling me that!" She bent over, grabbed her clothes and walked past me. "I'm going to bed. Alone! Goodnight!"

Do something you fucking idiot!

It wasn't how I'd planned it.

And that's when the epiphany hit.

Nothing about Nicole and I had ever gone as planned. Why would I expect it to change now?

I heard the zipper to the tent as she opened it.

"Marry me?" I blurted out on a growl.

The song of the cicadas, the rustle of the leaves in the trees, the lap of the water against the shore was all I heard for what felt like an eternity, but must have been no more than ten seconds before Nicole spoke.

"Michael, that's not funny."

I turned to face her. "I wasn't joking." I dropped to my knees on the blanket we had been sitting on moments before.

Well at least you're on your knees.

I reached into my back pocket and pulled out the small box I had there.

"You can't do this." I saw her tears.

"Honey," I sighed, "I know I'm a fuck up. Truth is,

you're all I'll ever want. You have no idea how hard it's been to resist you. I wanted this to be memorable."

"Well, you got that covered." She reached inside the tent and pulled a blanket to cover herself before closing the tent up and taking a few steps toward me.

"Nicole, I love you. You're my life, my everything. You're my best friend, my partner, my lover, my future wife, and the mother of my unborn kids. I told you once that we'd be growing old and grey together, and I didn't lie." She moved closer yet again. "I thought I had more time." I looked down at the box in my hands. "I was planning on giving you this tonight."

Her feet took her the rest of the way so she stood right in front of me.

"You told me not to in the hospital. I had planned it to be special this time around and…"

"…I've ruined it!" she finished.

"No!" I swallowed the ball of emotion in my throat. "I've ruined it, Nic. I've made you think that I didn't want you when it's the furthest thing from the truth. I can tell you it's because of everything that's gone on over the last couple of weeks, but it's not entirely true. Truth is, I've been trying to work this," I looked down at the ring in its box again and back up at her, "in all day, but I couldn't find a perfect time. And now you feel rejected and–"

"Michael," she dropped to her knees on the blanket, in front of me, "ask me."

"Huh?"

Her lips pressed together as if she was trying to prevent a smile from breaking out on her face. "Stop rambling and ask me again, Michael."

I swallowed the lump in my throat and took a calming breath. "Marry me, Nicole. Let's make a life together. There's no one else I'd rather argue and make up with, no one else I'd rather make love to, to have babies with, to protect and cherish. There's no one else I can trust my heart to other than you. You're my life, my world, Nicole. Marry–"

She jumped into my arms and fused her lips to mine. "I'll marry you, Michael, on one condition."

"And what's that?"

"That if you have to argue with someone, it's me. If you have some making up to do, it's with me. For everything in your world, good or bad, I'm the one you'll choose to share it with, and no one else."

"It's the only way I want it to be, honey."

"Then my answer to your question is yes, Michael Withers. I'll marry you. I'll have babies with you. I'll grow old with you. Just don't make me wait too long for the first two."

"God," I cupped her cheek with my free hand, "give me a minute to pop this sucker on your finger and then we can get started." She giggled into my chaste kiss.

Pulling away, I hurried to remove the ring from its box and slide it onto her finger.

The woman stared at it for a moment. "It's gorgeous!"

"It'll never be enough."

"It's perfect, Michael. Now, stop worrying about how big you think my diamonds should be, and be the man you promised you would be."

She threw her blanket off to the side and made haste with my shirt while I got to work on my shorts.

She stood up with me, letting my shorts fall from my hips with my underwear. I wrapped my arms around her and undid her bra. Sliding its straps off of her shoulders, our eyes remained locked together.

My fingers caressed her soft skin on their way down. I dropped to my knees again. Her hand reached to cup my cheek as she peered down at me, her eyes dancing in the firelight.

I kissed her stomach, my fingers feathering out to pull her closer before reaching for her underwear. The smell of her arousal, the digging of her fingernails in my shoulders as she tried to find stability, and the shiver that overtook her body as I kissed above her pubic bone were intoxicating.

When I nipped her thigh, her knees gave out and I eased her down over my lap. I laid her down on the blanket and kept my eyes on hers.

"You're beautiful." I kissed the side of her mouth. "You're sexy as sin." I kissed the other. "And you're mine," I growled before my lips took hers in a hungry kiss.

She moaned into my mouth and I began to trail my lips down her neck. Her hand grabbed my face and pulled me up. "I want you inside me right now. Nothing more, baby, please."

I slid myself inside, hissing at the feel of her internal muscles clenching down on me.

"I love you," she said.

"I love you too."

She began to rock her hips with mine as I set the rhythm, the urge to explode building.

Nicole's moans filled the air around us and merged with the crackling of the fire we lay beside.

She arched high into me as I felt the first of her spasms. Holding onto her hips, I buried myself as deep as I could go.

"Michael!" she managed before we both fell over the edge.

My glide grew slower and slower until we were down from the clouds.

Pulling back to get my weight off of her, Nicole wrapped her arms around my neck and forced me back down. "Stay."

"I'm crushing you."

"No, you're not." She kissed my chin. "Let me hold you."

I laughed. "Feel free to do that whenever you want."

"Good. I plan on it. So, did you plan on us sleeping out here tonight?"

"Hmm…" I rolled over and pulled her into my side, covering us with the blanket she'd covered herself with earlier. "It is a nice night to do just that, but I was thinking about a midnight swim with my fiancée, and then seeing how warm we can get the tent."

"God, I love the sound of that." She looked up at me with

a smile. "I think I'll love 'husband and wife' even more."

It was then that I realized, that just like her, I preferred the final title a hell of a lot more than our transitional one.

CHAPTER 58

We spent the rest of the weekend eating and lazing around, making up for lost time. I couldn't keep my hands off of Nicole, much like she couldn't keep hers off of me.

Fires, sticks, and shotguns weren't needed to keep the critters at bay.

The moans, the cries, the growls and groans filled the air around us and ensured we wouldn't be disturbed by nature's residents, day or night.

"Do we really have to go?" Nicole asked as I loaded up the last of our belongings into the back of the car. She was sitting on the hood, pouting.

"We don't have to, but I doubt that you want to unpack and set everything up again." I laughed. "And then there's food."

"Yeah, you're right. So it's back to reality, huh?"

"I know you're dying to get back and flaunt that rock of yours." I grinned.

She grabbed my hands and pulled me so I stood between her legs. "I'd rather spend my days wrapped around you, wearing nothing but that rock of yours."

I cradled her neck and kissed her. "You like it out here, don't you?"

She nodded. "A lot more now with this." She waved the hand that sported my engagement ring. "I want to come back."

"How about we make it a yearly thing?"

"At the very least. Let's get going before I jump your bones again."

She squealed when I gripped her hips and pulled her toward me, rubbing my clothed cock against her covered heat. "I think we can spare a little time, don't you?" I said against the skin of her neck.

She arched back and opened up to me, moaning when my teeth pinched the skin below her ear. "You better not be teasing me right now."

"That's your job, honey." I pulled away and winked. "I only aim to please."

CHAPTER 59

"Have you thought of when you planned on telling Dan-ica?" I asked Nicole as she came into the living room with our drinks, after we'd finished removing the camping gear from my car.

"You mean she doesn't know about this yet?"

I took the glass of iced tea from her. "Are you kidding me?" I shook my head and Nicole sat down beside me. "She would have told you, or at least hinted about it, the minute I'd have turned my back. Ben's the only one that knew about my plans."

"Really?"

"Yeah, why?"

"I just thought that it would have been too much for him, that's all." Her face darkened.

"He's the one that volunteered to come with me."

"How is he?"

"I think he's warming up to the possibility of finding someone new. I told him that I could set him up with some-one from the office, but he's adamant to find someone on his own."

"I'm glad to hear it." She snuggled into my side. "He de-serves to be happy again."

"I know." I hugged her, still watching her face. "But I don't want to talk about that."

"What about then?"

Grinning, I said, "Marrying you."

"You can be such a girl sometimes." She laughed for a

quick moment and then her face assumed a very business-like look. "What do you have in mind?"

"How do you feel about a few months from now?"

"I was ready to head to that altar the minute you asked." She pressed her lips to my cheek.

"I figured I'd give you and Danica time to figure out what kind of wedding you want."

"Nothing big," she said right away. "We could have a backyard cookout and I'd be happy."

I laughed. "It doesn't take that much to make you happy does it?"

She shook her head and her eyes softened. "All I need is you."

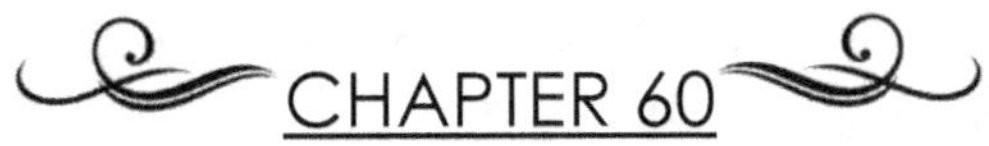

CHAPTER 60

I walked toward my office, the floor deserted with employees having long since left for the day. I was hell-bent on finishing up the last bit of work after another emergency client meeting had called me away.

Exhausted, all I wanted to do was go home to my fiancée.

Thoughts of work flew right out the window as soon as I opened my office door.

"Well, Mr. Withers," Nicole's tone was sultry, "I'm glad you could make it."

She was lying across the new leather sofa that had been delivered earlier in the week in nothing but strappy heels, a lacy corset, and underwear combined with garter and stockings. Her hair was down, framing her face in loose waves.

"Don't just stand there." She started to get up.

"No." I swallowed the ball of lust in my throat. "Stay!" I let my eyes assess her appearance again. "Just…stay there."

I loosened my tie and unbuttoned the top buttons of my shirt as I approached her. It had been a while since we'd indulged in my office.

The woman had been shopping. Her attire wasn't part of the items I had purchased for her after the fire, and good God was it a welcomed surprise!

My feet halted in front of her.

She sat up, leaned forward and began to undo my belt, popping the button on my slacks and lowering the zipper.

She got to her feet and kissed my chest as she released the remainder of my shirt buttons. I fisted my hand in her hair and pulled her head back. Her lips shone with a mixture of saliva and gloss, her eyes were dark with lust.

I couldn't hold back.

Crushing my lips to hers, and eliciting a moan, I took the opportunity and plundered her mouth with my tongue, her arms wrapping around my shoulders for stability.

My hands were less than gentle as I palmed her ass, picked her up, and sat her over my lap once I'd plopped myself down on my newly-acquired piece of furniture. I buried my face in her cleavage, enthralled with the taste of her, the feel of the satiny lace and her skin against my stubble.

"Just so we're clear," she sounded breathy, "this isn't me giving you the runaround on giving you my status report for the Fleishman project."

I pulled back and looked at her, grinning. "Didn't think it was."

"This is just a small detour because I barely saw you today." She bit my lower lip, soothing the sting with her tongue. "Now fuck me, Mike."

I groaned. "Honey, you won't have to ask me twice." I pulled at the lace ties on the sides of her underwear. "By the way, this is even better than going commando." I fingered the garter belt and snapped it against her skin. "These are staying."

Undoing a few clasps at the top of her corset, her breasts spilled out. I pulled the lacy thong from between her legs, leaving the rest of her attire on, including her heels.

In a swift motion, I had her kneeling on one knee with the other leg on the floor as she leaned over the armrest of the couch.

She gasped when my palm met the luscious skin of her ass. Seeing my handprint materialize, feeling the heat that radiated on that section of skin had me shoving my aching cock into her velvet heat.

"Oh God, Michael!"

I groaned at the tightness of her. "Give me your mouth."

She leaned into my chest and tilted her head backward

toward mine. My mouth ate at hers while my other hand headed south to massage her clit.

She bucked into me. "Please!"

I nipped at her jaw. "What do you need?" I pulled out at a slow torturous pace and glided back in.

"Yes!" She rocked back and ground her ass into my groin. "Hard!"

"Fuck! You undo me, Nic." I breathed into her neck as I plowed into her, the tension mounting.

"That's it!" She released a moan. "Fuck me hard, Mike."

I groaned. "I love that filthy mouth of yours." I bit her neck and she exploded.

My finger sought out her clit, feeling the nub throbbing. Her cries escalated as I continued on my frantic pace. She fell forward onto her hands and braced herself while I grabbed onto her hips and pumped mine against hers, hearing her mixture of grunts, groans, and moans.

My balls drew up, my skin felt too tight for my body.

"Holy shit!" Her core milked every last spurt from me.

Cuddled with Nicole on my lap as we regained our wits, she asked, "How long until you're ready to head home?"

"Let me get dressed and you cover this gorgeous body of yours and then we can go."

"What about work?"

"It can wait." I buried my face into her neck, soaking in everything that was her. "I need to get back to my fiancée. I'm sure the business won't fall apart overnight."

She laughed. "I can wait, handsome. Finish what you need to do." I gave her my best do-I-have-to look. She got up and leaned forward to cup my face for a sweet kiss. "I don't need you preoccupied with work this weekend." She tried to retreat, but the sight of her disheveled state made me want to take her all over again. I reached out for her, but she jumped out of my grasp, trying to tuck her breasts back in and doing up the clasps on her corset. "Work, then play."

"All right, you win. Now tell me about what you and George have cooked up with the Fleishman account."

⁓ CHAPTER 61 ⁓

"Michael," Nicole said, "what are we doing here? We're going to be late for the barbecue."

I parked the car on a side street and handed her an envelope.

"They can wait. This is more important, and it won't take long. I need to check up on something."

She remained seated in the car, looking at the envelope as if it was some foreign object that held secrets beyond her understanding.

I chuckled. "You can open it now."

"What is it?"

"Open it and you'll find out."

She didn't need more incentive than that.

Page in hand, her brows furrowed. "Michael?" She looked at me with a wounded expression. "Why?"

"Because I think you'll be rather too busy to entertain me around the office."

"Why'd you bring me here? We're parked on the side of a street, downtown, for Christ's sake! You could have done this at home."

"I have an early wedding gift for you and that, in your hands, is part of it." I gave her my best Cheshire cat grin. "Now, turn around. I need to blindfold you for this next step."

With a suspicious glance before doing what I'd asked of her she said, "What are you up to, Michael Withers? Why is it that I have my walking papers when I'm perfectly happy where I am?"

"Ah," I began with a sultry voice, "but are you really?"

She nodded. "Of course!"

"No, you're not." I made to exit the car before she could beg to differ. "Wait for me to come and open your door."

"Are you trying to start an argument?" I guided her out of the passenger seat.

I smirked. "With you, arguments are like foreplay."

I wrapped her arm around my elbow and escorted her down the large block and rounded the corner.

Stopping at our destination, I reached for the door and found it unlocked as I'd instructed.

The room was dark, but the emergency lights helped enough for me to see and guide Nicole around.

I grabbed her hand and led the way.

"Mike," she pulled back on my hand, "where are we? What are you trying to pull?"

I ignored her words, but paused to turn and face her with my hands clasped just below her jaw. "You have a dream," I moved to stand behind her, "and we both know that it's more than sitting in an office pushing papers for me."

"What are you getting at?" I began to remove her blindfold. "I told you that–"

A light snapped on to illuminate a lone guitar right as the blindfold fell from her face.

She gasped. "What's that doing here?"

Before she could take in too much of her surroundings, I turned her to face me.

"Nicole, you can't tell me that you're completely happy." Her brows quirked up in question. "You'll never be unless you're doing what you've always dreamed of doing." I cradled her cheek, kissing her chastely.

"And I told you..." She sighed out her annoyance. "Michael, can we talk about this another time? We need to get going."

I grinned. "What about your surprise? Don't you want to know what it is?"

She took a deep breath, realizing that nothing had been

revealed except for the fact that she stood in a strange darkened place she clearly didn't recognize, her guitar was on the premises, and I'd just handed over her termination papers moments earlier.

"Fine!"

"Now that you've got that insurance money of yours, I've been waiting for you to talk more about your plans to open your music shop again, but you haven't."

"What's your point?"

"You can't argue that it's a good time to make it happen."

Her breath caught and doubt filled her eyes. I saw the darkness, the fear, the excitement that lay there. The fear was most prominent, and I knew that she'd spout out a bunch of excuses as to why she hadn't moved forward with that part of her life as of yet.

"There's a lot involved in opening up a business, Mike. I have the overhead at this point, but I need a place."

"You have one."

She shook her head. "No, I don't."

I smirked. "Honey, you're standing in it."

Her jaw dropped. "Michael, I wish you'd run this by me first. There's so much more than just an empty space needed. The last place was perfect. Do you have any idea how much it costs to build a recording studio? How much the inventory–?"

"You mean instruments?" She nodded. "Which ones? Guitars?" A light came on and Nicole gasped when she saw the wall filled with an assortment—both acoustic and electric—from base models to the higher end ones. "Pianos and keyboards?" Another light came on, highlighting an array of Yamahas and Steinways along with other brands.

"What's going on, Michael?"

"I think you know what's going on, Nicole." The rest of the lights came on and the gang, who'd been hiding in the back storage area, appeared bellowing a loud *surprise* as I turned her to face them and held on to her hips to prevent her from toppling over from shock.

"You've got to be kidding me!" She looked all around. "This…this is my shop!" She whirled around to face me. "But…How did you–? It was rented out!"

So she had been looking around.

A pang of jealousy struck me that she hadn't shared that with me. With how things had fallen apart for her, I knew she wanted to handle this part on her own, as proof that she could make it.

I chuckled. "Wrong, it was purchased. I bought it."

"I can't believe you!" She smacked my chest and broke down, her face in her hands. I grabbed one of her hands and she stepped forward to bury her face in my chest.

"Nic," I whispered. "Honey?"

"This is too much." Her body shook with her sobs.

"It's nothing." I kissed her hair. "I told you I'd do anything to keep you happy and this is something that does."

Her arms came around me and tightened like a vice. "I can't…"

"You can, and you will." I delighted in the fact that she let me tilt her face up so she could see me. "Guys, give us a minute?" I waited until I heard the last of the footsteps fade into the stock room's direction.

"You shouldn't have."

"You don't like it?"

She shook her head. "No, I love it, but you shouldn't have. This was mine to do on my own."

"There's nothing wrong with a leg up, honey. Plus, you own the place now. No more rent and no mortgage. I paid it in full, it's in your name. All I ask is that you take this place and do what it is that you love."

"It's too much money."

"You're forgetting my net worth." I pecked her nose. "In case you forgot, I'm loaded."

She chortled. "You're crazy is what you are."

"And you belong here, with all of this," I gestured to our surroundings with one arm while the other held her close, "not in an office."

She began to look around. "This really is amazing. I'll never be able to thank you for this, Michael."

"You taking this place, doing what you love most, and seeing your smile every day is thanks enough. You've already given me enough by agreeing to be mine forever." I wiped the stray tear that trailed down her cheek. "Please kiss me and say that you'll keep it. I can always sell it and get you some bigger place."

"No!" She covered my mouth with her hand as if what I'd just said was blasphemous. "This place is where my heart is. You have no clue what you've done." Her eyes welled up with another bout of tears.

"I think I have a slight inkling. I saw how you looked when you brought me here and told me about when you first opened it up."

"So many memories are holed up here," she whispered. "Saying goodbye to this place was the hardest thing I've ever done."

I hugged her head to my chest and buffed my cheek on top of her head. "It's a good thing it wasn't a final one, even though you didn't know it at the time."

A sigh of resolve mixed with contentment escaped her. "I'll take it. I can't say no to this, Michael. The fact that you know me so well means the most, but this…" She pulled away and looked up. "This I can't refuse. I'll take it, but…"

I smiled down at her. "What is it?"

She grabbed my face and looked me in the eyes. "Don't you dare do anything like this again." Her eyes grew stern. "For one, I don't think you can top this, and two, you've given me more than a lifetime's worth of gifts and happiness with this place alone. I don't want anything else other than you…just you."

I laughed. "I can't promise you that."

Her eyes narrowed. "Seriously, Michael, I don't want anything like this again. You do know that men typically surprise their bride with jewelry or something of that sort."

Laughing, I let my forehead fall to hers. "I agree, it was

over-the-top crazy, but I'd do it ten more times to see the look on your face you have right now."

"Just so you know, you buy me another building, and I'll turn around and sell it to get you something nice in return."

I grinned. "That could be fun, but awfully expensive." My face grew serious. "Nicole?"

"What?"

"Kiss me."

"I was just about to." She pulled my head down and captured my lips with hers in a fierce kiss.

When she jumped up, I caught her, wrapping her legs around my waist as her hands dug into my hair and her forearms pulled my face closer to hers.

"I love you more than you'll ever know," she said over my lips.

I laughed. "I think that could be debated, but I'll call us even." Spinning us around, I yelled, "Get in here guys!"

Everyone came pouring in, hugs and kisses all around.

Jasper sat at one of the pianos and began pounding away, asking Paxton if he could have one, while Jordan was in the guitar section, checking out the electric numbers.

I watched as Nicole toured the shop and found a seat beside Jasper. The rest of the adults had gathered in the middle of the place and were busy catching up.

At some point, everyone's attention was directed to Nicole and Jasper. They were both playing *Chopsticks,* but it was cute seeing that within less than half an hour, the five-year-old had learned a few basic keys.

"Can you play me a song, Nikki?" the little guy asked. I saw the look of uncertainty cross her face—or was it anxiety? "Please!"

The kid's trademark pout did it. "Just the one." She looked up and crooked her finger at me. "Come here. This one's for you, handsome."

She played the baby grand and everyone corralled around the beautiful instrument to listen. I watched as her fingers tickled the ivories, love and passion pouring out while she played as if the music came straight from her soul. She made it look effortless and awed me, but also provided me with added conviction that what I had done for her had been the best decision I'd ever made, next to asking for her hand in marriage.

By the time she was done, every man who had a woman had their arms wrapped around them.

"Is there anything you don't do?" Ben asked in awe.

She giggled. "I don't play the drums, and don't ask me to play a wind instrument."

"I can't believe that you've kept your singing a secret for so long," Danica said.

"You're amazing," Alissa added. The rest of the group nodded in agreement, pretty much surprised and rendered speechless.

"I don't know that song," Jasper said, scratching his head and he perked up. "Can you play something else that I know?"

"What do you have in mind?"

We left the store, making sure everything was locked up, and headed to Paxton and Alissa's for what was to be our engagement party à-la-BBQ style.

Jordan and Jasper were running around, playing with a football while Nicole, Danica and Alissa were tending to a baby each.

I found myself tuning out the guys as I was taken with the image of my fiancée holding my niece.

"Mike," I heard, "did you hear me?"

I turned toward Ben.

"Huh?"

"I think we need to get you away from Nicole," Jake said and the guys laughed.

"I should remind you that you and my sister are still that way."

"Just wait until after two years of marriage. It never felt

like it would fade, but it did," Ben said. The guys and I turned to look at him. It was the first time that he'd spoken so openly about his dead wife. I detected a bit of resentment? "What?"

"It's just…" I began.

"I'm not that broken that I can't talk about her, bro."

I shrugged my shoulders. "I'm just surprised that you brought her up, it's all."

"It's better that way," Ben said and set his gaze on my fiancée. "Sure, we had our moments, but who doesn't, and she deserves to be remembered. You have a great woman, Mike. Nicole's the one that's reminded me that the accident wasn't the only thing that should be remembered about her."

I know that the man still felt guilty for what had happened, but whatever it was that Nicole and he had discussed, I could tell that he seemed to be working toward forgiving himself. Survivor's guilt was a constant demon of Ben's.

Jake excused himself to help Danica with the twins. Paxton followed, deciding that he should get some of the food on the grill, leaving Ben and I alone.

"I owe you an answer," Ben started.

I looked at the man I'd asked to be my Best Man and he smiled. "You're sure? I know it's not easy."

"I'd be honored to return the favor." He clapped a hand on my shoulder. "Plus, I kind of thought it was a done deal after you talked to me about giving her that ring anyway."

I was dressed to the nines and pacing the spare bedroom at Paxton's, where the ceremony would be held.

It was hard to believe that a month and a half had gone by since my rather unorthodox proposal, and I'm happy to say that things have only gotten better.

Nicole's leaving Withers had been a major adjustment for us.

Where I anticipated the decrease in seeing each other as being a bad thing, I found that our evenings meant more. Seeing the twinkle in her eyes and the smile lighting her face as she spoke about her business only confirmed that making her dream a reality had been the best decision for both of us.

As I waited for my cue to head downstairs, I peered out the bedroom window.

I took in the look of the Lowell's back yard and the transformation it had undergone in just a matter of days. The tents and dance-floor were set up, and so were the dinner tables and chairs. There were miniature lights garnishing the ceilings of each structure, waiting to be lit, adding to the allure of romance as they mimicked twinkling stars. Freesia and lilies made up the floral arrangements.

It was simple, elegant. It was perfect.

My eyes stopped on the archway that was covered in tulle, or so I think that's what I overheard Allie and Nicole discussing the other day. Flowers and lights were part of the mix there as well. There was a table off to its side which would be for the registry signing after Nicole and I were married.

"They're fifteen minutes out," Jake said as he entered the room with Ben. "We should get you down there."

My head bobbed.

"Everything okay?" Ben's hand landed on my shoulder.

I smiled to myself. "Perfect."

"Nervous?"

"Not even in the slightest."

"It's a good sign." He chuckled. "Only a few more minutes of freedom left. How does it feel?"

Amazing.

I greeted the guests on the inner portion of the aisle as I headed toward the altar. The justice of the peace shook my hand and then I waited.

Seconds felt like minutes, minutes felt like hours. I had only been there for two minutes before the soft sound of Pachelbel's *Cannon in D Major* began to play.

Danica walked down first and I was amazed at how beautiful my baby sister looked. She gave me a dazzling smile and a wink before assuming her place opposite me, leaving room for the woman I would soon be taking as my wife.

As soon as the song ended, a familiar tune began to play, but without its lyrics.

Our song.

I felt Ben's hand on my shoulder and looked down the aisle to find the most beautiful creature that would ever walk this earth.

Her gown, although simple, was amazing. Satin was gathered at her bust, hugging it down to her waist, a sparkling brooch adding to the fanciness of her attire where the skirt flowed flawless and moved as she moved, pooling to the ground. Her hair was pinned only at the front, leaving the rest of it to flow loosely curled around her bare shoulders.

She winked at me when she reached the halfway mark and I heard Ben chuckling. "Lucky bastard!" he whispered.

That I am.

Nicole came to a stop in front of me and handed her bouquet to Danica. "I figured you'd enjoy your song."

"You look beautiful."

"So do you."

The justice of the peace cleared his throat and the people in the front rows laughed, clearly having heard our exchange.

The ceremony was short and sweet and I thanked my lucky stars because I couldn't wait to kiss my wife, when permitted to, of course!

All right, so I wasn't exactly patient. The man had barely begun to utter *husband and wife* and I had Nicole in a scorching lip-lock while everyone laughed at the befuddled man who had muted himself instead of uttering his *you may now kiss the bride* line.

CHAPTER 63

I needed some alone time with my woman something fierce, but alas, it was picture time, and once that had been done and dealt with, we had guests to greet, dinner to eat, and the rest of the evening ahead of us.

"Why is it that I agreed to a whole evening?" I whispered in Nicole's ear before kissing her just below it.

"Because when we look back on this day, you would want to see all of this." She pulled back to look at me. "You, my dear husband, will have your wife to do with as you please for the rest of your life. And if you feel so inclined, there's always the barn."

Loads of laughter and some tears later, I was beckoned to the dance-floor by none other than my wife.

Wife.

I knew that I would enjoy calling Nicole that, but I never knew the full extent of pride I would feel, until this day, when I looked upon the stunning woman standing before me.

"DJ, how about a little music? I'd like to dance with my husband please."

She backed away, holding her hand out for me to grab. I heard the beginning of the tune and laughed. She and I had argued between versions while we were planning our big day, but to my surprise, she had given into my choice.

I spun her around and pulled her into me, holding her snug.

"So you gave into *Train*, huh?"

"I figured we had enough country plus, let's face it, I only argued with you for the making up." She winked.

I cradled her neck in my hand and pressed my lips to hers as our bodies rocked to the music. Hoots and hollers could be heard in the background as I pulled away and nuzzled her nose.

I spun her around again and dipped her, making her giggle. "Look at you all Astaire-like. I've been waiting for you to twirl me around like that since Austin."

"Then hold on tight, honey." I smirked. "I'm not done with you yet."

The song was at its end and was replaced by the Righteous Brothers' *Unchained Melody*.

I dipped her down low as those famous first words left the sound system, knowing that she would follow my lead.

"So that's how you want to play it?" She grinned as I pulled her pelvis tight against mine.

I nipped her ear. "If I can't make love to my wife right now, I might as well get her all warmed up for later." A groan escaped her. "I'm hoping she might call it an early night."

She laughed. "You think you've got it all figured out, don't you?"

"What do you mean?"

Her hand went up and next thing I knew, my little trick had been turned around with the tune shifting to something more upbeat in nature. I recognized it as the same song from our trip to Austin—that sultry Mediterranean tune.

I smirked. My vixen was coming out to play, and so play I would.

Nicole backed away, swinging her hips and I found myself wishing that her dress was shorter so I could delight in her fancy footwork.

My prayers were answered moments later when she unfastened the brooch at her waist and revealed a shortened version of her dress which hung loosely above the knee.

Everyone cheered. Boy, did she know how to heat my blood!

As she twirled by herself, I grabbed her hand and pulled her hard into me.

"I figured we were due for a repeat," she said. "After all, the barrier of employer and employee hindered us a bit in the midst of our hostility, don't you think?"

"Hmm…" I spun her around so her back met my front and I trailed my fingertips down her neck to between her breasts and to her waist before spinning her back to face me.

"Show me what you've got, stud."

By the time the song was over, it appeared that our salsa had left everyone in a mood to party, not to mention the heat factor had ratcheted up a notch for both of us.

I grabbed Nicole's skirt off the floor and pulled her along with me, covering the front of my pants.

I didn't stop for a drink or for any small talk, pulling my wife behind the wall to the tent our table was at and rushing us to the barn, hoping no one would come looking for us. The woman giggled the entire way.

Swinging the barn door open, we were quick to discover that we hadn't been the only ones with the same idea.

We witnessed the literal meaning to being caught with your pants down.

Paxton was over his wife, giving it to her good and proper by the sounds of it. "Oh shit!" I said and Nicole gasped.

"I told you we'd get caught!" Paxton told Allie who was giggling into his shoulder, her legs still wrapped around his waist and all private bits hidden with the exception of his lily white ass.

"Hurry up in here. The next poor sucker might want to join in," I said while shutting the barn door.

"I don't share!" Paxton bellowed out with possessiveness.

A deep breath whooshed out, causing Nicole to giggle. "Well that wasn't what I had in mind."

"Makes for a great story though." She held out her hand. "Come on, husband of mine, let's get us a drink and go make out like a couple of horny teenagers on the other side of the house."

I laughed. "If you keep this up, I'm throwing you over my shoulder and taking you to bed."

"Not before the garter toss!" She turned and winked at me.

I'd be making sure that long skirt was back in place for that portion of the evening!

EPILOGUE

I lay in bed, my wife in my arms. The salty sea breeze came pouring through the open window.

Italy was beautiful at this time of year, but Nicole wouldn't know that because we hadn't left our room since our arrival, much like on our first trip here for our honeymoon.

No, it hasn't been a year yet, but it's been six months since the day we wed.

If you were to tell me that things faded in the intimacy department, I would call you a liar. Truth is, it had gotten better between Nicole and me, and I had no inclination to believe that the heat we shared would be on the decline any time soon, Ben's warnings be damned.

Nicole's lips pressed against my chest. "Good morning."

"Good morning, beautiful." I kissed the top of her head. "Feeling better?"

"Much." She came to a hover over me.

My hands roamed her bare body as her mouth connected with mine for a deep sensual kiss.

Today was our last day in Naples and we were heading back home. I planned on maximizing my alone time with Nicole before reality's infringement.

I rolled us over, my body covering hers.

My mouth trailed down, stopping to pay attention to her breasts. Her nipples were already hardened and I didn't hesitate to take them in my mouth.

She let out a loud cry and arched into me. I let the nipple

go and did the same to the other one, gaining me the same reaction.

"I think I'm going to love making you scream this morning." I grinned down at her.

I continued and my lips found her ribcage, leaving a path of fire as I got to her stomach. I spent an indiscernible amount of time, licking, nipping, and kissing around her navel, reveling in her body's response.

"Michael." It came out breathless.

"Nicole." I looked up at her. Something in the way my wife looked at me prompted me, so I moved until we were nose-to-nose. "I have a proposition for you, honey."

"And what's that?" Her fingertips traced my jaw and met my lips. I kissed them.

"Well, there's no way around this, and I know this is the most fucked up time to be mentioning it. It's pointless to beat around the bush–"

Her hand came to hush my words and her eyes reflected humor. "Honey, you're rambling again. This must be big."

"Let's make a baby," I blurted out.

I hadn't expected that reaction, but I can tell you that I'd rather hear a belly laugh than get smacked over the head. Still, her reaction had me studying her.

"It'll be hard to do that," my brows arched at her words, "seeing as it's already been done."

Huh? My body stiffened with shock. "What do you mean?"

"I think I'm pregnant."

My heart beat miles a second. "Please tell me you're not joking." She shook her head. "Have you taken a test?"

She shook her head again. "I'm two weeks late, my nipples react to the smallest of breezes, they're so sensitive, my nose is like a bloodhound's, and I don't think this whole week has been about the food or a stomach bug."

I got up and rushed to my pants.

Nicole sat up, using the sheet to cover her naked form. "Where the hell are you going? I thought…"

I rushed to her and smiled as I cradled her face in my hands. "I'm ecstatic! I'm just going out to the drugstore."

"Take those pants off right now, Michael Withers, you're not going anywhere! What you're going to do is call room service, see what those five-stars of theirs are made of, and have the concierge deliver the pregnancy test along with our breakfast. Between now and then, you're going to finish what you started."

"I love it when you're bossy." I pressed a tender kiss to her lips. "Let me make the call and then I'm all yours."

By the time I sunk deep into Nicole, feeling the residual tremors of her first orgasm around my dick, I froze, worry all of a sudden invading my mind.

"Don't even think it, Michael. You can't hurt me or the baby, and that's if I'm actually pregnant."

"How is it that you know what I'm thinking?" She tried to roll us over but I put a stop to it. "Nuh-uh, this is my time."

Slow and deep, I began to thrust, making sure to be thorough as I loved on her.

We were lying in the buff, basking in the afterglow of our lovemaking, when the knock came at the door.

My heart began to race as I pulled myself from the bed and donned my robe.

When I closed the door, I wheeled the trolley with our breakfast and the box containing what would soon enough hold our answers.

Nicole jumped up, snagged it and ran to the bathroom.

She came out a minute later.

"So?"

She rolled her eyes but looked humored at my impatience. "Give it a few minutes!"

I paced the room, excited and nervous all at once. Damn does two minutes feel like an eternity when you're waiting on something so life-altering!

Nicole stopped me in my tracks and gave me a soothing kiss, her hands on my chest. "It's time."

She left the room and after a minute, she came back, holding the plastic stick. She had tears in her eyes, but the rest of her face held a blank mask.

Was she in shock? Disappointed? Terrified?

"Nic?"

She handed me the test. I looked down, saw the result and dropped it on the floor.

"I guess we should start calling you Daddy!" She squeaked in excitement and launched herself into my arms.

My words were blocked by the ball in my throat, so I just held on to Nicole and our precious package that grew inside her.

She pulled back a bit and I set her on her feet. "Mike, are you okay?"

"Fine." I swallowed hard. "I'm better than fine actually. I never thought you could make me happier but…" I had no words to express myself, so I laughed.

Her hands came up to cup my face and I felt her thumbs rub my cheeks. "Leave it up to a baby to render you to tears," she joked. "Now, Mama needs some food before you jump her bones again. I might as well take all the sex from you now, because there's no way you'll want to touch me when I'm as big as a whale."

The thought of her round with our child stirred something in me and I looked down at her stomach with a sense of pride and possession. "I think you might be wrong about that."

When I looked at her face, her grin was back, and her eyes were leveled on my rising appendage. "Maybe a little fun before breakfast wouldn't hurt."

I guffawed. "I don't think so! You're eating, even if I have to feed you myself."

"That could be fun."

As I fed her pieces of fruit, I thought back on my life and realized that I had everything I'd ever yearned for.

I had love, a wife who adored me about as much as I adore her.

I had the means to care for more than me and my family.

I had friendships that ran thicker than blood.

And now, as pieces of my wife and I meld together, I had my legacy.

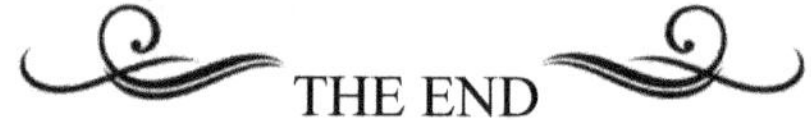

THE END

ABOUT THE AUTHOR

Born and raised in small town Northern Ontario, Canada, Carey Decevito has always had a penchant for reading and writing.

More than a decade later, with weeks of sleepless nights, where exhaustion settled into her everyday existence, she finally gave in and put pen to paper (more like fingers to keyboard!) She submitted to the dreams that plagued her. And the rest, as they say, is history!

A member of the RWA, Carey Decevito enjoys spending time with family and friends, the outdoors, travelling, and playing tourist in Canada's National Capital region. When life gets crazy, she seeks respite through her writing and reading. If all else fails, she knows there's never a dull moment with her two daughters, her goofy husband, and cat who she swears is out to get her.

Play Me to Infinity is the third book in *The Broken Men Chronicles* series.

FIND CAREY AT:

www.careydecevito.com
carey.decevito@gmail.com

ALSO BY CAREY DECEVITO

The Broken Men Chronicles series:

Once Written, Twice Shy
Almost Forgotten
Play Me to Infinity

www.ingramcontent.com/pod-product-compliance
Lightning Source LLC
Chambersburg PA
CBHW072030220726
48293CB00016B/614